MW00578897

# THE ROAD TO CHUMBA

# THE
# ROAD TO
# CHUMBA

**Leoda Buckwalter**

Evangel  Press

2000 Evangel Way
Nappanee, Indiana 46550-0189

Cover design: Brett Putnam
Cover artist: Kevin Ingram

Library of Congress Catolog Number: 94-71563
ISBN: 0-916035-60-3

Printed in the United States of America

4 3 2 1

To Andy,
because to me, your Aunt Leoda,
you symbolize every Woodstock student
who, like you,
loves the Garhwal Himalayas.

# Contents

# 1

# Sukhdev's ultimatum

The sound of the motorcycle caused Sukhdev Lall, fiftyish, with hairline receding, and mouth usually grim, to throw his newspaper on the verandah of the Swiss-style chalet. It was a crisp December evening, with twilight turning to velvety darkness. In the distance Himalayan snowcapped giants became shrouded in mist, but little friendly lights sprang up in the valleys and hills below.

"That you, Mahendra?" the man called.

"Yes, Dad." The Indian lieutenant—on extended sick leave from flying spotter planes on the far eastern border—now bounded up the steps.

"Sit, son. I want to talk to you."

So it's come, the young man thought. Last night of the year...the day before my sister Daya's engagement. Wonder what's on his mind.

The experienced real estate dealer sat back firmly, placing his hands behind his balding head. Tilting his chair, he said in clear, clipped tones, "Time for some parameters around here."

Oh? He thinks I've exceeded set boundaries? Well, perhaps he's right. I've been quite open about my love for Jesus Christ, and for Pansy. As for Zep, that's gone back years. I wonder....

Mahendra, scholar despite his vocation as a lieutenant in the Indian army, looked out over the hills and valleys he and Zep, his bosom friend, son of Kushwant Singh, had trekked. It was on those trails, meeting villagers, climbing with pilgrims to the famous Hindu shrines, that both he and his pal had learned to bypass temples for the wide open spaces. They loved the high mountains, the pastures, the play of wind and snow, the challenge of rain forests and razor back climbs. Yes, both he and Zep had gone beyond their families. Was that the issue? Hardly.

The older man continued, "Even though you're twenty-five—old enough to remember—it seems you forget that first and foremost we are Hindus." He gave his son a quick glance.

"Beg pardon, sir? My impression has been that you trained Daya and Raja and me to make our own choices. Sorry if I have misread you."

Sukhdev's anger flared. "Shut up, boy!" he shouted. "It's your very impudence that gets you into trouble. Be still, and listen to what I have to say."

A quiet smile played around his son's mouth. The discipline of the years took over. All his life he had known his father's wrath and studied it carefully. He felt that underneath the volcanic eruptions there resided a warm heart, but seldom peace. Father and daughter could spout off anytime, but then, Dad was partial to Daya. It seemed to bother him that his elder son should resemble his mother. Raja, coming along some twelve years later, seemed a healthy mixture of both. In a way, that's good, Mahendra decided.

His father cleared his throat several times, then said firmly, "Now, if you're ready to listen, I'll have my say."

The young man nodded.

"First and foremost, I inform you, son, that we're Hindus! You'll find wide enough parameters within the Hindu fold, but why do you insist on going outside to select your wife? This is ignominious!" Sukhdev pounded his fist on the arm of his chair and his eyes blazed.

Hmmm. It's Pansy after all. I might have known.

"Not only do you go astray, but you spinelessly follow pariahs. Bah!" Mahendra's father spit a long line of red beetul juice from the *pahn* he had been chewing. It landed on one of the flower pots bearing prize pansies, a fact that made Mahendra smile broadly. His father seemed at loss for words. Opposition he could handle...but indifference? The young man waited.

"Speak, boy! Don't sit there mute! Are you dumb?"

Mahendra chuckled, then said, "Thanks, Dad. I take it you have Pansy Michael in mind since you aimed so expertly at the flowers bearing her name?"

"By all the gods! You are brilliant!" he said sarcastically. Just like your mother, too. I keep egging her on, and she doesn't respond."

Mahendra laughed outright. "A real compliment, Dad! I think Mom's the best ever, and I'll bet you do, too."

"Humph! I thought this was a man's world."

"But it takes two, you know. You made a great choice with Mom. I hope I can do as well."

"Apparently you think you have. I'll concede Pansy's very attractive, but she belongs to the wrong religion. She's a Christian!" He spit again, aiming for another pot, this one bearing petunias.

"But what's wrong with taking the Lord Jesus Christ for a guru? Ever study his life, Dad? You'd go far to find anyone as self-less as he."

Sukhdev Lall didn't answer immediately. Both perused the vista that seemed to stretch to eternity in the darkness. One peak, however, shone white and clear, catching glints of moonlight. Was this prophetic? Mahendra wondered. His father spoke, "I don't understand you. Why talk about right and wrong...moral values? Son, you're crazy, and I blame Kushwant Singh for this. He allowed Manorma to come into his home as a daughter-in-law. That did it! You should hear the talk."

"What, Dad?"

"The town gossips say the entire family is becoming Christ-ian."

"Hmmm...interesting."

"Devastating! And when that poison touches your eldest son, that hurts!" He shouted, "I ask you, haven't you seen that star on the verandah? That's a Christian symbol. Who's running the Singh household, anyway? The lawyer, or a girl with a pretty face and smooth tongue?"

"Dad! Be fair!"

"Huh, why should I? Don't you see what's happening to you? Mahendra Lall, you're placing yourself under an impossible sys-tem where moral values count. Something is either right or wrong, good or bad, fair or unfair. So, what happens? Automatically, judgment begins. You're a sinner, and you're guilty. So you need a savior! Oh, yes, I know. I studied the Bible in college. Don't tell me anything!" He stood, and concluded, "I'd much rather be a Hindu, where what you believe is immaterial, but social struc-tures count for everything. After all, we have to live in this world!"

"Meaning?" The young man stood, facing his father and studying him as closely as he would a new species of orchid.

Sukhdev stopped, then with a half-grin, added, "Sorry I got out-of-hand, son, but...well...don't you see we've got to maintain caste? I really don't mind your maneuvering within our belief system, but you *can't* break caste rules."

"So what, Dad?"

"You can be friendly with Christians. But you can't marry one." He shook his forefinger in Mahendra's face and said, "Get it straight, my boy. You are a Hindu. You marry a Hindu. Yes?"

"I get the message, Dad."

"Is Pansy coming tomorrow?"

"She expects to. Daya and she are pretty chummy, as you know, and Daya wants her. The Singhs are entertaining the Michaels, so they can't come, but I encouraged Pansy to represent the family."

"You fool!"

"Why not, Dad?"

"She's wearing the diamond ring you gave her! Do you think I'll ever acknowledge that Michael girl as my future daughter-in-law? Think again, boy! She's out!" The set of his father's jaw made Mahendra turn away sadly. He wondered how he could spare his effervescent Pansy from heartbreak tomorrow.

But he could do little more than pray for her. His parents' demands kept him occupied from early morning until an hour before the fifty chosen guests would arrive. All was ready, with Daya's engagement ceremony planned to precede afternoon tea on the spacious tennis court amidst well-manicured gardens. Hopefully the sun would shine on this, the first day of January 1974.

By three-thirty, dressed in military uniform, Mahendra Lall jumped on his trusty Royal Enfield motorcycle and hastened the half-mile to Kushwant Singh's home to get Pansy. Perhaps they'd be late enough that he would escape performing the Hindu rites demanded of the elder son. He hoped so. He mused that one of these days he would have to make some outright choices. But until then he was content to live at home and try to preserve peace.

He turned up the familiar lane to the grey stone house set on a hill. As at the Lall's, so here, too, flowers and trees abounded— tall poinsettias, cosmos, roses, and a profusion of perennials spilling over in window boxes. Lush green grass and a gentle breeze invited lingering, but he hastened to the bungalow to be met by an exuberant Pansy.

"Happy New Year, Squirt!" she called as she hastened onto the verandah to meet him.

"Happy New Year, darling," he responded. Parking the motorcycle, he bounded up the steps, looked around and said, "Where's everyone? Vijay...Manorma...Uncle and Auntie Singh?"

"Left about half-an-hour ago for town with Dad and Lionel doing the honors. Dad wanted me to join them, but I told him I promised Daya and you I'd attend the function there today."

"Oh, my love!" He drew her inside the living room, took her in his arms and kissed her. She drew back, looked into his pain-filled eyes and asked, "What's the matter, Squirt? Is something wrong?"

He smiled and said, "Not with you. Pansy, you're my heart's desire. Isn't that a new *saree*? It suits you."

"I saved it for today," she said, giggling. "Dad gave it to me for Christmas. Remember? I told him this would be sort of like our coming-out party. Won't it, Squirt?"

"I wish I could say yes." Mahendra drew a deep breath, then placing his hands on the girl's shoulders, said seriously, "Look, love, I must ask you to be patient. I'm not sure I should even take you today."

"Why not? Are you ashamed of me, or is there someone else?"

He smiled slightly, and drawing her close, said, "Take my word for it, Pansy Michael. I shall never rest content until I give you my name at the altar. There is none other."

"Then, what?" Puzzled, she walked over to the front dormer window, and sitting down said thoughtfully, "Something's on your mind, Squirt. Spit it out."

"Yes, darling, but I wish I could spare you more pain." She brushed her eyes with the back of her hand, her face lovely even in repose. The rose-colored silk *saree* with its delicate gold border accentuated her olive skin and black curling hair that fell gently around her shoulders.

He walked over to the girl. Mahendra knew that her mother's eloping with another man had hurt Pansy deeply. But through it, father and daughter had found Jesus Christ as Savior and Lord. Tilting her face upward, he looked deep into those black eyes, brilliant with pain. "I know this hurts," he said softly, "but my Dad has given me two ultimatums. He says I must remain a Hindu...and I must marry a Hindu."

Her immediate response surprised him. She jumped up. "Oh, Squirt," she cried as she touched his arm, "how selfish I am! Why you're suffering, too, and here I am, thinking only of myself. Please forgive me, won't you?"

Mahendra smiled at her impulsiveness and said, "Look, love, I thought you would be devastated, and here you're thinking about me. We can weather this together."

"But now what?"

"I don't know. Dad's got a fierce temper. I don't know what will happen when he sees us today."

"Should I stay home?"

"I told him you're coming, so let's brave it. We'll sit back during the engagement ceremony, then we'll have the chance to congratulate Daya and Ramesh. I'll bring you home as soon as possible, if they'll let me. Honestly, love, my parents kept me so busy all day I didn't have a chance to see you earlier."

"When did your Dad tell you?"

"Last night."

She drew a deep breath, and said, "So that's what kept you! We had such a beautiful family evening, seeing the old year out and the new year in."

"Doing what?"

"Reading Scripture, singing, and praying."

"I might have known."

Within ten minutes the couple had arrived at the Lall residence to find that the ceremony had begun. They heard the familiar drone of the pundit reciting the mantras as he sat on a grass mat at the far end of the tennis court. Sukhdev Lall, with a younger brother, sat to one side representing the bride's family. The groom's family were on the other side, and the audience watched the proceedings. This initial legal contract between two families had followed weeks of preliminary routines. Today would finally conclude the first stage of finding a groom for Daya.

On cue from his mother, Raja kept taking items to his father and uncle who received them each one—money, rice, *sarees*—symbols of their authority over Daya. Sukhdev Lall placed each on a pile as promise of renunciation to the girl. In turn, the groom received them one by one, thus lessening Daya's ties with her own family.

The final cleavage came when Ramesh Chand, the handsome young entrepreneur from New York City's Indian community, tied a red cord around Daya's wrist to remain there until the wedding rites took place ten days later.

Ordinarily it would have been Mahendra's place to lead the merrymaking, but today Raja and the four cousins from Bombay took over, a fact that covered up the elder son's abstinence. Mahendra and Pansy quietly mingled with the guests, offering their congratulations as quickly as possible. Then they met Sukhdev Lall and a friend face to face.

The father of the bride stopped conversing, and said shortly to Mahendra, "Son, the bus must have been late. We finally went ahead, as you can see. Take your cousin into the house. Your mother will care for her needs."

Before Mahendra could respond, he turned to his friend, Mr. Kailash Rana, bank president, and said, "Our niece, Shakuntalla Lall, has just arrived, sir, from Hyderabad." Then to the girl he said, "Your plane must have come in very late, my dear, but we're glad you made it on time. Have you seen Daya?"

"Yes, sir," said Pansy, her black eyes gleaming mischievously.

"Whew!" Mahendra whistled softly as they reached the safety of the rose arbor, away from the crowd.

They clasped hands. With a whimsical smile Mahendra asked, "Shakuntalla, my cousin, may I have the honor of taking you home?"

The girl drew a deep breath. Her lips quivered, but she managed to say, "You and no one else, sir...not even your esteemed father."

"What a bungling fool I am!" he exclaimed. "Forgive me, love. Look, Pansy, what would you like to do?"

"Go home and cry."

"You do that, sweetheart. I'll take you, then come back and change into something casual. Okay? You change, too—something suitable for the botanical gardens. We must find a quiet place to talk."

She nodded, and pressed his hand.

The botanical gardens lay just beyond the Singh residence. In fact, the road ended there. Outside the gate a dozen or more rickshaws awaited passenger loads. Cycles, motorcycles, and at times cars filled another area. Mahendra, nattily dressed in dark brown slacks and matching windbreaker, looked in approval at Pansy's blue jeans, dark blue turtleneck sweater covered with a lightweight red jacket. "Much, much better," he said with a quiet smile before he paid the attendant for the motorcycle.

It was late afternoon, with the setting sun shining on the snows. The couple walked quickly to their favorite rendezvous, and settled in the cleft of the rock, away from the wind. In the quiet of the eventide they set some goals.

"I think I should go home," Pansy said. "Dad and Lionel leave tomorrow morning, Squirt."

"I was afraid you'd say that. Already I feel an empty feeling in the pit of my stomach."

"I know," she said. "I do, too. But Squirt, it's good for us to be apart sometimes. We'll get a better perspective on things. Don't you think so?"

"You sound like Mano," he said with a grin. "Where did you get your wisdom?"

"From her," she admitted with a giggle. How could she be sad in his presence?

"Bless you, love. We'll count the days...only three weeks until the family comes to Delhi for the Republic Day Parade."

"But a lot can happen in three weeks."

"True, but let's cover it with prayer."

Later that evening Pansy told the family about the day's adventures. "I'm coming home with you, Dad," she said seriously. "Both Squirt and I feel it wisdom to be apart for awhile, especially with his father's attitude so pronounced against me. I grant you, this afternoon it hurt—badly—but tonight I see the wisdom of leaving. May I come home with you, Dad?"

Captain Michael got up from beside the fireplace, and coming over to the dormer window where Pansy sat, he said, "You've made my old heart glad, my girl. I get pretty lonely, you know."

"We'll miss you," Kushwant Singh commented, while Susheela wiped away tears. But it was Vijay, Mahendra's bosom friend who bore the heavy nickname of Zeppelin, Zep for short, who voiced the general opinion, "Squirt will be after you, lass. Don't forget. He loves you, and so do we."

When Mahendra bade Pansy goodbye the next morning, he whispered, "Don't write me at home, love. Send everything here."

"More trouble?" she asked.

"Dad told me last night there's an alternate arrangement in the offing. But never mind, sweetheart. I'll be coming to Delhi in three weeks for the Republic Day Parade."

"Oh, Squirt." She hastily wiped a tear and said, "So much can happen in three weeks."

"Trust me, Pansy. Remember, I have the right of veto."

With Pansy out of the way, Sukhdev Lall brought on pressure for an early engagement with the second daughter of Kailash Rana, the bank president in Mussoorie. Mahendra's father called his son into his inner sanctum hardly a week after Daya's wedding and said, "You couldn't do better, my boy. Your mother and I know the Ranas through business contacts. We saw the girl at your sister's wedding.  I would have pointed her out to you, but...."

"Sorry, Dad," Mahendra said softly, "I'm not interested right now."

"But you don't understand! There's a heavy financial deal connected with it, my boy. Money talks, you know, and you'll never lack if you get into that family. Take my word for it."

Mahendra, studying his father, sensed the older man's uneasiness. His hands moved restlessly, and his eyes shifted, never looking directly at his son. Could it be that Sukhdev Lall, his father, felt guilt at having disposed so thoroughly of Pansy?

# 2

# Lakshmi's threat

Susheela Singh clutched Manorma's maroon-colored New Testament as she tossed and turned on that mid-January night in Happy Valley, North India. Her wooden bed felt hard, her arthritic knees hurt, and her eyes burned from the incense that hung heavily within the small room.

For the first time since she had publicly confessed faith in Jesus Christ, Manorma's mother-in-law felt strangely alone. If only her husband was here—but he wasn't! How could she expect him to be when theirs had been a Hindu marriage—one of convenience, a business venture? In this man's land, her lawyer husband lived according to his own whim and fancy, fulfilled in his precious books, his travels, his own quarters.

So here she was in her bedroom behind the kitchen. Even Vijay and Manorma stayed upstairs—an area forbidden to her, except on demand. Susheela sighed again and again. Could Jesus Christ change this family, even as he had touched her heart? Was he truly greater than Lakshmi, the porcelain goddess of wealth whom she had worshiped for the past thirty-five years?

Lakshmi still sat on Susheela's worship shelf, an idol somewhat neglected for the past three weeks, yet with incense burning as usual. She could see the flickering dull light above its gleaming brass holder, but the incense burned her eyes and nostrils as though menacing and lethal. Susheela felt dizzy, and clutched the little New Testament for protection. Against what? She didn't know, but she sensed impending disaster and cried, "Oh, God, where are you? What is happening to me?"

She heard a mocking voice. "God? Which god? Take your choice if you don't want me. There are millions out there, all with the divine essence pervading every tree, flower and animal. How about the Ganga, woman? Ha! Ha! Take your choice."

Vijay's mother shivered in fear, but managed to murmur, "I have already chosen." She pulled the sheet over her head.

The voice came closer. "Oh? And to whom do you bow?"

"To Jesus Christ, my Lord and Savior."

"So that's the reason I've been neglected?"

Who was speaking? Here in the darkness, suspended somehow between two worlds, Susheela Singh felt throttled. Was this a dream? She must find out. Impulsively she threw the sheet back to gaze in horror upon Lakshmi, life-sized, in form and appearance like the eight-inch porcelain figure that sat upon the shelf.

Lakshmi towered over her, saying, "So you follow another? You belong to me, and I demand your loyalty. If you refuse to serve me, I'll kill you and all in this house."

"Oh, no!" Susheela covered her head again and began to wail. The menacing voice laughed—a mocking, hollow tone. Bound by fear, Vijay's mother found thoughts racing through her mind....

God? Which god? There were millions, weren't there? Gods lived in every tree, flower, and animal. They permeated everything. How could anyone escape? She was in their land—the Garhwal Himalayas—the place where it all began! Look at these mighty snowcapped peaks, home of the gods—Shivaling, Nanda Devi, and a host of other giants soaring upward. From within this impenetrable whiteness the sacred Ganga flowed, Shiva's gift to a needy world.

Susheela visualized Ganga, goddess of the sacred river Ganges, daughter of the Himalayas, riding her alligator to water three worlds. She could see those four arms outstretched—two pouring out blessing, one holding a lotus, the fourth watering the earth.

God? Which god? Hadn't she painstakingly trudged the pilgrim paths to all four holy sites? Yamunotri? Gangotri? Kedarnath? Bradrinath? And lest she bypass a deity, she had stopped at temples and shrines along the way.

But Manorma had brought another religion into this house. Was Jesus greater than all others, or had she, Susheela, been tricked into accepting a Western faith? By daylight—and in fact for the past three weeks, she had been sure that Jesus Christ was stronger than any Hindu god or goddess. Now, in the dead of night, caught between consciousness and subconsciousness, she wasn't sure. But one thing she knew. Lakshmi had threatened her and her family.

In terror and confusion, Susheela Singh wailed.

Manorma and Vijay slept in the front bedroom of the grey stone house he had called home since boyhood. Exhausted from going to bed late, and entering her fifth month of pregnancy, Manorma awoke to her husband's urgent whisper, "Mano! Listen!"

A mournful cry pierced the silence, one wail following another. The girl turned over, sat up, and with a shudder asked, "What is it?"

"The neighbors! Somebody must have died!"

Her pulse quickened. "No, no, Vijay!" she exclaimed. "It's Mama's voice coming from downstairs. It's here...in our house... and Papa and we are upstairs. Mama's in trouble!"

"Are you sure?"

"Positive."

He jumped out of bed, grabbed shirt and trousers and said, "Stay here, darling."

"Can't I help?"

"After I check." Vijay opened the hall door, to meet his father emerging from the opposite bedroom. They ran downstairs.

Manorma glanced at the clock. Half-past-two. What an unearthly hour! She rose, put on her bathrobe, filled the electric teakettle and plugged it in. The wailing continued and Manorma began to pray aloud:

"Lord Jesus, help! What's happening? I don't know, but you do. Please, Lord...take care of Mama. She's been so beautiful the last three weeks, ever since she trusted in you. Please, Lord, oh, please!"

Tears flowed unheeded as she prayed. She moved to her favorite spot by the big front window that looked out on the snow-capped ranges, many peaks rising to over twenty thousand feet in height. To the slip of girl standing there, they represented God's faithfulness to his promises. She could count on him.

How many times she had stood here to pray? How could she tell? When she first arrived with her groom in Happy Valley some three years before, this had been her trysting place. Even as she now prayed and watched, silvery moonshafts glinted like iridescent beams on those white-capped sentinels that protect India's northern boundaries. Peace settled upon her, and Manorma drew a deep breath. "You're faithful, Lord," she said with a quaver in her voice. "I've had to walk a hazardous path, but I've watched you bring this precious family to yourself...and I thank you."

A wispy shadow caught Manorma's attention. Who was that running away from the house into the bushes at the edge of the lawn? The wailing had ceased. Vijay and Papa would come soon. She'd better fix tea. Instead, she heard someone coming up the stairs, so she rushed to the door. Father and son were carrying their arthritic patient. "Mama!" Manorma cried. "What happened?"

"It's all right, darling," Vijay said, panting somewhat. "She got frightened, but Dad's taking her into his room now."

"Oh...I've...the kettle's boiling. Won't you have some tea, all of you?"

Kushwant Singh, distinguished lawyer who had served in the Supreme Court until retirement five years earlier, smiled. After aiding Susheela to stand, he said, "Always serving, aren't you, daughter? No, thank you, we'll not stop for tea. I must get Vijay's mother to bed. Thanks, son, for helping." Little crinkles deepened around his eyes. "Go back to sleep, you two. See you in the morning." Then leading the confused woman into his bedroom across the hall, Kushwant Singh closed the door.

Vijay chuckled. "The end of an era," the tall Indian soldier observed. "Dad knows it."

Manorma giggled. Her husband picked her up lightly and across the room to his favorite wicker chair. "You sit. I'll get the tea."

"Why all the attention?"

"Can't let Dad get ahead of me, darling. Would you believe it? That's the first time in my whole life that I've ever seen him take Mom into his room. Does that say something?"

She giggled again, remarking, "It's the Lord, Vijay. He's making some needed adjustments, I'd say." She watched his assured manner as he easily made tea and served it with aplomb, even finding cheese crackers and saying, "Jolly good I brought these home. I knew they'd come in handy." And she laughed outright when Vijay plopped down at her feet and said, "You get more beautiful all the time!"

"At this hour of the night?" she queried.

"Definitely...clear olive skin, naturally wavy brown hair, and ravishing hazel eyes. I missed you so much, Mano, out there in my little pup tent in the rain forest. I'm so glad to be home."

"Tell me what happened to Mama. I'm dying to know."

"Maybe morning would be better. Night magnifies things."

"I can take it, Vijay."

"I'd say Mom's had a nightmare, but she calls it real. She says the goddess Lakshmi is threatening to kill all of us."

"But Lakshmi's not real! She's a mythological figure. And don't you remember my life verse? 'I will trust, and not be afraid.'"

"Ah, yes." Her husband jumped up to stride awhile as his father did when struggling with a problem. Coming back, he stood near her and said, "Mano, my love, I learned a lot on the Indo-Burma border. Remember, I experienced Hidden Valley! Those days showed me that the powers of evil are very real, and I respect them. We're not battling a porcelain idol on Mom's shelf."

Manorma nodded, and stroking her hair he continued, "Nevertheless, we are being attacked. Demons devise evil, and they hate God. So what do they do? They attack his children...and that's why this threat is very real. We daren't bypass it. We must stay alert and trust the Lord Jesus Christ to see us through."

The girl drew a deep breath, then said, "Vijay, darling, I do trust him. We're in this together."

He pushed his wavy black hair back and smiled. "You're great," he said, "I don't know what I'd do without you."

"Well, let's pray that dear Mama won't revert to Hinduism. She's so new in her faith, so vulnerable."

"And therein lies the danger."

"But that's where all of us come in. As family, we strengthen each other."

"True, darling. Now, let's get to bed. Morning will be here before we know it."

At seven-thirty Manorma tiptoed to Papa's bedroom, carefully carrying a tastefully arranged breakfast tray. A bouquet of fresh pansies, faces upturned, spoke of faith and trust. The girl knocked on the door, and pushing it ajar with her shoulder, entered. "Good morning, Mama," she said softly. "I've brought your breakfast."

Kushwant Singh had drawn the heavily brocaded maroon drapes before leaving the room since it was already sunny outside. Manorma stopped to accustom her eyes to the dimness, then moved forward to place the tray on a sidetable. Susheela turned over, rubbed her eyes and murmured, "Where am I?"

"In Papa's bedroom. He told me to bring your breakfast tray. Now, there, I'll just fix your pillows so you can sit and eat. And I picked beautiful yellow pansies for you. See?"

"Pansy...where is she?"

"My cousin? Don't you remember? She returned to Delhi with Uncle Syd and Lionel after New Year's. Mama! They're preparing for all of us to come next week. Remember? We're going for the Republic Day Parade where your Vijay receives his medal from the President of India! Aren't you proud of him? I am!"

The tall woman with the high cheekbones and rather severe features nodded with a hint of smile. She watched the girl pull the curtains back to let sunlight come streaming through the panes. A squirrel stopped his routine search for food to preen himself on a branch of the evergreen just outside the window. Manorma laughed and exclaimed, "Isn't he adorable?"

Susheela spoke slowly, as though piecing a puzzle together, "Vijay...medal...Delhi. You're going too?"

"Indeed so, Mama, and so are you."

But the older woman's eyes suddenly opened wide. In fear she murmured, "She's angry. She threatened to kill all of us. We can't go to Delhi."

"Tell me about it," the girl said as she poured a cup of tea. "Was it a nightmare?"

"No, no, daughter...it was real. I saw Lakshmi." Susheela labored with her breathing, but proceeded, "She stood over me... so evil...not beautiful! And I have served her so long." A tear trickled down her cheek.

Manorma caressed her hand. "The goddess can't do anything to you without our Lord's consent. Why, Mama! Jesus conquered evil! He's greater than anyone...everyone. Remember? Now, shall I pray before you have your breakfast?"

"But I must tell you what Lakshmi said. Then you pray."

"Yes, Mama."

"She said, 'So you follow another so quickly?'"

"How did you know her?"

Susheela put her hands over her eyes and whispered, "She was just like the goddess on my shelf, only life-size. I couldn't bear it...like the time your father-in-law bent over me when I had poisoned you. Oh!"

The girl laughed lightly, and in surprise Susheela looked at her. "Why do you laugh?" she asked.

"That's past history. Oh, dear Mama, aren't we glad that the Lord Jesus loves us? We can trust him. See? I brought you pansies, and a nice verse that says, 'I will trust, and not be afraid.'"

"But you don't understand. The goddess says she'll kill all of us...the baby too."

Vijay's wife leaned over the bed and declared, "Yes, I understand. We don't have to believe Lakshmi. See? We belong to the Lord Jesus Christ, and Lakshmi can't touch us. Can she, Mama?"

The grey-haired woman gazed long and hard at her daughter-in-law, as though probing the depths of this declaration. Manorma prayed inwardly, *Now, Lord Jesus! Now!* Release Mama's simple faith and let it grow, in the face of all that Lakshmi says.

In that sacred hush the girl saw fear recede from Susheela Singh's eyes, to be replaced by hope. She heard her whisper, "Daughter, I want this house to belong to the Lord Jesus, and not to Lakshmi."

"Ah!" Manorma wiped Susheela's tears and kissed her. "You have chosen," she said, "and so have Papa and Vijay and I." She stood, drew a long breath and said, "Now I can pray, and then you must eat."

While Susheela ate two *chapatis* (Indian bread) and drank tea, the girl chatted cheerfully. But soon the older woman pushed her tray back and said with a yawn, "Take it, daughter. I'd rather sleep. Could you help me back to my room now?"

"Papa says you're to rest here today."

"But I'm not allowed—except to clean. This is the men's quarters, daughter."

"I know, but you're allowed. Papa and Vijay brought you last night when they found you crying, and Papa wants you here. You're to stay all day, and we'll take care of you. Don't worry, Mama. Just sleep. Look, I'll darken the room."

Susheela lay back and relaxed with a contented sigh. Manorma placed the bouquet of pansies on the sidetable, took the tray and tiptoed out.

Father and son awaited her at the foot of the stairs. "How is she?" the elder asked while Vijay took the tray to the kitchen. "Sleeping, Papa, but she ate very little. She asked me to help her return to her room."

Kushwant Singh seemed startled. "Why?" he asked.

"She said she isn't allowed in the men's quarters."

"Hmmm...this house needs considerable changing. We must hold a family conference. Come, daughter, to the library."

Manorma felt weak. Were Lakshmi's threats real after all? Why was Papa so serious about them? Did he believe in the goddess? Of course not! "Mind if I sit?" she asked. "I'm very tired today."

"How thoughtless of me. Yes, daughter, sit. I'll have Rani bring you breakfast. You haven't eaten yet, and you need sleep, too." Kushwant Singh hurried to the kitchen while the girl sank thankfully onto the sofa at the end of Papa's library.

"Lord," she prayed, "this, too, is a miracle. Papa's opening his library—his inner sanctum—to me, a woman? Surely you're doing something. I'm so glad!"

# 3

# The angel of the Lord

Manorma soon realized that father and son had already decided a momentous issue: Mama Singh must never sleep in that back room again. This occasioned changes that profoundly affected the entire household. After the girl reported on her conversation with Susheela Singh, the lawyer looked around the commodious room in which they were sitting. "Hmmm," he said, then began pacing, hands behind his back. Only the ticking of the grandfather clock in the corner broke the silence.

Vijay and Manorma sat close to each other on the sofa, waiting. He stopped and took a chair near the young couple. Crossing his knees and matching his fingers precisely together, Kushwant said, "Listen, you two. I think we've found a solution. We should move your mother's clothes out of that back room today. She may not sleep there again. But being a wheelchair patient, I don't see carrying her upstairs all the time. Moreover, she should come and go as she pleases. Would you like to hear my suggestion?"

He paused, then smiling broadly, added, "With your permission, son."

"Why the drama, Dad?" Vijay asked, chuckling.

The lawyer's eyes twinkled, and his white mustache twitched. "First chance to try out the new arrangement, Lieutenant. I've signed this property over to you. You and your lovely wife are now the legal owners, and Mrs. Singh and I live here with your permission. See?"

"Dad!" Vijay jumped up to hug his father. "You don't have to give this place to us! I do love it, as you know, but...."

"It's my pleasure, lad. It's yours, and now, I'd like to exchange the library with your mother's present quarters to make this the master bedroom. I'll move down, and my room upstairs can be the official guest room. How's that sound?"

"Dad!"

Father and son faced each other, and Manorma noted how alike they were. Vijay queried, "You're giving up both your bedroom and your sanctum for Mom? You're moving in permanently with her?"

The lawyer laughed lightly. Placing his hands on his son's shoulders, he said, "That's as I see it. Your mother is my personal responsibility as long as I live. We can't go our separate ways any longer."

The family conference continued until the approaching throb of a motorcycle brought Vijay to his feet, exclaiming, "I forgot! Squirt's coming." He looked at his watch. "He said he'd be here by nine-thirty."

"But where are you going, Vijay?" Manorma asked.

"Out Tehri Road to Chumba, darling, if Dad doesn't mind."

"Go ahead, son. I'll take care of matters here. And daughter, you take the day off and sleep."

To reach Chumba, a nondescript hill village in the lower Himalayas, Mahendra and his pal would have to travel some thirty-five miles out Tehri Road. But first they must traverse Mussoorie, the popular hill station some two hundred miles north of Delhi, India's capital city. Mussoorie stretched a good twelve miles along a ridge that for over a century encompassed three bazaars— Library at the far end, Mussoorie in the middle, and finally, Landour Cantonment. Landour had been built one hundred fifty years before by plainsmen who migrated to service the needs of British convalescent soldiers.

Needless to say, this area of the Garhwal Himalayas possessed rich legends. During the British era, lords and their ladies escaped the blistering heat of the Gangetic plain to walk the Mussoorie Mall. These Englishmen worshiped in Christ Church and sheltered in the opulence of the Savoy and Charleville hotels. Gossip had it that liquor flowed freely, causing some rather undignified actions, and the general populace soon concluded that Christianity was indeed Western, to be shunned.

But in 1947 the British government left. Now the hill station would have become dreary and forgotten, except for a new clientele—a rising middle class that both Mahendra's and Vijay's family typified. Knowledgeable and affluent, these world-class citizens built vacation homes in and around Mussoorie. Tourists also abounded, mostly brown-faced, speaking one of the eighteen major languages of India. And the occasional foreigner still mingled with the others, but the general air was now Indian.

Squirt and Zep approached Library Bazaar first. The square in which the bandstand stood thronged now with laughing children, haggling parents, intrigued tourists, and the gentle mountain folk that peopled the surrounding villages. It took Squirt's careful maneuvering, along with honking his horn, to make a safe path through this ten-o'clock morning crowd.

In Mussoorie they fared better, for the street was wider, the action less hectic. They cruised steadily past Bata's, down the steep hill and out onto the Mall road, turned the corner at Picture Palace, climbed past the Union Church and on up to Landour Bazaar.

This began with the clock tower that changed color each year, from pink to purple, to grey. It chimed out the hour, as do all the clock towers in such towns in North India—on whim or fancy! But whether slow or fast, it nevertheless kept all of Mussoorie and Landour on one time—its own! That in itself was worthy of note.

Landour Bazaar stretched a mile of curves and climbs from the clock tower to Mullingar Hill where Tehri Road began. Its one lane, built originally for pedestrians, mules, or perhaps rickshaws, now was stretched by the occasional truck, the more familiar jeep and huffing-puffing coolies bearing lumber, produce, kerosene or other staples on their backs. They were the merchants' lifeline.

Sights and smells abounded in Landour Bazaar—from the clink, clink of the silversmith pounding out his wares to the whir of the ancient treadle sewing machine where the turbaned tailor earned his honest day's living. Bengali sweet shops did brisk business in hot *jalabies*, fresh *samosas*, and mouthwatering curries. South Indian and Tibetan restaurants vied with their ethnic dishes while cloth merchants called prospective buyers in to examine their well-filled shelves.

By anyone's count, Landour Bazaar deserved more than Squirt and Zep could give today. The duo puttered gaily past, even making the steep climb up Mullingar hill without effort.

At last they reached Tehri Road, and soon the heart of beautiful Garhwal spread before them as they cruised down the blacktopped highway that snaked around mountains and ridges at an elevation of approximately seven thousand feet. Breathtaking views made up for their oftentimes hazardous trip. The road had no guard rails, and a bus or mule caravan could suddenly appear around any corner.

Vijay, riding pillion, leaned forward to exclaim, "Squirt, I've missed this."

"Pansy and I did it several times while your Manorma was in hospital. Pansy's a natural on the motorcycle."

"You're made for each other."

"Wish Mom and Dad thought that. We had another round of it again this morning. It's worse since Daya's gone. She can control Dad. He listens to her."

"But what's the root of the trouble?"

"Caste rules." For several minutes only the sound of the Royal Enfield broke the pristine stillness. They could hear the soughing of the wind through the pines, the call of the Whistling Thrush, the chatter of monkeys. Mahendra finally said, "Funny thing, Zep. I can be as friendly as I like with Pansy. Nobody says anything, but I've transgressed as soon as I ask her to marry me. It simply isn't done!"

"What happened this morning?"

"Dad informed me last week they're making an alternate arrangement—somebody with big credentials and bank account. Ugh!"

"Have you no say?"

"Yes, of course. I can go independent, and pay my own way. I'm ready for that, except that I haven't regained full health yet. Moreover, I hate to break contact with the family. I long to see them come to the Lord, even as yours has done. I was praying about that again this morning, and then the big upset came."

Squirt veered off to the side of the road as a passenger bus rumbled by. Its capacity load of Garhwalis laughed and waved at the two young men and motorcycle pressed close to a rock. Vijay waved back. Then he asked, "What came of it?"

"What came of what?"

"The big upset you mentioned, Squirt."

"Oh, nothing. I escaped for the day. I hope Dad cools down before I see him again. One thing I know...I'm of age, and I have veto powers."

"You said it, man. Sorry, pal. We sort of had a bad time too, but ours was last night. Mom had a nightmare...began wailing. Says Lakshmi appeared to her and threatened to kill all of us because Mom's following Jesus Christ."

"Hmmm...interesting. Demons must be working overtime. Don't you think so?"

Before Vijay could answer they approached a curve and met a mule caravan head on. Mahendra swerved to avoid collision when one of the mules panicked and headed toward the middle of the road instead of hugging the mountainside single file. Laden with bulky sacks of potatoes, one sack lurched, just grazing Vijay's arm. An inch more and he would have been thrown off balance. He drew a sharp breath. To his immediate right he saw a sheer drop of shale and stone that most certainly would have meant disaster! The three muleteers driving the caravan called the animal back into line.

Perspiration broke out on Mahendra Lall's forehead. He almost lost control of the vehicle, but it swerved back onto the road and the men continued on in silence. Each realized a miracle had occurred. Several minutes later Zep asked, "How far do we go today? Dad's calling a family caucus at five."

"Then we'll shoot for Chumba instead of Tehri City. I do want you to meet a friend at a new little tea shop we found, and perhaps climb to a pilgrimage spot nearby. Remember Sukhanda Devi temple? It's becoming popular these days. Want to see it?"

"Fine with me."

They soon emerged onto an open ridge and felt the full blast of the chill January breeze. Near the far end stood a tea shop with two dozen or more people milling around the rest area. A rickety red and white bus awaited its load. The driver honked.

"Let's wait until they leave," Zep suggested as they parked the motorcycle. "Man, I'm hungry! Hope some biscuits are left."

Squirt grinned and ventured, "You've got a big hulk to fill, Zeppelin. Now, take me, for instance...."

His buddy chuckled and said, "What's the matter, Squirt? Can't you grow up?"

Mahendra's eyes flashed as he said, "Fat chance with you around. I have to share my goodies with you, but then, no problem. Mom gave me extra for our lunch."

Both laughed, then Vijay said seriously, "Thanks, pal. I didn't eat much this morning. All three of us—Mano, Dad, and I—were too worried about Mom. But good will come of it. Would you believe that Dad took my mother into his own quarters last night? Moreover, he has decreed that she dare not maintain her former patterns anymore."

"Meaning?"

"They're going to share a room together. That's what I mean." Mahendra whistled softly. "Wow!" he said.

The bus started noisily, and everyone piled on. Waving them off, the two friends turned to the pleasant Garhwali who exclaimed, "Mr. Lall! How good to see you! Where's the lovely lady today?"

"Home in Delhi, Daula Ram. But I've brought you my closest friend, the one who brought me to Jesus. I want you to meet him. This is Vijay Kumar Singh, and between you and me, he's receiving a medal for bravery from the president of India next week."

The proprietor had put on the teakettle for a fresh pot of tea. He came from behind the counter, bowed, and said with a smile, "What a pleasure, sir. I am indeed fortunate."

Vijay shook hands with the stocky young man, perhaps in his early thirties. Black closely fitting trousers held in a nondescript grey flannel shirt covered by a sleeveless jacket. The smell of pomade mingled with other odors hard to define, outstanding among them, the crispy smell of pine cones burning. Daula Ram stoked his wood fire, then turned to Mahendra to say, "I've been reading the book you gave me, sir." He pulled a Hindi Gospel of John from his pocket and continued, "I can't express the peace it gives."

Mahendra chuckled. "Perhaps you'll accept three more?" he queried. He unzipped his dark brown leather jacket, and handed the other three Gospels over. "Here, friend," he said with a smile, "these also tell about the Lord Jesus Christ."

Vijay slapped Mahendra on the shoulder. "Pal," he said with a grin, "I didn't know you were witnessing."

"Every day, Zep." Mahendra looked up with a chuckle and said, "I figure others are just as hungry for the Lord as I was. Remember when I saw you pray the first time? I asked whether you would share your secret with me, and you did. So can I with others."

"Mr. Lall gave me a wonderful gift," Daula Ram remarked as he pulled a box of Monaco biscuits from the shelf and arranged several on a plate. "He didn't know it, sir, but I felt very depressed the day he came."

"Why?" Vijay asked.

"Oh, something had happened, and I was longing for a friend with whom to share. In Mussoorie I used to talk things over with an elderly Christian evangelist, but he died suddenly last October." The man talked as he worked. He filtered sweetened hot milk through fresh tea leaves directly into the boiling water, then taking two gleaming brass glasses from the shelf, he filled them and handed them to his guests. "This is on me today, Mr. Lall," he said with a vigorous shake of his head. "I owe much to you."

"Why, thank you. By the way, would you like to tell my friend why you left the city?"

The Garhwali waved his right hand toward an enchanting view that encompassed a hill village nestled among magnificent pines and giant sized rhododendrons. Beyond lay the mist-filled hills with valleys layered and beckoning. And to the far north were the snows. "I got homesick for this," he stated. "I much prefer it to city life, but making a living here is difficult."

"Soil not good?" Vijay asked.

"Potatoes. Otherwise it's not much good for anything, and it's backbreaking! But we have something of more value than money. My people are honest. We don't mind working hard, and we love peace. But the city is different, sir. The last man I worked for expected me to cheat, and I've never done that."

"So you left?"

"Yes, sir. At least I'm free here. About two months ago I set up this tea shop with the earnings I saved over the years. Business is a bit slow right now, but it will pick up when the pilgrims come."

On seeing four mules and their drivers rounding the corner Daula Ram concluded, "Climbing again to the temple, Mr. Lall? I'll watch your cycle...and please have a good hot meal with me before continuing your journey."

Zep and Squirt glanced at each other quickly. "Thanks, friend," the latter said reading his pal's mind. The caravan arrived, and the muleteers tethered their animals beyond the motorcycle. Ten minutes later Mahendra and Vijay began their trek up the mountain.

It was a rugged climb, with the path well-defined by pilgrims. Sukhanda Devi Temple, a small shrine, sat on top, providing an excellent view of the high snows which all Garhwalis believe to be the home of the gods—a land both mysterious and unfathomable.

About halfway up, the whipping wind intensified. "Let's sit," Squirt suggested. "My strength's variable since the illness. I do pretty well on level ground, but this is steep."

"Here, pal...just the place." The men chose a pile of rocks in a sheltered spot and enjoyed the superb panorama before them. Several minutes passed in silence, then Squirt said, "Zep, you know something? I was dead scared when that mule charged us."

"Yeah?" Vijay picked several twigs off of a bush nearby and began breaking them into small pieces. "That sack of potatoes, or whatever it was, it almost threw me off balance. Man! That was a close call. Did you see that sheer drop?" He breathed sharply, then asked, "Remember the jeep that rolled over the *khud* near Landour Bazaar? This was fully as steep as that. It could have been us, Squirt."

"But you know something? God's grace worked overtime, I'd say. I know my nerves aren't very strong yet, but...." He looked over the wide open vista and concluded, "We would have gone over—both of us—except that someone's hands covered mine. I could feel them, but didn't see anyone."

"You don't say! Hmmm...what do you make of that?"

"Very simple," his friend replied, "the angel of the Lord."

"Uh-huh," Zep grunted. "So Lakshmi tried...but failed? Thank you, Lord."

# 4

# The idol's fate

Seldom had Kushwant Singh spent such a morning, one in which eternity seemed to have intervened in time. Not that it was long in the hours he spent studying and praying—actually only a bit over two, he thought ruefully—but inestimable in its depth. Last night Susheela had seen Lakshmi; today her husband met the Lord Jesus Christ.

Not given to dreams or visions, the lawyer preferred to find direction from the Word itself, and to this end he studied the fifth chapter of Ephesians. At times he wrote, then he would pace the floor, and once he knelt, hands folded in petition, to say aloud, "Oh, God...I'm not worthy to be the head of this family. You've entrusted me with a task far beyond my abilities or understanding, but, dear God and Father of our Lord Jesus Christ, I thank you for your Holy Spirit, my Guide and Comforter." At this point the man raised his hands, stood, and said solemnly, "With all that's in me, Father God, I ask the fullness of your Spirit this hour. Guide my steps, and cleanse my heart. In Jesus' name, I pray."

His pulse quickened; his heart filled with joy. He paced back and forth, muttering, "Walk in love...walk in light...walk in wisdom." He reflected that the rules for a Christian family are clearly etched. He, Kushwant Singh, was expected to be the spiritual head of this house, subservient, however, to his Head, the Lord Jesus Christ. Secondly, his relationship to Susheela, his wife, needed a great deal of attention.

A scene flashed through his mind, something that happened during Manorma's time in Delhi.

Vijay had returned from serving on the Burma border, and after seeing Manorma, visited his parents. They sat together in the dining room—father and son chatting during their meal, mother sitting in her wheelchair, listening. Twilight had come, and twittering birds heralded another night. It should have been a cozy family gathering, but it wasn't.

Susheela's angry exit and scathing denunciation seemed etched in blood upon his heart. After their son witnessed to personal faith in Jesus Christ, she had pulled herself up and shrieked, pointing her finger at Vijay like some witch.

Could he ever forget? She wore a light grey punjabi outfit, her usual garb, but it was her face he remembered. Distorted and gaunt, with hate-filled eyes, his wife had yelled, "No son of mine becomes a Christian! Do you hear? No! Never!"

He had tried to intervene—in futility of course. Who can control an enraged woman? Her tirade poured forth, ending with, "I'm going to bed. Enough of this nonsense. There's not another sane person in this house." And Susheela had left, spitting out, "Go ahead, you two. Hallucinate together!"

What had Vijay done?

He must have been deeply wounded, yet he exhibited a sweet forgiving spirit, the same as Manorma later showed when Susheela poisoned her food!

Vijay's father now shivered as he recalled the emptiness he felt, the white-hot anger, the hatred. Out of his deep inner sense of failure he had asked his son, "Why can't I share the same spirit that both you and Manorma have?"

"You can, Dad," the young man had replied. How handsome and collected he looked in his dark blue safari suit, his face serene although his eyes betrayed inner pain. Vijay had said, "You're talking about Jesus Christ in our lives. He'll come into yours, too, but on his terms."

"But, son, I believe in Christ," he had said. "I keep the Holy Bible with all my other sacred books."

And Vijay had stood, walked over to the window and looked out. Was he praying? Kushwant felt sure that in that moment his son had sought spiritual wisdom from above. Finally he turned with a smile to say, "Yes, Dad, it's true your Bible sits on your top shelf. Perhaps that's the reason you're missing the treasure."

He had talked of Christ's exclusiveness, his claims to deity, his insistence that Jesus, alone, could lead a person to God, and concluded, "Dad, you can't bypass Jesus Christ. Either he's Lord, or he's a liar. It's all, or nothing!" He had paused, then added, his face aglow, "I believe he's God Incarnate, and I love him. Dad, I've given him my heart...and my life. I am his."

Father and son had faced each other, and Kushwant remembered how he burst out saying, "Vijay! You're a man! How can you give up your independence? You have the right to rule!" To which his son had answered, "But you and I have always been close. I've never found it hard to obey you, because...well, I love you. Somehow we seem to understand each other. If you and I can be like that, Dad, why not my God and I?"

The grey-haired lawyer stopped pacing, and now bowed his head in shame. "Oh, my God, my son has far outstripped me spiritually. I've been so proud...proud of my ability to rule...proud of my tolerance." He took a long breath, then added, "I might as well face it, my God. I haven't led my family; instead, I've consciously allowed each person autonomy—my son, my daughter, my servants, and most of all, my wife."

Other scenes flashed before him. He saw himself escaping on one pretext or another, never asking if it suited—merely announcing his going.

Kushwant Singh continued praying, "Lord God, your viewpoint is diametrically opposed to mine. You love everybody. Calvary proves it. To me women are inferior, and marriage a convenience. Susheela has borne my children, but frankly, I've never even thought her beautiful...not until three weeks ago."

Vijay's father stopped suddenly. He looked up, his face aglow. "This is amazing," he whispered. "Something has happened to her...or to me...perhaps to both of us. I've always thought her plain, sometimes ugly, always strong. But now? She seems years younger. She carries herself with new dignity, and I love her gentleness, even though her strength is still there. Susheela is like a bride, and I want to embrace her." He laughed lightly.

"Lord," he continued, "you've done this. When has she tried to please me by dressing carefully? Or conversing freely with the family after the evening meal? She does now, and I find my wife beautiful."

The grandfather clock struck eleven-thirty. Kushwant Singh rose resolutely and said, "Dear Lord, it's time for me to act."

He climbed the stairs, opened the door to his bedroom and called, "Susheela." He pulled the curtains back to let in light, placed a chair near her bed and noted the look of peace on his wife's face.

She stirred and opened her eyes.

"It's all right," he murmured. "Don't be afraid. I'm here to take care of you."

"Where am I?" she whispered.

"With me, Susheela, where you belong. Do you like it?"

Vijay's mother sat up, pushed her hair back and said with chagrin, "I...I...must have overslept. I'm sorry. Shouldn't I return to my room?"

"What's wrong with mine? Let's stay together, like Vijay and Manorma. It strikes me they enjoy companionship. Wouldn't you move in with me?" He concluded with a smile, "Please, my dear."

"But...but...Lakshmi?"

He laughed, little crinkles showing around the corners of his eyes. "Strikes me she's good riddance—like your fickle friends who turned against you. Lakshmi hasn't done you any good. Remember? You were terrified of her last night."

Fear crossed Susheela's face. "But she says she's going to kill all of us."

"That's what Lakshmi thinks," he said, chuckling, "but I'd say she doesn't have the final word. Move in with me. We can help each other."

"I can't climb the stairs."

"Don't worry. Vijay and I will manage. In any case, next week we go to Delhi. When we return we'll move into the master bedroom downstairs."

"I'm sorry, I don't understand," she said after a pause.

"No, of course not!" her husband said with a boyish grin. "While you slept, my dear, the rest of us held a family conference. I told the children that we'd move into the present library. That has easy access for your wheelchair, and it places you close to all of us. We'll make this a guest room."

"And my room?" she whispered.

"A delightful family area that opens onto the garden. My books and desk will go in one corner, but the room won't be exclusively mine." He touched her cheek and said softly, "See, my love? It can be done."

Susheela remained silent.

Kushwant bent over her and said urgently, "All I need is your consent before making changes. Rani and Leela can bring your clothes, and I'll hang them in my closet. There's plenty of room."

The woman covered her face with her hands, then looked up and laughed. "I think I have lost my senses, my lord. I'm not hearing properly. I've never heard you talk like this before."

"Ah," he said, "that's because something has happened to both of us." Like an abashed suitor he continued, "I do hope you'll approve of the new Kushwant Singh. I've...I've fallen deeply in love with a certain Susheela, five years my junior."

She extended her hand and said softly, "Yes, I'll move in with you...and you may destroy the idol. My lord, Jesus *is* greater than Lakshmi. Look at what he's already done for us."

In the kitchen Rani, the rotund little Garhwali, middle-aged and standing four feet ten inches on tiptoe, expanded with pride over "her family." "Too quiet today," she murmured. The Singhs were special people, and she worked hard, cooking favorite dishes to please them.

She wept when she had to take her husband home to the village four years ago. Despite her constant nursing care he had died within the year. Lung trouble got him, even though she'd fed him plenty of goat milk and garlic, like the doctor ordered. But, the gods be blessed, here she was back again. Kailash was running the farm, so she didn't need to stay in the village.

Her thoughts continued as she fried onions for tonight's meal, then added seasoning, potatoes, and peas. Turning the gas fire low, she heard her master call. "Yes, sir," Rani answered, "I'm coming."

The little Garhwali smoothed her red checked cotton skirt and lavender long-sleeved blouse covered with a sleeveless handknit sweater. She straightened the silver coins on her necklace, then drew her orange shawl over her head. Now acceptable to appear, Rani met Kushwant Singh at the dining room door. "Do you have a few moments?" he asked. "I need to talk about Madame."

"Why, yes, sir. Is she worse?"

"No, no," he said smiling. "Are you busy? We can do this quickly." He sat in his usual seat at the head of the table and she stood nearby, saying, "No need to hurry, Master. The curry's simmering."

"Very good. Now, Rani, I need you and your daughter, Leela, for a special task. Likely you heard that Madame had a bad experience last night. She's considerably shaken."

The little Garhwali nodded. "Yes, sir," she said, "all of us heard the wailing. We thought it came from the neighbors." Her thoughts whirled. Better not tell Master about that gossipy woman next door, Kailu's mother. Why, she told me this morning at the well that the goddess Lakshmi had visited Mrs. Singh and threatened the life of the entire family. And, she had added pointedly, that's what comes of tinkering with a foreign religion! Look at that Christian star out there—enough to anger any goddess.

Rani thought of all this, but simply said, "I've missed Madame today."

The lawyer nodded. "In my wife's present condition," he said, "I can't leave her alone at night. Frankly, I think it was a nightmare instead of being real, but...." He paused, then added, "whatever the circumstance, I must take action. I've moved her into my room."

Rani smiled. "Ah, yes," she said, "I noted Madame's room is empty. I went in to refill the incense burner as usual."

Kushwant Singh lowered his voice and spoke, "If you hear of any threats against us, or see suspicious actions, may I trust you to tell me immediately? I'm depending on you, Rani. That's why I brought you back when Vijay's young wife was poisoned."

The little woman drew a deep breath and clasped her hands tightly together.

"You heard of that, of course," and with a wry smile he added, "In this country nobody keeps a secret."

"Beg pardon, sir," she said looking up. "I can...and do..."

"Good! Hmmm...Madame insists that someone entered her room last night and threatened to kill the entire family. I reiterate, I think she was dreaming, but nevertheless, for her health's sake we must protect her. Understand?"

"Yes, sir. I agree."

"Today's rest has benefited Vijay's mother, thank God. We'll bring her down for afternoon tea and the evening meal. Serve her with the rest of us. From now on we'll eat together as a family. You understand, Rani? Madame will eat when we do, even though you may continue to serve two menus."

She smiled and nodded.

"Now, if you and Leela could bring Madame's clothes up to my room, that would help."

"Yes, sir. Please, sir...before you leave."

"Yes?"

"That boy, Kailu. I happen to know he snoops around doors and windows, and his mother is a big gossip."

The lawyer stood still, then said smiling, "I haven't misjudged you, Rani. Thank you. From today we'll have afternoon tea in the library instead of in the garden. Can you manage?"

"Yes, sir." She gave her master a look of pride. He was smart, just as she thought.

For the next half-hour mother and daughter carried Susheela Singh's personal effects to the big bedroom upstairs. Master himself relieved them of their loads and hung the clothes in his wardrobe. Rani could scarcely believe he would stoop to such a menial task, but then, Madame was still resting and shouldn't be disturbed.

The task completed, Rani dismissed her daughter but returned to the kitchen. She needed to be alone. She had a lot of thinking to do before taking her afternoon rest. Now, Hazari Lal...ah...Master could depend on him. He was smart, and honest. Loyal, too, but sometimes he liked to brag about taking Vijay and his friend on treks. Humph! That's nothing! She fed them.

Rani added a bit more ginger to the chicken curry for flavor and turmeric to keep it golden in color and decided that Kailu was becoming a problem. His snooping had to stop! He's a likeable ten-year-old, she thought, hardly more than mischievous, but his mother must be prodding him. How did Maya Bahadur find out? Huh? Her boy must have rushed over to the big house to spy on them. She must talk to Hazari Lal about protecting this precious family—privately, of course. Why shouldn't the Singhs have the freedom to place a star on their verandah if they so chose? Rani decided this world was getting topsy-turvy.

When she returned from her afternoon rest she looked at the clock, then decided to make some of Vijay's favorite cheese balls. She had barely completed the task when he bounded in, took a deep whiff, and said, "I believe it is. Yes, I know it is my special order. Cheese balls?"

"Yes, young Master."

"Bless you, Rani. Today's a very special day. Dad says we'll have tea in the library. Hazari Lal has already built a fire there, and Dad's gone up to bring Mom. We'll be ready by five. Okay?"

"Okay," she mimicked, the hint of tears in her gleaming eyes.

That tea smacked of celebration. Both the ladies looked attractive. Susheela wore a light blue punjabi outfit her husband had helped select, and Manorma matched Vijay's safari suit in her dark blue *saree*.

Kushwant Singh led his wife to his own easy chair facing the fireplace. When she remonstrated, he gently pushed her into it. He walked over to the window, glanced sharply around, then closed the curtains and smiled. Perhaps they could be assured of privacy today. Turning to his family, he said, "We're celebrating a new beginning. Now that we're united in serving and loving the Lord Jesus, it's time to set new patterns."

He took a chair beside his wife, and pressed her hand, a gesture that made Vijay tighten his hold around Manorma as they sat together on the sofa. Kushwant continued, "As head of this house, I now propose some changes with immediate effect. We'll be eating all meals together—not men first, women next. The ladies are going to eat with us, Vijay. Right, Susheela?"

As though in a daze, she assented with a nod. Her husband continued, "We will begin these changes now with my asking God's blessing on our food, and this will be a continuing practice."

Later, after Rani and Leela had cleared the dishes, Kushwant said seriously, "You wonder at the change? My beloved family, something happened to me today. It was good for me to be alone, because at last the Spirit of God could get through to me. I learned that we have fallen far short of God's plans for a family. I confess that last night's events hastened my spending time with God, so you see, good is coming out of intended evil—and that, my dear ones, is the Almighty at work."

He walked over to his desk, drew some half-a-dozen pieces of porcelain from his bottom draw, and turning, said with a smile, "Here's Lakshmi."

Manorma gasped, but felt Vijay's restraining pressure. She relaxed and listened. The lawyer continued, "Vijay, your mother told me I could do this. I know both of you will rejoice." He held a piece of the idol, laying the rest of it on the coffee table. He said softly, "Lakshmi can't feel, talk, or think. But these pieces symbolize something far greater. Hear me, family! Lakshmi and her kind represent spiritual forces arrayed against the God of heaven."

"But, Dad, weren't you scared to destroy her?"

His father chuckled. "No son. You see, I'm on the winning side. Jesus Christ is the Eternal Conqueror, and I'm glad to be a member of his army." He paused, then added, "Of course, being astute, I waited until Rani had gone for her daily break, then I not only took the idol but cleansed the entire room, praying in the name of Jesus. Lakshmi has ruled there long enough. I've taken it back."

Manorma could keep silent no longer. "Mama," she exclaimed, "how do you feel about all this?"

Susheela clutched the arms of her chair. Should she break with custom and speak openly of that which was on her heart? Why not? Custom must give way to a greater authority...and she and her husband were starting a new, exciting adventure. Susheela smiled, then said, "Daughter, we come from a long line of warriors. I served the wrong commander all these years. I'm convinced that your Jesus has power over Lakshmi and all she symbolizes, so I told your father to get rid of her." She paused, then concluded, "I believe in Jesus. He's forgiven my sins, and I know he loves everyone—even me."

"Oh, Mama!" The girl jumped up to embrace her mother-in-law. "You're both beautiful and strong. I love you!"

Susheela wiped a tear, then said, "Thank you, Manorma. In you I met a force stronger than hate. I've never loved Lakshmi. I've bargained with her, hated and appeased her, but now I know something superior. God's love has come to me. I love Jesus...and all of you."

"Pray, son," Kushwant Singh said with glistening eyes. "The Lord is here. I sense his presence."

"Let's stand around Mom's chair and hold hands," Vijay suggested. His burst of adoration, praise, and commitment solidified what had been a fragmented family. Bonded, now they were ready to walk in obedience to the Lord's commands. Battle? Hardship? Probably. But one thing they knew; their Lord was with them.

Under a waning moon crossed by wispy, ghostly clouds, with the snowcapped Himalayas showing faintly on the horizon, Vijay and Manorma threw Lakshmi's remains—piece by piece—over the *khud* from their vantage point in the botanical gardens. When the last piece disappeared, Vijay noted with a chuckle, "The end of an era, darling, and the beginning of another. The Singh family is united at last, thank God."

In Library Bazaar, three miles away, an excited ten-year-old sought out his father, Tej Bahadur, cloth merchant who was attending a club meeting in Whispering Windows Restaurant. The man looked up in surprise to ask, "What brought you here, son?"

Kailu, hair falling over his forehead, shifted from one foot to the other and said, "Mama Ji said I could come because it is important. Papa!" The boy pulled at his father's sleeve to get his undivided attention and said, "You know I told you this morning that Mrs. Singh wailed last night because the goddess Lakshmi threatened to kill everyone in the house?"

The merchant frowned, conscious that discussion has ceased. All hushed to hear the boy. "Yes?" his father said. "Probably a dream."

"No, Papa! I stopped on my way home from school this afternoon, and would you know? The goddess has gone! She always sits on the worship shelf in Mrs. Singh's room. The incense is there, but she isn't! I know. Papa," and the boy drew a deep breath before concluding, "she's angry! Did she leave because she's angry?" His eyes filled with fear.

A murmur went through the room. Somebody muttered, "That star's still there. Kushwant Singh, fine as he may be, is fooling around with a foreign religion."

# 5

# Gur Bachan breaks the news

On their return from the botanical gardens, Vijay and his wife stood for a moment under the soft light of the Star of Bethlehem that shone above the front door. Manorma looked up and said, "Shine on, you beautiful star. Let the whole world know that the Redeemer has come."

They turned to find Kushwant Singh awaiting them in front of the glowing fire in the living room. Seated in his black vinyl armchair, he perused the latest issue of *India Today*. He looked up as the young couple joined him. Vijay said, "It's done, Dad. We've dispensed with the goddess of wealth."

The lawyer threw his magazine aside and said, "My news, son, is that the story has broken."

"How could it?"

"Both of you sit down. Let me brief you before the action begins," he said with a twinkle in his black eyes. Manorma perched on the edge of the sofa, and warming her hands asked, "So soon? We've just thrown her away."

The lawyer chuckled. "Hand it to Kailu. I always knew he was smart, and Rani warned me about him. He's been spying on our movements, telling his parents."

"Oh, no!" Manorma looked up, then said, "I think I saw him last night when Mama was wailing. I was standing at the window and I'm sure I saw someone running and ducking."

"Probably."

Perplexed, Vijay asked, "Did he follow us to the gardens? I didn't see him, Mano. Did you?"

Kushwant Singh rose to stir the fire. He turned before the girl answered, and said, "No, he wasn't following you. He was too busy delivering the news to the whole town!" The lawyer chuckled.

"Come on, Dad, what's it all about? And what about Mom? Is she all right?"

"Very much so, son. I escorted her to bed immediately after you left and we prayed together for the first time in our lives. Then she turned over and went to sleep." He drew a deep breath, then said, "The phone's been ringing the last fifteen minutes."

"Really? Who?"

"Oh, a friend of yours, Vijay. Gur Bachan, he says, staff reporter for the local weekly. Then your mother's former friend, Mrs. Gupta called." Manorma looked up as the lawyer continued, "She's very solicitous."

Manorma smiled remembering the woman who had glibly reported her as immoral. No doubt she could capably repeat the performance. Oh, well. Where once she hated Mrs. Gupta, now she could love her. Manorma asked, "Papa, what did Mama's friend say?"

The lawyer laughed heartily. "Well, if you want to know," he said with his eyes gleaming and his mustache twitching, "she gushed her sympathy for my wife and offered to take her to the temple tomorrow to appease Lakshmi."

"Papa!"

"I confess to both of you it gave me particular delight to tell the lady that Mrs. Singh is indisposed and already in bed, not to be disturbed. That's that."

"But, how did Mrs. Gupta find out?"

"Our little friend, Kailu, cycled to Whispering Windows this evening where a club meeting was in session, and he informed his father—and all listening ears—that Lakshmi had disappeared, that she's angry, and that our lives are threatened. Apparently Ram Gupta was present, as was the staff reporter, Gur Bachan."

"Whew!" Vijay whistled in astonishment. "What did you tell him, Dad?"

"That I consider it a nightmare, and that everything is under control...to just forget about a little boy's fancies."

"Very diplomatic, sir, but Gur Bachan has a nose for news. I know. When we were in high school together he'd walk around looking for a scoop for his precious school paper. We couldn't find Gur Bachan without his pad and pencil. Dad, he'll be here with his camera and flash before we know it. What do we do? Any strategy?"

"No, son." Kushwant Singh smiled. "Let's not meet trouble until trouble meets us."

"But Papa," Manorma jumped up, her eyes gleaming, "we can prepare for emergencies by praying and making a cup of hot tea. It helps. It really does."

Vijay chuckled and said, "See Dad? She's invaluable, and I happen to know her favorite recipe never fails." He pulled her down, saying, "Darling, prayer first, then tea."

"Okay, Vijay."

"Agreed," said the lawyer with a wide smile, "and since the story may break in the *Mussoorie Weekly*, we'll ask your friend to share that cup of tea. Let's start witnessing. Why not on the front page of the local newspaper?"

"Bravo, Dad! You're great! Come, let's pray."

Ten minutes later their golden haired Tibetan terrier, Sherpa, first picked up the motorcycle noise. Snoozing beside the warm fire, he suddenly pricked up his ears and began thumping his tail. Then, as though disappointed, the dog relaxed. "It's not Mahendra," Manorma observed with a laugh. "But someone's coming. Sherpa says so."

"Gur Bachan, darling. Go, make tea." Vijay rose to greet the newcomer.

Ram Gupta, wealthy cloth merchant from Mussoorie Bazaar, left Whispering Windows abruptly after the club meeting and walked home rapidly. Dressed in his usual handwoven tunic and trousers with woolen sweater overlayed, the portly gentleman pulled his large grey woolen shawl around his shoulders like a blanket. A brisk wind made him clutch his bright yellow turban that marked him. He wore it wherever he went.

The whole Lakshmi incident had left him more shaken than he dared admit. Why listen to a boy who had disrupted their meeting? One could scarcely credit his assumptions, the man thought belligerently. Yet the niggling doubt remained. What if Lakshmi was angry, and her wrath would be vented not only upon the Singh family but on all the area merchants as well? If she had left one household, was there any reason to believe she wouldn't leave others?

He didn't consider himself a religious man. His wife made up for that. Leela worshiped Lakshmi daily, while he preferred to make money instead of pleading for it. Now, levelheaded as he was, he hurried home to confer with Leela about this, too troubled to note the beauty of the night with the twinkling lights of Dehra Dun piercing the darkness like diamonds on black velvet. Passing through crowds walking the Mall between Library and Mussoorie Bazaars, he finally turned in at the side door next to the shop bearing his name.

"You've come quickly," his wife began as he entered. "Here, my lord, is the evening paper. I'll serve your meal within ten minutes."

"I'm exhausted! I'll rest till you call." He sprawled on the divan in the dining room. The voluminous woman in the dark grey punjabi outfit asked, "Are you all right? Here, I'll rub your back." She bent over and began to massage him, an action that tended to mollify his damaged spirit. In his house, at least, he was king. Why worry about Lakshmi?

Half-an-hour later, after finishing his meal alone, he went to the minuscule back verandah that held but one wicker chair. A light bulb hung from the porch roof. Taking the evening paper with him, the man awaited his wife, reflecting that his daughters-in-law would serve their husbands when they returned from attending the movie at Picture Palace, down by the bus stand. He felt his two sons spent far too much money on cinemas. Didn't they know he worked hard to produce it?

Leela soon joined her husband. She squatted on the door sill, pulled her dark grey woolen shawl around her shoulders and asked, "Why did you come home early? Any special reason?"

"Be still, woman! What right do you have to ask?"

"Beg pardon, my lord," she replied, but he could tell by her tone that she resented his command. Well, maybe he wasn't king in his own domain after all, just the consort of the queen. Ram Gupta sighed, then decided to talk.

The woman listened without making comment. When she finally spoke, she burst out, "They have it coming to them! It's that hussy married to their son. She's corrupted the whole family!"

"Why so?" he demanded. "Kushwant Singh is highly respected in Delhi and here. Better be careful of your words."

"Oh?" she shouted. "I've done my part. I warned his wife, and there was a day when I considered her my friend. But she's cut me off completely! When I try calling her she says she can't talk. I hear she keeps to herself like a hermit, allowing that daughter-in-law to do whatever she wants. Why in the name of sense did they bring a Christian into the family? Now I ask you."

"Shh, Leela. Keep your voice down. The girls are listening."

"At least they're docile. They don't boss *me* around like that daughter-in-law of Kushwant Singh's." The woman raised her hands as she looked up in a gesture of thankfulness. "I say, the gods be praised."

"Well...hmmm. I know you're regular in temple attendance, but how about a special offering tomorrow morning to placate the goddess? We can't afford her ill will spilling over on us."

"Oh?" The woman stood up, then said, "Yes, I'll do it. And what's more, to prove my goodwill to the lawyer's wife, I'll offer to take her along. I'll phone her now, and we can go first thing in the morning. If you'll excuse me, I'll make arrangements."

Ram Gupta's restlessness lessened. Perhaps his wife's religiosity would exempt him, but just in case.... He drew a deep breath as he rose to go to his room and determined to place a special flower garland tomorrow on Lakshmi's picture in his cloth shop.

Next morning at six-thirty, with dark skies threatening rain, Ram Gupta hastened downstairs to the tea shop across the road. His wife had already left the house for her special trip to the temple, and he had assured her he would buy his breakfast before opening the shop for the day. Crossing the street, he joined three businessmen gathered in front of the stall.

"Hear about the boy who disrupted our club meeting last evening?" he began casually.

"You were there, sir?" one asked. "You mean over in Library Bazaar at Whispering Windows?"

"Why, yes. How did you know?"

"It's here—in the *Mussoorie Weekly*. We've just been discussing it."

"Here, my good man." The newcomer pulled a coin out of his cloth money bag that he kept in a side pocket and offered it to the proprietor. "A newspaper please, and fresh *samosas* and tea." Taking the paper with him, he walked to an empty table in the corner and by the light of a dim bulb hanging from the ceiling Ram read the account under the heading, "Goddess of Wealth Threatens Local Family." Once again the man decided that he could scarcely credit a little boy's assumption against the word of the well-known lawyer Kushwant Singh. Mr. Singh apparently felt the entire story to either be fabricated or merely a nightmare. Fair enough! But the big question remained: What if the little boy's words are true?

Ram Gupta hastened to open his cloth shop, and settled himself on the dais that served as platform, display area, and work space. Behind him well-fitted shelves of materials rose from floor to ceiling, displaying all manner of prints and plain textures—enough to suit the most fastidious of tastes. He prided himself on his good selection, even in midwinter.

The man glanced around the shop that represented his life savings. His hand fell on the tin box in which today's accumulation would go, and he frowned. This Singh family! Why should they endanger the entire community? Why should they displease Lakshmi by displaying a Christian star on their verandah? It all stemmed from them bringing a Christian girl into their home.

Really, this was going too far for even friends to accept. Not that he called Kushwant Singh a friend, but their wives had seen each other regularly in the past. In fact, if he understood Leela correctly, it was the temple that drew the two ladies together. Hmmm...perhaps he'd better turn the business over to an assistant this afternoon while he personally offered something to appease the angry goddess. Yes, that's what he would do!

Ram Gupta adjusted his bright yellow turban, then got out his ledger and pens and settled himself for the first customer of the day. He simply must make a sale, even at financial loss, since a first sale was a good-luck omen. The man assumed a lotus-like position on his dais and glanced hastily at the imposing row of framed pictures on the wall opposite. Yes, Lakshmi's was still there. He hoped she wouldn't leave.

Throughout the entire area—in Library, Mussoorie and Landour Bazaars, even in Sisters' Bazaar high up on the ridge above Tehri Road—merchants read the news item with varying degrees of trepidation. That day Lakshmi's temple did a thriving business as eager worshipers sought to appease her wrath, begging the goddess to strengthen the economy, not to wreck it.

In the bank meeting that morning the president, Kailash Rana, commented to his underling, "Look, Mehta, we'd better change our minds. Remember? Yesterday I thought of inviting the lawyer, Kushwant Singh, to sit on our board of governors. But," and he pointed to the story in the paper and continued, "now I'd say we'd better be careful. Why get involved with this? If the boy's word is true, all of us may be threatened by the indiscreet action of this man."

Mehta, desirous to please, rubbed his hands together and said, "Yes, sir, I would say so, too. You're right, Mr. Rana. I read the account in the paper, and I'm sure we'd do well to bypass the lawyer." He paused, then with a burst of inspiration added, "Beg pardon, sir, but Mr. Singh could very well become the ruin of us all."

"Humph! Maybe. Time will tell." With which word of wisdom Kailash Rana closed the matter, at least for today.

But the subject erupted in Mahendra Lall's home. Squirt had risen early, as was his practice, and after spending an inspiring hour in prayer and Bible study at his favorite trysting place on the hillside facing the snows, he walked home for breakfast. He felt an inner uneasiness, and prayed for strength to meet courageously whatever came today, but he scarcely anticipated the wrath in his father's voice that rang out, "Mahendra! Where have you been? Come here immediately!"

He sprinted up the path and into the house. The elder Lall's eyes flashed as he ordered, "Get into my office, chump! I have something to say to you."

"Yes, sir," Mahendra managed to answer. A quick prayer for grace somewhat quieted his fast pulse as he followed the irate man into his inner sanctum.

"Close the door!" Sukhdev Lall ordered. "Now stand there."

"What is it, Dad? What's the matter?"

His father waved the newspaper at him and spit out, "You and your Singhs! You're ruining us! Bad enough for you to lock yourself in with Vijay Kumar Singh as your bosom friend without getting engaged to his wife's cousin! Without our consent, young man! No horoscopes, no pundits, no dowry! No! You take things in your own hands. Who do you think you are?"

Mahendra answered quietly, "Sorry, Dad, but I need to know the reason for this outburst. What has happened?"

"Here, idiot, read for yourself! Can't you see that the goddess's wrath on the Singh household affects all of us, particularly those close to their family?"

Mahendra perused the item then answered, "Dad, Vijay told me about this yesterday. Both he and his father think Mrs. Singh suffered a nightmare."

"Nonsense!" Sukhdev Lall stood, his spare frame filled with indignation, his eyes flashing as he said, "Make your choice, young man. Fool around with a Western religion, and you get burnt. Come under the rules of this house and we find a wife for you in the prescribed order. Otherwise, you leave. Hear me?"

"Dad! Are you serious?"

Sukhdev Lall pounded his fist on the table. "Yes, sir!"

"How long do you give me to consider?"

"One week. You'd better think hard if you want to be my son...."

Mahendra bowed his head for a moment, then looking up, said, "All right, Dad. I'll let you know by Monday morning."

A sober young man walked out the door, but again, even as on the road to Chumba, so now—he felt another with him. He didn't walk alone, and already he knew his answer.

# 6

# Mahendra Lall's choice

Sukhdev Lall's thriving real estate business functioned from the office in his home, entered by a side door that faced the busy road leading into town. A sign bearing his name and credentials hung a bit awry to the left of the door. The steady stream of clients faced seeming disarray as they stepped into the large room, but to the two clerks, trained by their boss, the more hectic the day, the greater their sense of fulfillment. Hence, like Sukhdev Lall, they felt important.

The room resembled a government office with its piles of correspondence, files, ledgers and books stacked on tables and shelves. Mahendra, the essence of neatness, often wondered how his father accomplished anything in such disorder, yet he seemed to possess an uncanny sense for finding whatever data he required.

However, the small anteroom that opened into the larger area was much more prestigious. It carried a luxurious touch—the sphere of an executive, an effective spot for clinching big deals, for getting signatures and making decisions.

It was in this inner sanctum on Monday morning that Sukhdev Lall fingered a letter, delivered moments ago by the milkman, Mama said. She stood in front of her husband's desk, her face etched with lines of pain. She seemed to have suddenly aged twenty years, he thought. The little woman dressed in the green *saree* said softly, "Sukhdev...please...will you allow me to speak?"

"After I read the letter," he growled. Mahendra's father opened it to read:

My respected parents,
   This is a difficult letter to write, since I owe so much to both of you. I wish I didn't have to make a choice, but since life is demanding it of me—and I am forced into a position of deciding between two religions and two prospective brides—I now exercise my legal right to vote. From today, I go on my own. Thank you for giving me a beautiful home and a sense of security. I'll miss you, particularly the family times.
   Early tomorrow morning I leave for Delhi, to return in about ten days. I have taken a room near Mullingar Hotel, and you can contact me by phone. My number is 298-9614. Please feel free to call. My highest joy would be to maintain contact with you.
                          Your loving son, Mahendra.


"You said the milkman brought this to you? *Where is that boy?*"
"I tried to get him to wait until today to move out, but he took his clothes last evening."
"Last evening, when I wasn't here?" The man looked crushed. "But...but..." he stammered, "what about this big business deal tomorrow—with the girl included? Just when it's ripening, he does *this* to us?" The man ran his fingers through his hair.
   Shanti Lall hesitated, then said softly, "Please don't take this so hard, my lord. Mahendra's a good boy. Perhaps he'll change his mind, especially if you show him a sympathetic attitude."
   Sukhdev's temper flared. He shouted, "What do you mean, woman? Do you dare to take his part? I have a mighty mind to disown him—and give everything to Raja!"
   "But, my lord...pardon my reminding you that our eldest is legally of age. And remember that Lawyer Kushwant Singh has very strong connections with the leaders of this land. What hopes have we if we raise our voices? My advice is to please watch your temper and give your son his rightful freedoms."
   "*Get out!* There's the door!" Sukhdev Lall stood gaunt and haggard, pointing to the exit that led into the dining room. On watching his wife leave, he slumped into the overstuffed executive chair and covered his face with his hands.

The dread of leaving home had hung heavily over Mahendra these past ten days. Now that the time had come, he experienced a sense of astonishing peace. Was this special measure of grace for this specific moment, he wondered, or would it stay? It certainly mitigated the pain, making the severance bitter-sweet. Moreover, he now understood more clearly his Lord's rejection at the hands of those he loved, and the joy of one day soon being joined to his beloved Pansy thrilled him. They would serve the Lord Jesus Christ together.

But first he must become a true disciple, and that meant preparation for taking baptism. However earnest his desire, or his love for Jesus Christ, his world would never accept the fact of his conversion until he was baptized. So Mahendra decided to stop at Dehra Dun Bible College on his way to Delhi to investigate the possibility of enrolling for a semester.

Late Sunday night, prior to leaving Landour Bazaar, he telephoned Vijay.

"Hello, Zep," he said. "I'm in my new quarters."

"You don't say. How did it go?"

"Better than I expected. Dad wasn't home. Mom was weepy, of course, but she helped me. She seemed apprehensive at what Dad might do when he found out I moved in his absence."

"Meaning what?"

"Who can say? But some day I must go back to get my books and records, Zep, so it isn't a final goodbye. In any case, I have given my parents my telephone number."

"That's good."

"I leave in the morning, pal. How about you?"

"Not until Tuesday. What's your hurry?"

"I'll tell you when we meet. Pray for me, won't you, please?"

"Sure thing, Squirt. Lord, bless him and protect him.... Don't let him make a misstep at any point. Amen."

"Okay, buddy. We meet at Captain Michael's. Right?"

"Right on, Squirt."

The festive air that gripped the Singh family on Tuesday made Manorma marvel—so different from her last trip down this hill to India's capital city. Not only did Papa insist on sitting with his Susheela, but he regaled them with one funny story after another while Vijay drove his Dad's newly purchased Standard to Delhi. And where did Manorma sit? In front, beside her husband!

What had happened to the Singh household? Were Papa and Mama just discovering each other, as do honeymooners? Manorma giggled at the thought and conceded it could be so. Manorma glanced swiftly at Vijay. She saw him chuckle. He knew too. "All well, darling?" he asked.

"Very much so," she said.

They laughed then—and often—during their eight-hour journey to Delhi. True, the usual harassments of the long, dusty road were there—slow, lumbering oxcarts, cowherders utilizing the highway to take animals to pasture, casual pedestrians, the ubiquitous cyclist tinkling his bell. And always, oncoming busses and trucks, careening down the center of the road, playing chicken.

Sights, sounds, smells! An old man huddled on his door sill hoping for a ray of sunshine to warm his cold bones...a mother and six children running across the highway like a hen surrounded by chicks...vendors selling, buyers haggling...sightseers sauntering while munching peanuts...temples, towns, crowded sidewalks and tea shops...wide open spaces with exotic flowers and trees, delightful villages amid mango groves or lush wheat fields...piles of red chilies next to fresh green vegetables...the scent of jasmine garlands sold near Hindu shrines, the lure of curry and spice from open-faced restaurants....

All of this had been here on her former trip to Delhi three years previous, the girl reflected, but somehow, today was different. She whispered, "Isn't the Lord good to us?" Vijay smiled, sensing her joy.

Vijay's parents awoke from napping as the car neared Old Delhi. Papa Singh, now refreshed, assumed the role of tourist guide, and after an hour of driving through the city, they reached Captain Sydney Michael's residence about three o'clock.

Mahendra rushed out, followed by an exuberant Pansy. "Uncle, Auntie," she called, while Squirt ran down the steps to greet Zep.

Vijay jumped out to embrace his friend. "You look dashing in that light grey safari suit!" he said. "New beginning?" A meaningful look passed between the two. "When did you arrive?"

"Last evening."

"I suspect you had big business on hand."

"Man, did we ever! We've almost set our wedding date."

Pansy, smart in her dashing pink punjabi outfit, hugged the lawyer and said, "No running away this time. You're staying with us. We've got plenty of room for you and Auntie."

"Well," he said with a chuckle, "since you're willing to put up with us, we accept. How about it, Susheela?"

"Of course," she murmured. "I've missed you, Pansy."

"Oh, I'm so glad you've come." She clapped her hands, then ran to embrace Manorma, who asked, "You've been lonely?"

"Rather! With Dad at the Secretariat, and Lionel working, you know."

The two girls helped Mama Singh up the steps to a wicker arm chair on the verandah, and Susheela gazed wonderingly over the expansive compound. Despite being in the heart of the city, lawns and flowers surrounded them. A six foot high wall assured privacy, and arched pillars on this attractive white bungalow suggested luxurious living. Susheela said in surprise, "This was your home, Manorma? You came to a palace after living in our humble quarters?"

"Not really, Mama. This is nice, but I love our Happy Valley home. Pansy and I did have good times together here, as we did when she came to live with us."

"Yes," the older woman said with a sigh. "I've missed her."

"Oh, Auntie, how sweet of you." Pansy bent over and kissed Vijay's mother, then said, "I love these old British bungalows, the way they catch every breeze blowing and make the best of living in a hot climate. But frankly..."

"Yes?" queried Manorma.

"I've been very lonely here, especially since I returned from Happy Valley. I've counted the days, haven't I, Squirt?"

He laughed and said, "Every letter, folks."

"Is your father home?" Kushwant Singh asked as he brought the wheelchair over to the ladies.

"No, uncle. You arrived first. Dad said he'd try to leave office early, but...well, you know how it is this close to Republic Day." She clapped her hands and continued, "Mano! Dad changed our parade tickets so all of us can sit together as a family. Thanks for giving us your numbers, so we could do that. Who wants to be separated?"

"No way!" Vijay responded with a grin. "I'll spot you easier as a group when I go by...."

"On the back of an elephant...yeah! The conquering hero!" Mahendra said. He ducked as Vijay made a pass for him, exclaiming, "Sweetheart, come! It's dangerous out here! We'll alert the servants to bring in the luggage. Mano can handle Zep."

"Sure, Squirt." Pansy grabbed her fiancé's hand and said, "You know your way around, Mano. Please see Uncle and Auntie to their room." Manorma decided that Mahendra already had found his niche in the Michael family. His insistence on detail, combined with his quiet wit, surely complemented Pansy's effervescence.

The bungalow had much the same design as British-built ones throughout the land. Double doors opened from the wide verandah into a spacious living room, which, in turn led to a like-sized dining room. An enclosed screened-in back verandah served as pantry with storerooms on either side, and some ten feet beyond, a separate small brick building functioned as the main kitchen.

Six other rooms of varying dimensions, four of them with adjoining baths, clustered around the two main rooms of the house. Manorma and Vijay now entered the living room with Papa pushing the wheelchair, a task he would give to none other.

The girl stopped and stared. "Look, family! See what Uncle Syd's done!" she cried.

Gone were the ostentatious white overstuffed settees and chairs, symbolic of Aunt Rose's longing for status and position. Now a divan invited a person to curl up with a good book. Its rich Persian rug cover blended in nicely with the maroon-colored overstuffed settee and easy chairs. Persian rugs brightened the dark red wall-to-wall carpeting that the Captain had installed, as did bright colored cushions.

"Yes, daughter, what do you think?"

"Oh, Uncle Syd's hurting, deep down inside. Aunt Rose meant a lot to him, and her leaving him for another man must be galling. But he's facing his trouble by doing something positive about it, and I'm glad. Look! He's turned this into a family room!"

"I think you're right, my girl," the lawyer said. "I suspected as much at Christmas time and decided we'd come here instead of using my personal quarters that I keep in the center of the city. In fact, I think I'll give that up. Perhaps our Lord has provided this instead, so that we can mutually help each other."

Pansy and Mahendra's approach, followed by two servants in white uniforms, stopped further reflections. "Ram Chander!" Manorma exclaimed, "I'm glad to see you."

The elderly man in the lead saluted smartly and said, "Welcome home, Miss Manorma. This is your husband?"

"Yes, and his parents, Mr. and Mrs. Singh."

"Greetings. We're honored," he murmured, then hastened to bring in the luggage. Manorma sensed that both Vijay and Mama and Papa had passed Ram's test. She smiled.

But after leaving the others in their quarters, the girl suddenly began to feel nauseated. She turned to her husband at the door of their spacious bedroom and said falteringly, "Sorry, darling...but I wish they'd put us somewhere else. This room...this is where I hit bottom."

Viiay gave her a quick qlance, then quietly closed the door behind them. His perusal showed high ceilings and whitewashed walls dating back to British days. A commodious bed at one end was flanked by dresser and closets. At the far end, an attractive fireplace promised cozy evenings. A padded wicker chair and settee with a coffee table and hanging lamp beckoned. French doors opened onto a wide verandah and gardens at the back. Even with the doors closed the room suggested outdoor living.

Perhaps it was the nature scenes on the walls that set the tone, or the off-white drapes now pulled to show their bold green patterns of bamboo stalks, leaves, and singing birds. A beautiful potted palm highlighted the impression of quiet, good taste, as did the bouquet of rosebuds on the side table. Vijay scrutinized it all and said, "It's pleasant, Mano. What do you fear?"

She turned to him, placed her arms around his neck and said with tears in her eyes, "Darling, I'm sorry. It must be just me. I don't know why I feel like this, as though Jesus is far away, and I'm about to be pulled down again like when I lived here before."

"Come, let's talk." Vijay led her to the settee, and sitting, drew her close. "Tell me what happened, love. I tried desperately to find out from your letters, but you hid your feelings very well."

"Well, I enjoyed this privacy at first—teas in the garden, servants doing all the housework. All I had to do was read!" She sighed, then continued, "But I was alone all day, waiting for Pansy to return from college."

"Aunt Rose?"

"She followed a busy schedule of shopping and lunching out with friends, then worked at Claridge's Hotel from midafternoon until about midnight."

"So you got lonely?"

"And depressed. And I'm ashamed of it. But..." she wiped a tear, then said, "little by little I grew spiritually cold. Oh, Vijay, I've confessed my sin to the Lord and he has forgiven, but I don't want it to happen again."

"When did you begin to feel this way today? We had such a happy time until we reached here."

"Come to think of it, it's something that slapped me down when we walked in the door."

"Hmmm.... Yes, I see." Vijay rose and said, "You lie down and rest, darling. I've got some work to do."

She looked up, alarmed. "What work?"

With a whimsical smile he asked, "Remember another room? One that Dad cleansed? I think some little imps have been using this place for their purposes, and we've had enough of that!" He pulled her up, led her to the bed and said, "Now rest and don't worry. I'm taking this room back in Jesus' name."

Thoughts whirled through her mind. What's he going to do? She watched as he paced back and forth, hands behind his back like a true son of his father. Then he drew himself up as though for combat. He looked up and said, "Lord God Almighty, I now confess again that you alone are God. Beside you, there is none other! And in your mighty name I now rebuke the spirit of depression and any other evil spirits residing here." His voice deepened as he commanded, "In the mighty name of Jesus, out you go! You have no control over us, and we renounce you!"

Vijay stood quiet for several moments, then with outstretched hands, palms uplifted, added, "Now, sweet Spirit of God, come and take my Mano and me again, and sanctify both this room and us to your own purposes. I ask it in Jesus' name."

Manorma jumped up, ran to her husband, and with her arms around him, said, "Yes, Lord! This is from both of us, not just from him."

They began to laugh and cry together, experiencing a holy presence such as they had never before known. An hour later they joined the group on the lawn, unaware that their faces glowed.

Mahendra watched them closely. "Zep," he finally said, "what are you hiding? You look like you've struck gold."

"Yeah, I guess that's right," his friend answered. "We'll tell you sometime." But Captain Sydney Michael's arrival kept Mahendra from pressing the issue.

Pansy's father looked very much the sea captain in his white immaculate uniform, bowed legs suggesting many a deck, and much climbing of masts. His leathery skin and greying hair reminded one of sea and sky. His stories regaled them with hearty laughter.

Mahendra finally voiced his curiosity again. "Zep," he said, "what gold did you find?"

"Tell them, love," Vijay said turning to Manorma.

She began shyly, "You all know me...how the Lord has brought me through deep waters in the last three years. My husband and I just went through another such low—when we walked into our bedroom I was hit by depression. And Vijay took victory over it. That's all, except to say that the Lord moved in like never before. We're glad."

"You cleansed the room, son?" Kushwant asked.

"Yes, Dad, like you did Mom's room. Thanks for showing me how. It's a valuable lesson."

A servant appeared, saying, "Mr. Kushwant Singh? A telephone call for you, sir. Just follow me."

When he returned he said, "Phulmoni. They're with friends near Cannaught Circle, and we've arranged to meet them at Kwality Restaurant tomorrow noon at one o'clock. Any dissenters?"

Susheela murmured, "Phulmoni...I wonder whether she'll accept me. I have a lot of changing to do, and mending."

Her husband patted her hand and said, "We'll vouch for you, my dear. She'll find all of us changed for the better."

"Bravo, Dad!" said Vijay.

But neither Phulmoni nor anyone else anticipated the new Susheela who met them with her husband the next noon. For the first time in decades she had visited the beauty parlor to have her long grey hair washed and set in an attractive hairstyle that accentuated her queenliness. "Mother!" Phulmoni gasped. "You're simply beautiful. I'm so proud of you!" Mother and daughter sat together both at the luncheon and that evening during the investiture that took place at Rashtrapati Bhawan, the president's palace.

The latter was a grand affair, attended only by invitation. The Michaels and Singhs sat together as family. To Manorma, the evening passed as in a daze, with speeches, medals, and music leading up to that one climactic moment when her Vijay's name was called. She listened, amazed, at the citations for bravery, sixteen in all, that related his exploits piloting an unarmed spotter plane over enemy lines, flying low to get pictures. Special mention of his finding a cache of guns and ammunition, singlehanded, in Hidden Valley in Burma brought forth thunderous applause. Manorma watched her husband receive the *Vir Chakra* medal for outstanding courage, along with the raise to the rank of Colonel. Her heart felt it would burst with pride, and turning to the others—his parents, sister, and friends—she found her own feelings mirrored in their faces.

That night, alone in their bedroom, Vijay led her to the settee and said, "Let's talk awhile and pray. I must tell you something."

"What, Vijay? I thought it perfect! A wonderful day!"

"True, Mano. But all that hoopla is merely cake. I want to tell you about the icing."

He threw some fresh chips on top of the charred wood to bolster the smoldering fire, then leaned over to blow new life into them. Straightening, he said, "Darling, when I heard my name it was as though the Lord Jesus Christ called me forth from all others, and I wondered what my eternal record holds."

He paused. Manorma waited quietly until he said, "I'm proud to be an Indian in the service of my country, but tonight I heard a higher calling. The Lord wants me to work for him."

She clasped her hands together, reading the intense desire for understanding in Vijay's outstretched hands and dark burning eyes. She murmured, "What kind of work?"

"Darling, I don't know, but I'm sure the Lord will tell me. Maybe in the military, or perhaps he'll ask me to leave the army and study for Christian ministry."

"Hmmm...no steady income...and the baby's coming?"

"It's all or nothing, gal. Pray about it, Mano. In fact," and he pushed her back to look into her face, then chuckling said, "I'll bet you know already."

She giggled, hiding her face against his shoulder. "Couldn't fool you, could I?" she murmured. Then looking into his shining eyes she whispered, "I've been praying for this!"

# 7

# Uncle Singh's stranger

The night before the Republic Day Parade, Kushwant Singh stood tall and dignified in the midst of his extended family gathered in Uncle Syd's living room. Already the acknowledged head of the clan by common consent, the lawyer looked around, saying, "Someone's missing?"

Chatter and laughter subsided. Pansy asked her father, "Dad, where's Lionel? He ate with us."

Captain Michael chuckled as he sat in his favorite chair in the corner, with lampstand, sidetable and magazines at hand. He said, "Top secret. He has a prior engagement."

"Mavis?"

"Yes, why?"

Seated on the divan beside Mahendra, Pansy clapped her hands and said, "Oh, family, I'm so happy! I must tell you, secret or no. Isn't that what families are for?"

"Go ahead, lass," the captain said with a nod. "Uncle Singh can wait several minutes. Right?"

The lawyer sat, nodding, and Pansy continued, "My brother's been chasing a non-Christian gal, thinking he was in love with her. Dad and I didn't like it."

"So that's off?" Manorma asked. "When I lived with you he was hot after Usha."

"Like many other suitors, Mano. Sometimes I could hardly stand it because I don't trust her. She's too slick." She drew a deep breath, then added, "Well, Dad and I kept praying it would stop. Finally we took victory over it in Jesus' name, and now Lionel is coming to church with us, and he's dating a nice Christian girl. Oh, I'm so glad!"

Manorma's eyes glowed. Susheela pressed her husband's hand and murmured, "They found out Lord Jesus has power?"

"Yes," the lawyer said. "Effective prayer comes from following the rules."

"Ah," Uncle Syd spoke up, "now we're ready for our prayer, Uncle Singh."

Kushwant Singh stood, much as a family priest would have done. Lifting his hands, he said, "Lord God, the Almighty One, we come corporately to you to praise you for who you are, and we thank you specially for the great deliverance you have given Lionel. Tonight we pray your abundant blessing on him, that he shall follow you wholly, and live for you fully."

He paused, then continued, "Lord God, our heavenly Father, you understand my heart. As we approach Vijay's moment of recognition at the Republic Day Parade, as his earthly father I ask for more than mere personal pride. Could all of us enfold one that is needy? Perhaps lonely and afraid? We have experienced your divine comfort in our hearts, and we long to share that with another. Sovereign Lord God, send us someone who needs us. I thank you in Jesus' victorious name. Amen."

Pansy pressed Mahendra's hand and whispered, "Does that mean we look for a stranger?"

"Probably."

Vijay said, "I wish I could stay with you, but I'll be on duty until evening."

"We'll share with you, Zep," Mahendra said. "In any case, you're the reason for it all," he concluded with a grin.

"Isn't he, though?" said Pansy with her infectious chuckle, to which everyone laughed.

Next morning at the YMCA Tourist Hostel on Jai Singh Road, in the heart of New Delhi, Terry Pennell, newly arrived from Australia, turned over in bed and wondered why that alarm had wakened him so early. Then he recalled his surroundings—he was in India's capital city and this was January 26, the day of the spectacular Republic Day Parade.

The newcomer jumped up and showered quickly. Dressed in his grey jeans, long black tunic, and a heavy grey woolen shawl thrown casually around broad shoulders, with sandals for his feet,

Terry felt ready to take on Ashrams and shrines in the Himalayas. But first, for nostalgia's sake, he'd go to the parade.

He pulled his shoulder length fair hair back with a rubber band, even while remembering parades he had seen here as a boy.

Known to Australian fans as a famous soccer player, Terry hoped he could burrow into India's millions for awhile, not for display, but to find an answer to inner turmoil. He feared being recognized; perhaps his newly grown beard, long hair, and mustache would help him avoid detection. Moreover, he hadn't alerted any former friends. After all, ten years' absence is a long time, he mused, and he was a different person today than when he left India with his missionary parents as a ruddy-faced sixteen-year-old.

Terry ran downstairs, gulped a quick cup of coffee in the restaurant and asked for a donut.

"Sorry, sir, we don't have any. We can give you French toast or hot *samosas*, and, of course, we have eggs."

"Can't wait for eggs. Bring me whatever is ready."

Over the soggy pieces of toast, the young Australian swore under his breath. The tea was so strong it would stand up! Face it, he told himself, and take what you get. It's probably a million times better than what you'll find when you're trekking from one Ashram to another.

Terry Pennell sighed. If only Suzy was here, life would be perfect. Or would it? India being India, would she fit?

Bother! Suzy wasn't here! Three months ago she had jilted him for his close friend, Mac Dougal. Why? Because Mac took the soccer honors while he recuperated from an injury.

Fair enough...and best to find out what made the gal tick before their wedding day. But why couldn't he get her saucy face out of his mind? Those flashing eyes taunted him, her vigor, her ringing laugh.

On going to the foyer, Terrence Pennell informed the desk clerk he'd return by evening, and went outside to see what transportation was available. "Nothing but taxis, sir," a burly Sikh informed him in impeccable English.

"*Tab taxi bulaiyiae, bhai Ji*" (then please call a taxi, brother), he said in clear Hindi and smiled slightly to see the immediate reaction.

"Yes, yes, sir," the Sikh said, and added, "You speak our language very well. You're been here before?"

"Born here...attended school in Nainital."

"Ah, that's why you love our country. Have a good day, sir."

The Sikh's comment became a recurring refrain, singing itself in a minor jangling key as Terry traveled to the parade route with four other passengers. "That's why you love our country." Had love for India drawn him back? Perhaps the Sikh was right, perhaps not. Did it matter?

Nothing mattered! Amazing...this jostling, pushing, shoving, these masses of people. Had he ever really known this vast land with its glamor and mystique, its blatant search for material benefits on one hand, and soul peace on the other? Somehow, today he felt like a lost child searching for his mother.

Terry sighed, then pushed and shoved as did the others to find a good seat close to the parade route. By showing his tourist pass he finally reached a section reserved for dignitaries and foreign guests, just a block from the president's reviewing stand. Terrence Pennell plopped down in the one available seat at the end of the front row. Beside him sat an Indian couple, clean cut, the man in military uniform. Terry barely glanced at them, not until the girl's infectious laugh pierced him through. She sounded like Suzy!

"There, there. See, Squirt?" she cried, pointing to someone she recognized.

Terry drew a long breath, then gazed unashamedly at her. Mischievous eyes must accompany such a laugh. Yes, he was right. But her olive skin, onyx-colored hair, shoulder length instead of short, combined with her bright orange punjabi outfit with green scarf marked her distinctly Indian. No, this wasn't Suzy.

He slumped in his seat, hoping the young man at his side wouldn't receive the same treatment he had received from Suzy...nor, for that matter, from Marcia before Suzy came on the scene. His world had somehow turned sour.

But not for long, for his neighbor turned to him with a winsome smile and asked, "You're from the States or Canada?"

"Australia, now...but born in India."

"Hmmm, that's interesting, friend." The soldier, dressed in a lieutenant's uniform, extended his hand and said, "Welcome back. I'm Mahendra Lall from Mussoorie, and my fiancée, here, is Pansy Michael from Delhi. And you?"

"Terrence Pennell, better known as Terry," he mumbled.

His neighbor sat up straight, looked at him, then with a grin, said, "Not *the* Terrence Pennell, famous soccer player?"

Terry swore under his breath, then said glumly, "I come to India to get away from it all, and run into a guy who knows my past! How come?"

Mahendra chuckled and said, "Not really, but I do happen to be a soccer fan. I've followed everything I could find about you since your Nainital days. I thought your face looked familiar, but the beard and mustache sort of threw me."

"Part of my pilgrim endeavor," the Australian said. He sat up to examine his new friend and remarked, "I didn't think my record worth following."

"Rather, man! You should be in soccer! How long have you been out? Hopefully this pilgrim thing is just a digression?"

"Don't know...have to sort out a lot...." Terry drew a long breath, then sank back in his seat in an effort to end the conversation. But the lieutenant kept up a running commentary, and within five minutes Terry volunteered, "Strange—this meeting you right away. Mind if I call you Squirt?"

"Please."

"Sort of unusual nickname for an officer."

His companion chuckled and said, "Got it long before becoming a spotter plane pilot in the Artillery. My buddy, Zep, gave it to me when I nicknamed him Zeppelin over fifteen years ago. You will see Zep riding on an elephant as one of today's national heroes."

"By all the gods! What did he do?"

"Served with me on the border, flying spotter planes under impossible conditions—treacherous weather, dangerous missions, and more...much more."

"Like?" Terry asked idly, engrossed in watching wiggling children sitting on rugs at the line of march. As Prime Minister Indira Gandhi approached, they shouted in chorus.

Squirt answered, "Oh, the big personal favor Zep did was to pray me back to health from a virulent attack of cerebral malaria."

Terry sat up straight. "What? What? I'm sorry. I was watching the kids."

His companion chuckled and said, "My buddy Zep did me a great big personal favor when he prayed me back to health. I was dying from cerebral malaria."

Was this man telling the truth? Terry thought cerebral malaria to be fatal. What power did this Zep possess? As though reading his mind, Squirt grinned and said, "Yeah, you're wondering, aren't you? That's the way I felt about it, too, being a Hindu."

Isn't he a Hindu now? If, not, then what?

Squirt continued, "Well, I came on home leave, but Zep stayed on to get the honors, and today I'm celebrating with him."

"You mean you don't mind his walking away with everything?"

"Great day, no! He's my buddy."

Pansy interrupted the conversation with an urgent, "Squirt! See? They're coming!"

With the advent of the first military contingent, all further conversation focused on the immediate—India's military might on parade. The line of march would move down Rajpath, Terry learned. It would go to India Gate, then turn westward into the heart of New Delhi. Squirt told him it would end in front of the historic Red Fort, capital of the famous Moghul Empire of three centuries ago. He said the entire route covered at least five miles, with the tribal dancers and children's divisions marching the first mile only.

Pansy, the most effervescent of Terry's neighbors, amused him with her comments, but he soon learned that the entire Singh and Michael families were engrossed in the parade for one major reason—to see their Zep riding on the elephant. Magnificent floats passed, interspersed by Army, Navy and Air Force bands. Military weapons were followed by the Camel Corps, the elite Presidential Guard, the famous Gurkha regiments (heroes of Terry's boyhood) and infantry wearing gaudy uniforms reminiscent of the Moghul Empire extravaganzas.

"Here they come!" the exuberant girl exclaimed. "The elephants!" She leaned far forward and cried, "Toby, Toby!" The zoo ranger leading a baby elephant turned and smiled. "He attends our church," the girl told Squirt and Terrence Pennell, and the latter thought, so she's a Christian.

Now Kushwant Singh and his daughter, Phulmoni, had cameras flashing, taking pictures of Vijay, their handsome and assured hero. He rode on the first of two magnificent beasts that bore the six national heroes. Two smaller elephants carried selected honor students, children who had won first place in the land.

"He's facing us!" Squirt gasped. "See? The one on this side." Upon which Mahendra Lall stood at attention and saluted the man waving from his seat on the richly-decorated howdah. In that proud moment Terrence Pennell glimpsed the power and strength of the family system, and he felt bereaved, lost and alone. Squirt and Zep sharing the glory, even as they had shared numberless experiences during the past fifteen years; Zep's wife and mother, quietly wiping tears; his distinguished father, vivacious sister and her family, their cameras flashing, ensuring future memories.

His hurt intensified and the glamor of the parade lessened as Terry sank into depression. He wished he had never come. Of course this might be jet-lag, he mused, but really, he'd have done better to stay home and sleep.

Only at the grand finale did Terry rise above his thoughts to enter somewhat into the excitement of the crowds as wave after wave of fighter planes zoomed overhead in V formation, belching out orange, white and green—the colors of the flag. They flew high overhead, then suddenly dived toward the reviewing stand, only to climb abruptly skyward in an amazing display of dexterity and control. The watching throngs gasped! Simultaneously, orange, white and green balloons rose skyward from near the Secretariat, announcing the triumphant end of yet another Republic Day Parade.

Terrence thought he'd slip out, but the immediate throngs that filled the road made him stand aside. He felt Squirt's hand on his shoulder and heard him say, "Come with us, friend, for a picnic lunch. We'll be eating on the grass behind the bleachers."

Captain Michael strode over and reiterated the invitation, asking, "Are there others with you?"

"No, sir. I'm alone." Terrence Pennell thought it an understatement.

"Then you *must* stay," the Captain boomed. "You are our guest, sir."

"My pleasure," the Australian said with a slight bow and a wry smile.

That evening in his sparsely furnished room at the Tourist Hostel Terrence Pennell tried to express his feelings, the churning within, the thoughts that raced through his mind.

He sat at the small table and wrote in his journal: "I'm torn! Fragmented! Coming apart. I don't know where I'm going, only that I'm running away. My past haunts me—Marcia, so naive, tender, and beautiful, enamored by that Indian guru! My disillusionment with our marriage, and my consequent wrong choices.... Then Suzy.

"O my God! Why did Mom and Dad die in that plane crash? Why? Leaving India was bad enough...to be left an alien in a foreign land...devastating!"

Terrence Pennell pushed his notebook aside and wept—something novel, like much-needed rain breaking up fallow ground. The nostalgia of this day coupled with black, dancing eyes and exhilarating laugh that pierced his thirsty soul—these, and much more broke the resistance Terry had built between himself and a harsh, uncaring world.

At last he began to write again: "I'm afraid to say luck placed me in the heart of an unusually beautiful Indian family. Providence is more accurate. I met two Indian girls—Pansy, Mahendra Lall's fiancée, and her cousin, Manorma, sweet-faced and madonna-like, wife of Vijay Kumar Singh. The two couples are extremely close, with the two men answering to Squirt and Zep. Squirt loves soccer. He extended me friendship when I felt like boxing him, but somehow he managed to persist. Then I found a treasure chest of family harmony that scintillates and glows. I wish I had met these people earlier. Perhaps my life would have been different.

"In a way, the Singhs remind me of my parents—integrated and purposeful. Yet they're Indians, *not* missionaries! Great God in heaven, are you there? Why did you allow me to walk such a rocky path? What have I to show? Quarrels...hangovers...a divorce that still galls...Suzy....

"Great God! Why do you torture me?"

## 8

# A different dimension

Friday, the day after the Republic Day Parade, Terrence Pennell showered and dressed early, expecting to leave town for Hardwar, a famous pilgrimage spot at the foot of the Himalaya mountains. When the phone rang, he wondered who would find him here. "Yes?" he said. "This is Terry Pennell."

"Hello, man. This is Squirt."

"Squirt! What a surprise! How did you get my number?"

"Easy, friend. I just called the central desk and asked to speak to you. Look, man! We want you to move in with us over the weekend. We're planning lots of interesting things, and Pansy's Dad insists you're part of the family. How about it? When can Pansy and I pick you up?"

"Oh...very kind of you...but I thought I'd head for the Himalayas today."

"Terry, no problem. Save it for next week. Those mountains won't go anywhere."

He heard Mahendra Lall chuckle and responded, "You've got me there, lieutenant. I guess you're right."

"Sure! Come on over, meet Zep and all of us in our home setting. Will nine o'clock be all right?"

"Man! That's super! I'll meet you with my gear in the lobby."

For five beautiful days the lonely Australian sponged in everything—listening carefully, assimilating much. He found special rapport with Lionel, Pansy's brother, a shy young man who had lived in Penang all his life and now found the change to this Indian city confusing.

Lionel, about five feet ten inches tall, worked for an export firm and loved motorcycle riding. Terry, of the same physique, often found himself riding pillion with Lionel, thus allowing the other couples to gravitate together.

When the Australian first met Squirt's buddy Vijay, he tried being formal and said, "Glad to meet you, Colonel. Congratulations on your receiving the *Vir Chakra* medal."

The newly-acclaimed hero laughed. Placing his hand on Terry's shoulder he said, "Friend, just call me Zep. I'll come running."

Five days of watching Zep assured him this wasn't a stance, rather an indication of true inner humility, something Terrence Pennell had found in limited quantities until now.

In fact, both couples impacted the newcomer. Take Squirt's inner pain, the rejection by his personal family, something that came out incidentally. That must hurt, Terry mused. Yet here he was, seemingly joyful and at peace. He must have found a place in this extended family already, by all appearances. And then, Pansy. Terry loved her laugh, but there the initial likeness to Suzy ended. This vibrant girl lived in terms of others; Suzy for herself. Terry cast his vote for Pansy!

He wrote in his journal: "An interesting family, this. They're neatly divided—elders, two couples, and Lionel and me (singles) tagging on behind. But we're not fragmented! Somehow we each belong to the whole. Each strengthens the other. I find security, the joy of interaction, open communication with one another and with the God they worship. I wish I could stay."

Manorma and Vijay also considered these days precious, like holding fragile treasure. Proud of her husband, she thrilled to both the Investiture and Republic Day Parade, albeit sensing an aloneness that cut deeply. Mama had Papa, and Pansy her Mahendra. Vijay? Where would he be when she most needed him? Both Vijay and Manorma wondered.

Festivities interspersed with family times climaxed with their attending the famed "Beating Retreat" on Monday evening. From prime seats overlooking Vijay Chowk, normally a busy intersection now converted to center stage, Uncle Syd's enlarged family prepared to assimilate this extravaganza of music, drama, and color.

In the late afternoon the elite camel corps stood silhouetted on the ramparts of the Secretariat buildings. The president's entourage arrived. A thousand spectators hushed as martial music sounded in the distance. Soon, smartly uniformed Army, Navy, and Air Force bands arrived to present an hour of superb ethnic and martial melodies. The afternoon sun gently tinted the pink limestone buildings to coral and gold; the turrets provided an oriental touch, a reminder of India's Moghul past.

Now the crowd awaited their favorites: the lullaby from North East India, the drum beats, and finally, Gandhi's favorite hymn, "Abide with Me."

Manorma scanned her program. She glanced at her husband. Sensitive to her needs, he clasped her hand and smiled. The stalwart Sikh conductor stepped aside as a slighter man mounted the podium. "He's Christian, darling," Vijay whispered. "He traditionally directs when Gandhi Ji's hymn is played."

From the turrets two bugles began the plaintive melody while the massed bands below provided muted harmony. Manorma struggled with tears. She had sung it so often: "The darkness deepens; Lord, with me abide." Vijay's next appointment, another separation, the pending birth of their first child—all this and more flashed through her mind. The song's prayer seemed made for her.

Then came taps, and the withdrawal of the troops up Rajpath, back to the presidential palace grounds from which they had come. But nobody left. In the expectant hush Manorma, too, waited for the climactic turning of darkness into a fairyland with thousands of lights outlining every building, dome, and turret.

"Whew!" Vijay whistled softly, adding to the audible gasp from a thousand throats.

That night, while her husband slept, Manorma reviewed the week that had passed. She dreaded tomorrow. What would her husband's appointment reveal? Would he be a thousand miles away when the baby arrived in mid-June? She finally fell asleep around four in the morning.

Vijay pulled the curtains when he arose and said, "Stay in, Mano. You deserve a good rest. I'll have breakfast and lunch sent in."

She murmured, "Thanks," glad that her husband understood her need.

By four that afternoon a refreshed Manorma rose to bathe and dress for tea. A half-hour later Vijay rushed in, calling, "Mano, Mano, darling! Good news!"

His joyous tone lifted her spirits, and she answered from the dressing room, "Coming. I'll be right there."

"You look smashing," he commented as she joined him on the settee. "I always did like that pink *saree*."

She giggled, saying, "They're wonderful, much more concealing than punjabi outfits. For obvious reasons I'll be using them from now on."

"You look all right to me, love. Now," he took her hand and said, "I want you to know first."

"You look flushed. How about a cold drink?"

"Sure, I'll get it." Vijay jumped up, poured two glasses of ice water from the thermos on the side table, then said, "Now, as I wanted to say, my next posting is Dehra Dun."

Her look of amazement made him chuckle. "You don't believe me, Mano? Well, headquarters has decreed that I teach at the Officers' Military Academy. How do you like the new prof?" he asked, handing her the water.

She took it, placed it on a coaster in front of her, then jumped up. Throwing her arms around her husband she said, "I can't believe it, Vijay! Only twenty-five miles from home? Why, we can stay in Happy Valley!"

"Yes, darling, that's as I see it. We have the option of married quarters, a home to ourselves." He grinned and added, "That looks attractive, but..."

"Someday, Vijay, but right now we shouldn't leave Mama. She's so new in her faith. Really, I should spend more time with her."

He released her, and as they drank, he said, "I agree. Mom wondered whether we should consult the horoscope before setting our leaving date for Delhi. More changes must come in this family."

"But Mama's already changed a great deal. Remember, Vijay, she lived in terms of pundits, temples and horoscopes until she met Jesus."

He drew a deep breath, then said, "Right, darling. But Dad! Look at the way he's beginning to lead the clan. That's thrilling!"

Manorma clasped her hands together, and laughed. "Dehra Dun? I can't believe it, Vijay—regular work hours, open evenings to spend with your wife and baby? Oh, darling! Dehra Dun? Who could ask for more?"

"You've been worrying?" He tilted her face back.

"I shouldn't, I know," she confessed, "but I did. Particularly last night. I dread another long separation, with you a thousand miles away...especially when the baby comes."

"Silly girl. You forgot your life's verse?"

"I know. I forget so soon."

"But, Mano, you're the one who taught me to trust."

"I know," she concluded with a sigh. He kissed her, then said, "Let's find Squirt and Pansy. By the way, we had a great talk together this morning. Darling, all sorts of things are brewing."

"Like?" They walked out the French doors into the garden.

"Persecution...."

"Yes, I know—his father. Papa says Sukhdev Lall has been trying to marry Mahendra off to Kailash Rana's daughter!"

"Really? But how does Dad know?"

"Didn't he tell you? He went to the bank the day before we left and Mr. Rana was in a talkative mood. So Papa encouraged him. It seems Squirt's father had led him to believe that the arrangement was agreeable, but suddenly fell through. Mr. Rana said Mr. Lall acted almost insultingly that morning, and said he's going to contact the Arya Samaj...that it's this Christian bug that's bit his son."

Vijay looked at his wife, amazed. "Dad told you all this?"

"Yes, Vijay, before you came back from the Republic Day Parade. The others had drifted off, and Mama was tired from her long outing, so Papa and I sat on the verandah in the quiet evening air and he shared it with me. We prayed about it, too."

"Hmmm...so you had a lot to think about last night, not just my next posting."

She smiled and nodded.

They had walked past the rose garden, onto the grassy lawns adjoining the tennis court where tables and chairs were set for afternoon tea. "Come, Vijay, let's sit," Mano suggested. "Tell me Squirt's version. He told us he's left home, that he's rented a room in Claremont Cottage, near Mullingar Hotel. That will be nice, won't it?"

"It gives him a base, a place to put his things."

"Isn't he going to stay?"

"He's decided to enroll for a semester at Dehra Dun Bible College, Mano."

"You don't say! How long has he been thinking of this?"

"Since his Dad began putting on pressure."

"Why just a semester?"

"He says he wants to prepare for baptism."

"Well, that's valid. When does he start?"

"Beginning of March."

"And you, Vijay?"

"About the same, perhaps the last week of February." He began to chuckle, then said, "Might as well let you in on it."

"What? You're hiding something?"

The breeze rustled the leaves, and the fountain gurgled in the gardens nearby. Vijay shifted, then said with a grin, "We have a dream, Squirt and I. We'd like to trek again for several weeks before getting tied down. Do you mind?"

Manorma's laugh lilted forth. "Zep, I might have known. You're getting itchy feet."

He chuckled, then said, "But not for long, love. I'm a family man, you know."

His new assignment to the prestigious Military Academy pleased everyone, particularly his mother. "You'll stay at home, son?" she asked as the group lingered in the garden after tea.

"Sure, Mom! I've been hankering for a motorcycle, and now I have reason to buy one. Later on, perhaps, if Mano and I so desire, we can take advantage of the married quarters detailed for officers, but as I see it now, I'd like to stay at home."

Her eyes lit up. "Oh, I'm so glad," she murmured.

Kushwant laid his hand on hers and said, "See, Susheela? I told you the Lord would take care of us."

Mahendra spoke up. "Pansy and I want to make an official announcement." He glanced her direction, and she blushed. "We have set July 20th as our wedding date."

"Super!"

"Bravo!"

"Do we get to come? Where will it be?"

"Congratulations!"

In the general hubbub that erupted with much laughter, the prospective bride and groom explained details. "Of course you must come," Pansy said. "Hopefully baby Singh will have arrived. That's a *must*, since we want Zep and Mano to stand up with us. No dillydallying around, Mano!"

Mahendra continued, "As to where...likely in Delhi, here at Centenary Church."

"Why not sooner, rather than later?" Manorma inquired.

"Better one thing at a time," he said with his quiet smile. "I'm enrolling for a term at Dehra Dun Bible College."

"You're leaving the military?" Pansy's father asked.

"Yes, sir. I need structured Bible study right now for two reasons.

"Oh?" Captain Michael stroked his Van Dyke beard thoughtfully.

"My first reason is to prepare for baptism. In our culture, as you know, people consider me a Hindu until I take baptism. I have gone independent from home now, and I am making some big choices."

"Like what?" Susheela asked.

"Well, Auntie, my parents were trying to force me into a Hindu marriage. My father gave me the ultimatum to either agree, or leave. So I've left."

Susheela Singh's eyes filled with tears, and her voice trembled as she said, "That's hard."

"You understand, don't you?" Mahendra paused, then added, "My second reason for going to Bible College is closely linked to the first—I want to learn how to lead others to Christ."

"And would you believe it?" Vijay spoke up. "Already he's witnessing. I believe God has given him a gift for it."

"Hmmm..." Captain Michael said thoughtfully as he stroked his beard. Kushwant Singh encouraged him with a smile.

Two hours later, when a brand new Terrence Pennell followed by a grinning Lionel entered the dining room, Manorma gasped, "Zep, look!"

Pansy and Squirt cheered, and the Australian bowed, "Like it?" he asked.

He stood before them dressed in a brown safari suit, with his beard and mustache nicely trimmed, his hair short, his sandals covering brown socks.

"He's just my size, Dad," Lionel said eagerly. "Wait until you see him with my brown leather jacket, goggles, and helmet. He's neat! And what's more, tomorrow morning we're starting out for Hardwar and Rishikesh on my motorcycle."

The family barely settled long enough for Uncle Syd to ask the blessing over the meal. How had Lionel worked this transformation? Including a haircut? In such short time? "It's a miracle!" said Pansy.

Her brother's natural shyness seemed to have evaporated. Eyes alight, he explained, "You see, Dad, instead of sitting at home for the rest of the week, I decided to take Terry, and we'd do it together."

"Why, of course, son. For how long?"

"I'll be back Monday night, ready for work on Tuesday. That gives us several days and I can help Terry get the hang of the place, even though I can't keep on with him."

"Very good."

Squirt asked, "How's it feel to be in civilian clothes, Terry?"

"You should know, lieutenant," the Australian said with a grin. "Very comfortable, in fact, sort of like laying a disguise aside and being myself." He helped himself liberally to rice and chicken curry and added, "Five days with this family has turned me right side up. When I came, Captain Michael, I was in a bad dream, wondering about a million things. But all of you have taught me so much...things I needed to know. Thank you."

"Our pleasure, young man," the Captain said.

Kushwant Singh's voice boomed forth, "After your little jaunt to Hardwar and Rishikesh, why not come on up to Mussoorie and Happy Valley? We always have room for one more."

"Thank you, Mr. Singh. I appreciate your invitation."

"We can do it, Uncle!" Lionel exclaimed, then said grinning, "Tomorrow's travel, Thursday and Friday in Hardwar and Rishikesh, and Saturday on to Mussoorie. Sure, Terry, how about it?"

Before Terry could answer, Vijay said, "Great! That's good! We'll be looking for both of you."

Terry, not knowing what to say, said nothing. But Susheela wheeled her chair on impulse close to his as the others began to scatter. She had much to share about pilgrimages in general and the pitfalls awaiting unwary foreigners in particular. The young man felt grateful, but sure that he could handle any eventuality, Terry merely thanked the kind lady and decided to let each day bring its own adventure.

# 9

# Gur Bachan's news

In Happy Valley Kailu's mother, Maya Bahadur, sat at her favorite window overlooking the Singh residence. Her knitting in hand, her chair far enough back to escape detection, she loved to spend her off hours watching people, particularly the Singhs. When her son came from school he aided her thirst for news by eavesdropping around doors and windows, particularly after dark. But today had been quiet.

On this Tuesday afternoon Maya, the little Nepalese lady, looked in vain for some sign of Rani or Hazari Lal. Where had everyone gone? The family had left in the morning. Ah, yes, she thought with a sigh, when the cat's away the mice will play.

But she suddenly sat up with a start. A rickshaw was turning into her gate! Company? Now? She watched, and soon recognized Mrs. Ram Gupta, wife of the wealthy cloth merchant in Mussoorie Bazaar. What brought her here? At least two years had passed since Maya had seen the lady at the Singh's residence. It was February, she recalled, when Mrs. Singh and two friends lunched together in the garden. Two days later the young Mrs. Singh went to Delhi to live. Now, why was Mrs. Gupta coming to the Bahadurs, instead of to the Singh residence?

From her vantage point Maya watched the voluminous lady clamber down from her rickshaw, casting inquisitive glances at the big house on the other side of the oleander bushes. The stiff breeze blew the visitor's hair awry, and Maya noted she looked both cold and perturbed. Maya smiled. Whatever had brought her, Tej Bahadur's wife decided to listen rather than talk. She would hand out treasures for a price. The wife of the wealthy Ram Gupta didn't come to this humble cottage every day!

She waited until she heard the guest calling at the side door, "Anybody home?"

Saying, "Who is it?" Maya opened the door slightly to peer out.

"It's me, Mrs. Ram Gupta."

The little Nepali lady threw the door wide open. With a smile and bow she said, "I am honored. Please come into our humble house. You visited the Singhs quite often, but it's been some time now, hasn't it? I trust you're well?"

"Humph," her guest grunted with a toss of her head. "Nothing wrong with me. I want to know what's wrong with Susheela Singh."

"Oh? Ah...yes...please sit, and we'll have tea. It will be ready in a moment." She motioned to her chair by the window. Leaving the lady to her thoughts, Kailu's mother swiftly went to the kitchen where her teenage daughter, Shanti, was preparing vegetables for tonight's curry. "Leave that, and make tea and spinach *pakoras* immediately. That important Mrs. Gupta has come...only the gods know why...and listen...."

"Yes, Ma?" The willowy girl with braids down her back turned to look at her mother.

"Don't you 'Ma' me. Remember now, you're the cook. That lady probably has a houseful of servants. Keep your mouth shut. We'll make a poor enough showing at the best."

Shanti shrugged. Then, washing her hands, she twisted her braids into a knot at the nape of her neck and straightened her dark blue punjabi outfit.

"That's better," Maya said with a nod. "Now, use the best dishes. Hurry! I'll entertain the guest. She's probably taking inventory to see what we don't have."

She bustled into the dining room and pulled a rocking chair close to the padded wicker one in which her guest sat. "You have children?" she began, taking up her knitting.

"Two grown sons, both married." Maya heard the pride in Leela Gupta's voice.

"Grandchildren?" she asked.

"Three from the elder son. And you?"

"Well," the little woman said, drawing a deep breath, "we're not that far along, but our only son, Kailu, is somewhat a man-about-town already, despite his being only ten years old."

"Humph, my son mentioned him. Did you know the school has opened a Kailu Klub? That's spelt with a 'K' my son tells me. He's the math teacher, and he says your boy is quite a hero. Now," and Leela lowered her voice persuasively, "tell me how he learned the news about the Singh family."

Maya rocked back and forth for a little, thinking and knitting. She looked up to say mildly, "Nothing to it, Mrs. Gupta. We heard the lady wailing in the night. Sounds carry far, you know. Well, I sent Kailu over to see if we could help, but by the time he arrived, Mr. Singh and his son were in command. So Kailu came back. That's all."

"Humph! Then why all this talk about Lakshmi?"

"Probably a nightmare at the worst, or a bad dream."

Leela leaned forward and asked, "What do you know about Susheela? Every time I phone she has some reason—or shall I say excuse—for not seeing me. I want to know what's going on! Is that hussy still there? I heard she returned."

"Hussy?"

"Her daughter-in-law! Didn't you know she's a Christian?"

The little Nepali lady looked up and said, "I heard some rumors but never believed them. The girl has a sweet face. She certainly seems devoted to her mother-in-law."

"How do you know?"

"Well...after she returned from hospital, she and Mrs. Singh often spent time together in the garden. I couldn't help but see them while sitting where you're now sitting."

"Ah, more than hearsay? Not just Kailu, I take it."

Maya felt distressed but said nothing. Take it easy, her better judgment warned. Don't get irritated. Maybe the lady will tell why she came.

Her daughter appeared in the doorway carrying a tray filled with fresh *pakoras*, dishes, and a pot of hot tea. She set it carefully on the table while her mother said quickly, "Thank you, Shanti. I'll take care of everything."

"Yes, Madame." The girl turned. Maya rose and began serving her guest, thankful for this diversion from what might have become an uncomfortable situation.

But Leela Gupta would not be deferred. As she sipped her tea she said, "I understand that the Christian star still shines from their verandah at night. Is this true?"

"You can see for yourself it's still there. In fact, I rather like it...so cheerful."

"You do? Are you also converting to Christianity? You'd better watch out, my dear Mrs. Bahadur. Don't you know that that girl is influencing all of them? Take it from me, there's more going on over there than meets the eye."

"Like what?" Maya plied her guest with more *pakoras*.

"Oh," Leela Gupta added, "that's what I'd like to know."

Ah, thought Maya, and that's why you came. With a smile she suggested, "Why not stop over and see Mrs. Singh?"

Her guest peered out, then remarked, "Doesn't seem to be anyone there...very quiet."

"They're probably inside."

"Humph. Yes, of course. Thanks, my dear, for the tea.

After Mrs. Gupta left, the little Nepali woman wondered whether she had offended her. But why should she divulge information when the Singhs had always treated her kindly? Especially that young Mrs. Singh. Since her husband had returned from the Burma border the two of them often walked to the park in the evening, and like as not, the girl would wave to her as she sat on the front verandah and knitted. Maya reflected that with a face like hers, she couldn't be all that bad.

Maya smiled slightly as the rickshaw took Mrs. Gupta down the road and up the adjacent lane to the Singh's residence. She deserves what she gets, she reflected. Why should anyone be so nosy? Let her find out for herself that nobody is at home, that the entire family left this morning about eight o'clock by car. Where to? Maya wished she knew.

When Kailu returned from school his mother suggested he find out where the Singh family had gone. The boy threw his books down and said, "Sure, Ma! And, you know, we have a new club at school, and they've named it after me! That nice reporter from the *Mussoorie Weekly* came over and talked to us. Ma," and the boy picked up some *pakoras* and munched, saying, "you know, the man who came and talked with us after I went to Whispering Windows."

"What about him, son?"

"Well, he said he got his start carrying a pad and pencil every-where he went, and he thinks I'd make a good newspaper reporter." He drew a deep breath, then continued, "So we're to carry pads and pencils with us and jot down interesting things. See? Ma! They're calling it the Kailu Klub!"

"But it's not good to be so nosy, Kailu. It leads to gossip. That's dangerous. Son, you be careful."

He looked at her and grinned. He had already learned that ten-year-olds aren't supposed to mimic their parents. So why not prac-tice being grown-up? Much more exciting!

When Gur Bachan learned from the Kailu Klub the next day that the entire Singh family had gone to Delhi, he faced a big ques-tion. Had they fled from Lakshmi, as the boys shouted? Or did they have another reason? Gur Bachan felt it was related to the Repub-lic Day Parade, to be held, as usual, on January 26.

Therefore he rode to the capital the day before, and checked in to get a press card for his motorcycle, and an identification for himself as reporter for the *Mussoorie Weekly*. He hoped to provide the newspaper with a real scoop.

Gur Bachan joined other national and international media per-sonnel directly opposite the president's reviewing stand. Having stationed himself advantageously, he checked the parade pro-gram, marking it with his handy red pencil. Midway he stopped. There it was! "Vijay Kumar Singh, recipient of the *Vir Chakra* Medal."

His black eyes glistened. A wide grin creased his thin features as he inwardly shouted, Scoop! He'd always liked Vijay. Some-thing clean and different about him. Well, he had this coming to him, along with national recognition. If his hometown newspaper could help celebrate, it would be worth the hard ride down and back.

Bother! Now he'd have to beat it across Delhi to reach the Red Fort before the parade disbanded. He simply *must* capture Vijay dismounting, and get a personal interview. Then he'd hoof it back to Mussoorie to make this week's issue. Think what this would mean to the town!

Seldom had a news item stirred Mussoorie and surrounding area as did this one. Ram Gupta casually opened his copy to see an enlargement of Kushwant Singh's son, Vijay. A black caption read,

"Local Acclaimed National Hero." He reeled as though hit, then yelled, "Mohan! Is your mother there? Tell her to come immediately."

Leela Gupta hastily covered her hair with her grey shawl and hurried out of the kitchen to the front room where her husband perused the *Mussoorie Weekly*. "Yes, my lord?" she asked.

Ram's finger shook as he pointed and said, "Look here! What's all this nonsense about Lakshmi's being angry with the Singh family? Are you telling me? I say they've done something right!"

"I don't understand," she sputtered.

The wealthy cloth merchant slapped his knee, laughing, and said, "All that money I gave Lakshmi the other day—foolishly, woman! The Singhs don't bother, and see what happens? The lawyer's son becomes a national hero! Now, answer that."

Leela blinked rapidly, then murmured, "Perhaps the goddess doesn't pay all her debts at once, my lord. I think we'd better play safe and not doubt her abilities. The Singhs will find out...." She paused, then added firmly, "Let's wait and see before drawing conclusions."

Her husband closed the paper impatiently, threw it on the floor and said, "I don't have time to philosophize. I've got to open the shop. Have it your way, woman, but watch your temple offerings! We can't afford them!"

She picked up the papers carefully, then took them back to her bedroom for personal study.

In the bank office nearby, the president turned to his underling to say, "Mehta? Look here!"

The young man from Bombay obediently bent over the *Mussoorie Weekly* while his superior shouted, "Why did you dissuade me from asking Kushwant Singh to be one of our directors? We couldn't have done better."

Mehta stood, troubled at the outburst. Kailash Rana continued, "What with Mr. Singh's prestigious position in the Supreme Court and now with his son receiving national recognition, we simply *must* include him, somehow or other. Why...why...why did you dissuade me? You fool!"

Young Mehta began wringing his hands and stuttered, "S...S...Sorry, sir. I...I...I've come from Bombay...and I don't know the people here." He drew a long breath and thought, yes, that's it. I'm new here.

Grasping for anything that would place him in better light with his employer, he stood tall and said, "I admire your wisdom, sir. Lawyer Kushwant Singh is excellent. Nobody like him, but...but, sir? You've already filled the position?"

The heavy man glowered and muttered, "Don't you ever tell me again what to do. I'll give you one more chance, Mehta. Walk carefully, or you're out!"

"Yes, sir." The young man gulped with relief and resolved to stop by Lakshmi's temple with an extra gift for the priest. Perhaps one of these days the goddess of wealth would turn to look favorably upon him.

Over in Happy Valley Mahendra Lall's father sat in his inner sanctum, his chair pushed back, his feet on the edge of the coffee table. The telephone rang. He answered, "Hello...hello...yes? Who do you want? Sukhdev Lall? Yes? Yes...speaking."

"This is Ajit Kumar."

"Yes...yes...from the Arya Samaj office?"

"The same." The caller cleared his throat several times then continued, "We have noted your request, Mr. Lall, and we will take up the matter. But for the present...well...have you seen today's issue of the *Mussoorie Weekly*?"

"No, no, I haven't. What is it?"

"Take a look at the lead article on the front page, and you will understand why we are concerned about timing. We'd better wait for any outright action against Lawyer Kushwant Singh at this point. But we're keeping your request in mind."

"Oh? Is that so?" Sukhdev Lall slammed down the receiver, and stomped into his dining room. "Where's the *Mussoorie Weekly*?" he yelled.

A house servant came running. "Madame took it to her quarters, sir," he said.

"I want it! Right now!" the man thundered.

"Yes, sir, I'll bring it, sir."

"To my inner sanctum."

When Sukhdev saw the picture and caption, he understood. He threw the newspaper to the floor in rage. "I'd like to get my hands on that Singh family," he muttered, "and cut them down to size. They have no business spoiling my Mahendra!"

By contrast, a half-mile away at the Kushwant Singh residence, Hazari Lal, Rani, and the other servants expanded with pride on seeing the prize picture. Its incentive pushed them to fever pitch as they completed the task their employer had set.

By Friday the new master bedroom matched the creased magazine picture Hazari Lal carried in his pocket. "Beds made... sidetable with embroidered cover...blue flowers to match the blue and white curtains...potted palm by the window," he noted.

"It looks nice," Rani said nodding.

All day they scrubbed, cooked, and decorated. By the time the family arrived at four o'clock, a banner welcomed them saying, "Congratulations, young master!" Streamers crisscrossed the living room and balloons billowed on the verandah. The servants gave the Singhs a feast that evening that concluded with offering Vijay a gift.

With their families they crowded around as "young master" tore off the newspaper wrapping, and threw the string aside. As he drew out a framed photograph they waited for his response.

"Hazari Lal, where did you get this?" he exclaimed.

Kushwant Singh took one look and began to chuckle.

"*Where* did you get this?" Vijay demanded of the elderly man standing obsequiously at hand, dressed in impeccably white tunic and trousers. Joy creased his wrinkled features as he answered, "Babu brought it, sir. It was in the *Mussoorie Weekly*."

"Whew!"

"Hmmm...." The lawyer's eyes gleamed. "That means the town has the news," he observed. "How did that happen?"

"Gur Bachan, Dad. I met him at the Red Fort when I dismounted, but I didn't realize he saw me at the reviewing stand. That man!"

Rani's teenage son, Babu, said it best. He yelled, "Three cheers for young master!" and everyone responded three times, "Hip, hip, hooray!" It seemed a fitting ending to a memorable occasion.

## 10

# In the land of the gods

Fortunately for Terry Pennell and Lionel, his guide, their visit to Hardwar came between bathing festivals. Otherwise no vehicle, however sturdy, could have withstood the onslaughts of pilgrims' bodies. At such times masses panted and pushed through narrow streets to the river's edge to bathe in the sacred Ganges.

It's the river that makes the town. Its icy blue waters tumble through a gorge onto the plains. It comes from the land of the gods, the mystical, beautifully untamed area of the mighty Himalayas known as Garhwal. Indeed, Terry's brightly illustrated brochure read:

"Garhwal, home of the gods amid the eternal snows, is a land of thundering waterfalls, high crevices, sacred rivers and alpine lakes. Sages and pilgrims have walked its trails, seeking and finding spiritual fulfillment. Weary travelers forget life's struggles in this exotic land of myths and legends set amidst the highest mountains in the world."

"Ah," Terry had sighed when he first read the description. "I must go there." Now he wasn't so sure.

His bones ached from sleepless hours stretched out in his sleeping bag on the cement floor of a pilgrim shelter. Every nerve in Terry's body shouted that what he lacked was silence. Lionel snored softly beside him. He had quickly succumbed to sleep, but even though they shared a corner—out of the main line of traffic— the Australian remained conscious of incoming pilgrims stepping over humps of other sleepers.

One loud group particularly annoyed him with their chatter and chanting of mantras. Not until their enthusiasm touched him, on reaching Hardwar after two weeks of strenuous travel from some remote village, did Terry's irritation turn to interest. When they finally slept at about three o'clock, he too succumbed, only to awake long after the others.

Temple bells tolled on that frosty morning in Hardwar, the famous pilgrimage spot that venerates Vishnu's footprint on the nearby island in India's sacred river, Ganges. Terry awoke to read Lionel's scribbled note: "Sleep on. I'm bringing breakfast, and will be back soon." He looked around; the shelter was almost empty at seven-thirty!

He jumped up and joined a line at a raspy pump outside. His leather jacket felt good. Terry glanced in pity at the man behind him, frail and sixtiesh, who asked between coughs, "You American?"

"No, I come from Australia."

"Oh!" The man drew his blue shawl a bit closer around thin shoulders and said, "Yes, I know Australia." After coughing he continued, "I teach in high school in Bihar...but...cough... cough...cough...I spend each vacation here."

"Why, friend?"

"Because I'm ill. If I die with my feet in the Ganges my soul goes directly to heaven. No more rebirths."

"Really?" Terry looked incredulous.

The man nodded and said, "Varanasi is closer, and the water is warmer, but I love Hardwar...cough...cough...cough..... It's rugged country, sir, and holds...cough...cough...cough...promises, mystery. It is marvelous...cough...cough...cough."

"Look, friend, perhaps you shouldn't talk."

"No, it's nothing. The sun will rise soon...cough...cough...and I'll feel better." They moved forward, a foot closer to the pump.

The throb of an approaching motorcycle cut their conversation short. "Take my place," Terry said. "I can wait. My buddy's coming."

Reflecting that he could wet his towel with a bit of drinking water in his backpack, he left the line to quickly rejoin Lionel, who soon spread the food on a window ledge in the corner.

"Boy, I'm hungry," he remarked, helping himself to *chapatis.*

"Me, too. Did you get any sleep?"

"Not too bad. How about you?"

Terry shrugged and said, "Too much noise." He drank some hot tea then added, "Those fellows made me mad. I wanted to shut them up, but..."

"You didn't. Why not?"

Terry grinned. "I understood too much! Man! They all came from one village and traveled fourteen days to reach here. Who could sleep when you're that close to your life's dream?"

"I wouldn't know," Lionel said, reaching for more potato curry and another *chapati*.

"I know! I've lived in villages with my parents. Ordinary farmers save for years to do this trek."

Lionel laughed, then said, "Fortunate for us—we're in between festivals, otherwise we'd be crushed."

"Yeah? Well, I could have cussed those fellows blue last night except for one thing."

"What's that, pal?"

Terry grinned and said, "Let's face it. I've met the Michaels and the Singhs lately."

Lionel replenished their cups from the thermos, then said, "Kudos to you, friend. You're a quick learner, I'd say. Take me, for instance."

"What about you?"

Pansy's brother settled himself on his sleeping bag and reminisced, "My family worried about me while I chased a fickle female. Dad and Sis kept warning me I'd make a fool of myself with nothing to show, but something inside kept insisting that they were wrong, that one of these days all would become right. I should just work harder at it."

Terry drew a deep breath and asked, "What made you change?"

Lionel sighed. "My Dad's example," he admitted. "Instead of moping over Mom's jilting him, he's taken it like a man, a giant of a man! You'd think he would be bitter, but no, he just takes what happens and builds on it. He loves Mom. I know he does, and I'll bet he's praying she'll leave that other chap and return. But if she ever does, she'll find a whole new atmosphere at home." Lionel ate silently, a thoughtful look on his face.

But Terry prompted him. "What's different now, pal?"

"The front room...Dad himself...no more smoking, let alone drinking. He's reading his Bible, and he and Pansy spend long evenings studying it. I never realized there was so much in it."

"What did you think it was?"

Lionel shrugged and said, "What? The Bible? Not for me, man! Not my generation! Old-fashioned, with a few useful stories like David and the giant, or the prodigal son. Archaic, you know."

Terry chuckled, and asked, "Do you still feel that way?"

The younger man pulled a Gideon New Testament out of his inner jacket pocket in answer and Terry stared, incredulous. "You carry a copy with you? What for?"

"To read. I've got to study the map."

"What map?"

"This one...*my* life's journey."

"Blow me down! Why?"

"Because it has the answers, Terrence Pennell. Take all these religions, for instance. Dad showed me they're rooted here, all reaching upwards. But the Bible is *God* searching for you and me. That's different."

"So what?"

Lionel changed position, then said, "Well, that hit me, Terry. If God is looking for me, then I'd better show up. I've felt pretty dumb in my lifetime alongside of Pansy. It's time I woke up...so...."

"Yeah?"

"I finally asked the Lord's forgiveness and told him I'd be his. Real neat!"

"Incredible! You're an Indian!"

Lionel grinned and said, "So you think the Lord Jesus is Western, do you? I've got news for you, buddy. You'd better change your mind."

Terry rose and stretched. His thoughts raced...Lionel is really turned on. I thought he was a quiet guy. Oh, yeah? Just get him on the right subject, and he has plenty to say. But before the two left the shelter he had the grace to say, albeit with a yawn, "Thanks, pal. You gave me lots to think about."

Five minutes later, after tipping an attendant to watch the motorcycle and their backpacks, the young men sauntered the river's edge on their way to a little white temple decked with flags. Set on a hill above the town that mushroomed on the right bank of the river, it afforded a magnificent view of the entire terrain.

Morning mists hung low. Saivite sadhus (mendicants who worshiped the god Shiva) squatted naked before dying fires in niches below their temples. With only cowdung ashes for clothing, they sought what little warmth the embers could provide.

Farther along the river bank Terry and Lionel passed Vishnavite Namodaris (holy men who followed Vishnu rather than Shiva, a distinction marked by wearing three stripes on their foreheads—two white with a blood red one in the middle). These wore their hair in mud-packed beehives.

Barbers and clients plied their trade. "Want a shave?" Terry asked as he pointed, chuckling, to a duo squatted in the shelter of a wall.

"He doesn't leave much, does he?" Lionel responded, noting that the barber was shaving the man's head, ears, and even nostrils.

"I'm amazed at how public private life is here," Terry commented. "Look at those entire families bathing...and over there, some are washing clothes, others are worshiping the rising sun and the river. You know, Lionel, it strikes me that Indians can do this without any embarrassment because they live in extended families and communities."

"I hadn't thought of that. I guess I'm used to it."

"Well, in the West, we seek privacy. In contrast to this open worship, Christians tend to look for four walls."

"Hmmm...that's interesting."

The young men passed a small horde of middlemen making preparations for another busy day. Auntie Singh had warned against such, assuring Terry that these greedy Brahmans would read his horoscope and inscribe his name into their books for a healthy fee. "They'll even perform the ceremonial Ganges Puja (worship rites) over your head," she said. "Watch out for such."

The sightseers strolled past these tempters, some offering anointing oils, others selling sandalwood paste and ground up yellow clay to mark the forehead of the worshiper. They laughed at the ingenuity of intriguing brushwood rafts made more buoyant by dried gourds. Many people used such for transport, plying the craft up and down the river with long bamboos. A flight of ducks roared upstream into the mouth of the gorge, soon lost to view in the mists that suggested mystery beyond.

Now the path veered abruptly upward. Terry and his friend began climbing to Mansa Devi's temple. Puffing slightly, they reached the top, a vantage point that showed them the mountain gorge, the forest lands opposite, and the grimy reminders of civilization in the town below. Gaudy billboards screamed their products, the town clock struck the hours, and masses of people, each a minuscule unit of desire, followed his or her own choosing.

"Tell us about Hardwar," Terry said to an engaging English-speaking pundit connected with the temple. "I'm interested."

Fiftiesh and portly, wearing gold-rimmed glasses, his head bound in a heavy white turban, the man pulled his dark grey woolen shawl more securely around his shoulders. "Your first time here?" he asked.

"Yes," Terry answered. "I attended school in Nainital when young and often wished I could visit this famous part of the Himalayas, but never had opportunity. Now my friend from Delhi has brought me."

"Ah...yes, sir. Come, please sit. We can talk." The pundit motioned to a three-foot high stone wall nearby that encompassed the temple courtyard. Settling in a fairly secluded spot, he pointed out areas of interest, then said, "But I think you are more than a sightseer, sir. I quote from the oracle of Lord Shiva, from *Brahmavaivarta Purana*: 'The Ganga is the source of redemption.... Heaps of sin, accumulated by a sinner during millions of births, are destroyed by the mere contact of a wind charged with her vapor.... As the fire consumes fuel, so this stream consumes the sins of the wicked. Sages mount the staired terrace of the Ganges, on it they transcend the high heaven of Brahma himself; free from danger, riding celestial chariots, they go to Shiva's abode.'"

"Pardon me, Pundit Ji," Terry intercepted. "You're saying that a sinner has only to immerse himself in these waters to be freed from the past?"

The Hindu teacher smiled, nodded, and answered, "Not I, friend, but the sacred scriptures. Now hear some more. Lord Shiva says, 'Sinners who expire near the water of the Ganges are released from all their sins: they become Shiva's attendants and dwell at his side. They become identical with him in shape; they never die—not even on the day of the total dissolution of the universe.' That, my friend, is the good news we offer. Moreover, Hardwar provides you that opportunity."

"Hmmm." Terry looked thoughtful, glancing at Lionel who immediately asked, "What does Hardwar have that's unique?"

"Ah, we possess the footprint of Vishnu, right down there." He pointed to an island with a large concentration of pilgrims bathing. With a toothy smile, he added, "It is beautiful. In the evenings the river glows with small lights floating on its bosom, each bearing a wish to the gods."

Terry's brow furrowed as he sought to grasp an elusive memory. He tried to look interested and said, "Sir, you mentioned Shiva, and now Vishnu. What relationship is there? I understand both are very much revered here."

Their guide rubbed his hands together in a pleased gesture. "Yes, yes," he said, nodding, "a very open mind you have. I can tell, just as Swami Vivekanand found when he went to America."

That's it! A light flashed through Terry's memory and he remembered Marcia's guru sitting cross-legged on their living room floor, rubbing his hands in just such a pleased manner. The revulsion he had experienced in Australia almost overcame him now. Yet he must act civil. Terry forced himself to listen to the pundit's explanation:

"We have millions of gods, all emanations of the divine force. You, sir, have a divine force within you if you only knew. But unfortunately, you have no doubt been taught that you are a sinner and need a savior. We bring to you enlightenment—the great truth that all roads lead to God. Hinduism is not so much dogma as a way of life. Now let me answer your question."

The Australian martialled his thoughts. What had he asked prior to the blinding revelation that this man seemed part of another, one that brought ruin to his marriage? He battled inwardly. Was he being unfair to judge this man by that guru? At least hear him out, so Terry listened.

"You asked about the relationship of Lord Shiva to Lord Vishnu? Ah, yes...like you Westerners, we too, have trinity." He nodded and smiled, his tone silky and persuasive. "Our gods are Brahma, Vishnu, and Shiva. See? Three in one...Divine Force...Creator... other names only."

Lionel looked up, interested. "Is that right? I didn't realize," he said.

Their guide took off his gold-rimmed glasses, carefully wiped them with one end of his woolen shawl, then replacing them on his nose, continued, "Now, my friends, about *Trimurthy*—as you say, trinity. Brahma is the creator, Vishnu preserves life, and Shiva destroys it. Each takes many forms, and millions worship as they please. Many Hindus prefer goddesses...Lakshmi, Durga, Saraswati...."

Lionel gave his friend a quick, meaningful glance.

Terry drew a deep breath, then asked, "Your trinity finds many expressions?"

"Yes, yes. One worships one; another, a different form. What matter? All are true."

"Hmmm...as I see it, Pundit Ji, these many gods represent some facet of life, broken down into personalities with names and stories woven around each?"

"Yes...yes...very much so! We are one with nature, with the elements. You have very quick mind, sir. You must search for truth now that you have entered the door to God."

"But," and Terry felt confused. "I don't understand. Why do you think I have entered the door to God?"

"*Har-dwar*, my friend, *Har-dwar*—door to God. That's its literal meaning. For you, my son, I foresee its truth. You must keep seeking."

# 11

# Disclosure in Rishikesh

From the seclusion of the hilltop, Terry and Lionel descended into a very materially minded city, despite the fact that "Hardwar" literally means "the door to God." Terrence Pennell sighed often, the emptiness in his heart reaching out, seeking something to fill it, but he didn't find it here. Instead, he saw only grime, dust, and a religiosity that thrived on the pilgrim trade.

"Let's go," he said wearily to his friend after they had a hot lunch at a wayside stand. "I'm fed up with bathing *ghats*, masses of pilgrims, and all this commercialization."

"Fine with me, pal. Rishikesh should be better."

Their sixteen mile route passed sugar cane fields and mustard, then miles of forest lands filled with *sal* and *shisham* trees whose thin trunks, like elms, permitted glimpses of picturesque villages tucked into their shade. Ashrams appeared in abundance. Likely each had been established by some strong, authoritative figure, Terry mused. Each would propound some facet of truth...or was it truth? He felt too weary to answer such a momentous question.

After climbing the Swaliks range, considered one of the oldest formations of all time, by midafternoon Lionel and Terry entered Rishikesh, literally, the valley of *sadhus* or holy men. Here, too, pilgrims thronged the town but without civilization's encroachments badgering them as in Hardwar. It seemed more natural, with the sacred river flowing—sometimes turbulent, more often subdued—in this pastoral setting of rolling hills and valley. "Oh, I like it," Terry said with a sigh of contentment.

"Yes, this is nice."

"Pleasantly warm, too. But I thought we'd see higher mountains, like Nainital, you know."

"Probably tomorrow, on the road to Chumba."

"But look at all the temples, and bathing areas. Let's go out of town, Lionel."

They rode past busses and horse tongas, pilgrim shelters and rest houses, an array that catered to either affluence or simple lifestyles. So, too, with the variety of tea stalls. Finally they paused by a sheltered area overlooking the Ganges.

"Mind if I stay awhile?" Terry asked. "I'd like to rest. You can scout around and return in about an hour. Okay?"

"Fine, buddy. I'll book a place to stay, and probably bring food back with me." So saying, he returned to town while Terry sought a convenient seat under an overspreading oak on the banks of the river.

An Ashram gate beckoned with attractive gardens and flowers. It's good to be alone for awhile, he decided. Lionel's great, but this is life! Why go on? I think I'll settle for Rishikesh.

Resting by the placid waters, Terry heard the corby's deep notes answered by the indescribably sweet call of the Himalayan whistling thrush. His eyelids drooped and very soon he slept.

The sound of voices awakened him. He sat up, blinking rapidly to focus on the source, an approaching group of women walking single file. Six elderly, gaunt hags carried staffs in their hands and balanced bundles on their heads. They looked for all the world like witches bound for their coven, he thought hazily. But he noted that the seventh, though part of the group, differed from the others. She moved with grace, possessed youthful interest and wore clean clothes. He saw her more than casual glance in his direction as they neared.

As though mesmerized, he watched the tall leader veer off the road toward the tree under which he sat. Each woman followed, single file, throwing her bundle to the ground. A nod from the leader signaled the opening of their possessions, and for the next ten minutes the drama unfolded in uneasy silence. Given the Indian twilight as background, with the twittering and chirping of birds finding their night quarters, once again Terrence Pennell felt he had inadvertently invaded forbidden territory that these witches desired to claim.

Finally, he drew a deep breath and sat up with decision. Such nonsense, his reason shouted! These aren't witches, merely tired pilgrims. But why don't they talk? Their chatter awakened me. Are they playing a game?

Even as he watched, three teams went into action. Two took aluminum pots to the river while two others found stones for an hastily improvised stove. The third duo foraged for sticks to stoke the fire, and the young woman extracted greens from her bundle. She washed them thoroughly with river water, taking time to again examine the young Australian. As though satisfied, she smiled slightly. Terry sensed she wanted to talk, but in this unlikely setting it would have to be in the context of the group.

Well, he could initiate that, he concluded. He stood up and approached the leader. In clear Hindi he asked, "You're pilgrims? From where?"

Three women giggled, but the tall angular one looked up to say, "Yes, Sahib Ji. We're from Madhya Pradesh."

Relieved, he answered, "My fortune, mother. In this land of many languages, at least we can converse."

Some of the women pulled their torn *sarees* over their mouths to hide increased amusement, but the leader said with a nod, "Son, you do pretty well yourself. Where did you learn our kind of Hindi?"

"In Nainital where I studied as a school boy." He smiled as he added, "I suppose I spoke Hindi before English since I was born in India. You see, my parents were Australian missionaries."

Only blank looks met him, so he explained further, and soon everyone was sharing travel experiences.

"We're all related, and we've wanted to do this for years," the leader explained.

Another ventured, "We've been on the road now for over four months."

Her partner said, "We didn't get to all four shrines because of winter weather, but we've seen lots of temples, Sahib Ji, and we did reach Gomukh."

"What's there?" Terry asked.

"Very important place, sir," the tall, angular woman replied. "For years I've longed to see where Mother Ganges came to earth, and now I've done it." She looked around proudly, then said, "We've seen it with our own eyes...all of us but," and she indicated the young woman with a toss of her head, "she didn't see it. She came later."

One of the hags pushed the young woman playfully, much as grandparents enjoy a child. Terry noted that the young woman's eyes were fixed on him, and he wondered what she was thinking. Did she have something she wanted to say?

"Where is Gomukh?" he asked.

"High up in the mountains," another said. "You ride and ride by bus until you get to Gangotri."

"Then you walk another twelve miles to the cave out of which the Ganges flows."

"It's true, Sahib Ji! The *Ganga* comes from nowhere! There it is—a big river in front of you!"

Terry nodded, then asked, indicating the young woman, "Where did she join you?"

"Oh, on our way back," the leader said nonchalantly. "We got tired doing all our work after trekking hard all day, so she helps."

"Ah...yes," Terry nodded, then asked the young woman, "Your home? Is it in Madhya Pradesh, too?"

"No, I come from near Mussoorie."

"Really? Were you a pilgrim? How did you join these people?"

"Fate, Sahib Ji. The gods ordained it. One of my group fell from a cliff and died. Everyone said we were cursed, so they went back. But I wanted to see more, so I joined one group after another, then this one."

"Don't mind her, Sahib Ji. She doesn't know anything. She makes mistakes," one said.

"No, no, I don't...only once." Her face clouded, and Terry asked directly, "Mind telling me?"

"We were at a monastery high up in the mountains," she said. "It looked like a stormy night, so the priests urged all of us to sleep inside instead of on the verandah. That was after I joined this group. We went into the women's quarters—where the nuns stay, you know. And among them was a young woman with skin like yours." She giggled, embarrassed, and hid her face in her hands.

"A white woman? But surely you see many on the pilgrim trail? This part of the Himalayas is very famous, you know."

"Yes...yes...of course we see other white people."

"See, Sahib Ji? She does make mistakes."

"What was your mistake?"

"She tried to talk to me, but her Hindi wasn't very good. Not like yours, if you'll excuse my saying so."

"Parvati, get to your work," the leader said abruptly.

But the younger woman continued, "It's her face I remember, and her pretty red hair drawn back so tight. She was too young to look so sad, as though she's caught and wished to join us. But a nun called her away, and I didn't run after her. I should have. I think she needed a friend."

"Parvati! That's enough!"

Terry sensed the leader's intense displeasure, as though his informant had trespassed set limits. The young woman said no more.

In the midst of interesting conversation, the arrival of Lionel on the motorcycle turned everyone's attention to the newcomer. Despite the group's invitation to share their meal, the two young men rode off in the twilight to the Rest House in which Lionel had booked a room. Terry said with a grin, "Buddy, this is great! Imagine having hot food and decent beds!"

"Yeah, I thought we had it coming to us."

Lionel retired early, but Terry, refreshed by his late afternoon nap, decided to write in his journal. He donned his jacket and sauntered onto the verandah with his pen and notebook. Under the light of a hanging bulb he inscribed his varied feelings and thoughts.

A hush pervaded the sleeping town...no sound but a dog howling at the moon. Terry heard the gurgling of the river, and Parvati's story came back into sharp focus.

Was she trying to tell him something? Perhaps not true in all details, but firmly enough etched to let him fill in the blanks? Let's see...a white woman with red hair, sad eyes, in a monastery—needing a friend....

His mind leaped. Marcia? No! Of course not! She's in Australia! But then, who knows? I haven't heard from her in three years, not since the divorce! You know...it could be Marcia. She has pretty red hair, expressive hazel eyes and mobile features. Maybe she followed the guru back to the Himalayas. Why not? She loved these hills when she was a girl in Mussoorie. That's what initially drew us together. And this Parvati. She comes from near Mussoorie? That would draw Marcia to her, too. Hmmm....

Terrence Pennell straightened and drew a long breath. As he paced the verandah, thoughts tumbled through his mind. His pulse raced. A bitter sweet pain pierced his heart.

He had tried to forget Marcia in his infatuation for Suzy, but now? Strangely enough, he had somehow felt liberated by learning to know Pansy. Moreover, Suzy belonged to another. Nor did he desire her since he had learned to know one so superior and beautiful that the old seemed useless. No, Suzy could never attract him again. Nor did Pansy belong to him. Pansy had given herself to Squirt.

Marcia? Ah, she was different. Her tender, clinging ways called forth his manhood. He had loved her from the time they first met on the boat to Australia. Now he relived their courtship, their early marriage and happy days until the Maharishi appeared with his strange, infatuating devices.

And now? Had Marcia been drawn into some illusive web, a lie that sounded true but remained empty? Was she struggling for freedom in a monastery in these Himalayas? Something shouted that this was true. He heard her wistful, pleading voice within his spirit. Marcia was calling him. He could never delay in Rishikesh!

Tomorrow, he and Lionel would travel to Chumba where several roads intersected. His friend would continue on to Happy Valley but he, Terrence Pennell, must begin his search. How? He didn't know, beyond seeking out monasteries and Ashrams.

His heart pounded. Now he knew why he had to come to India! Surely more than mere coincidence. Face it, Terry! Mom would say it's God's hand, not Brahma, not Shiva, not Vishu, but the God of the Bible, the God of his youth.

He covered his face with his hands and sobbed as he sat in a wicker chair. For years he had spurned the Lord Jesus Christ, yet now he faced him as the Good Shepherd searching for a lost lamb. Terry breathed heavily and whispered, "Great God, God of love, you care enough about one lost lamb to send me to find her? Oh, Lord Jesus, my God, I'm not worthy."

How long he sat and wept he didn't know, nor care. A new Terrence Pennell finally arose. Exultingly, with outstretched arms, he said aloud, "I've come home, Lord Jesus! You've found me, too. Please tell Marcia I'm coming. You know where she is. Guide me to her, my wonderful Lord."

The world had righted itself. Just wait until he told his buddy, Lionel.

Next noon, after finishing a late lunch in a busy tea shop in Chumba, Lionel inquired of Terry, "You'll be all right?"

His Australian friend momentarily toyed with his earthenware teacup. He sipped the milky-white, sweet liquid, trying to resist the sense of loneliness that threatened. "I'd rather go with you," he admitted, "but I can't let Marcia down. I'm sure she's somewhere in these Himalayas needing me. I hope the family will understand, pal. Get them to pray, please."

"You bet I will." Lionel touched his coat pocket and said with a boyish grin, "Terry, I'll give your note to Uncle Singh as soon as I see him."

"Bless you."

Now, with Lionel's familiar form disappearing into the rush of Chumba's busy little bazaar that burgeoned with crowds gathering for the annual spring festivals, Terrence Pennell rose and asked directions to the Tourist Bungalow. He'd go early to book a room. Perhaps he'd meet some compatible person who could orient him to this new locale. Auntie Singh's warning sounded, "You've got a white face," she had said. "You make fair game for anyone who thinks you don't know India. Please be careful with your money and information."

He now remembered how casually he thanked her, grateful for her concern, but assured of his competence. Now, without Lionel, matters looked different. Terry felt the least he could do was to secure a good base.

Ten minutes' walk brought him to the Tourist Bungalow set back from the road and fronted by a pretty garden. Even here, on the edge of town, Terry booked just in time. A Canadian couple was signing for one room, and a busload of pilgrims arrived immediately after Terry. But he did get a room, about the size of a ship's cabin he thought ruefully. However, the adjacent private bathroom seemed luxurious.

He decided to investigate his surroundings. Chumba, just an ordinary hill village for most of the year, overlooked the valley in which Tehri City sprawled at the confluence of two rivers that then became the Ganges. Chumba, at six thousand feet elevation, abounded in fresh, invigorating mountain air. Tehri, on the other hand, was known to be sultry hot. True, Chumba lacked a river, but it excelled in glens and forests, and its importance rose from the convergence of three main roads: to Tehri and the high Himalayas to the north; to Rishikesh and Hardwar, southward; and to Mussoorie on the west. This, then, had become the important site for the annual spring festivals.

They would begin tomorrow, the houseboy informed Terry. "Ah, sir," the teenager enthused, "there will be a week of proces-

sions and feasting." He grinned broadly as he served the foreigner with tea and biscuits, and added, "But you must see the climax,
when everyone douses everybody else with colored water."

"*Holi*?" Terry inquired.

The boy's eyes gleamed. "You know, sir? Do they do that in
your country?"

The Australian chuckled and said, "Hardly. The police would
have something to say."

"Is that right? Don't you have any festivals?"

"Yes, of course, but very different from yours." He was glad to
be warned against *Holi*." This little hideaway might prove more
useful than he foresaw.

After an invigorating walk in the early evening, Terry returned
to the Tourist Bungalow to write in his journal. The sound of the
evening breeze in nearby pines formed a soothing background
for the clear call of the Himalayan Barbet inviting dialogue with
another. Yes, there it was, the brisk interchange of bird calls Terry
hoped to hear. He wrote:

"I'm a boy again in my thoughts, back in the cottage with
Mom and Dad when they spent summer vacations in Nainital,
and I was a day scholar.

"The insistent calls of the barbet take me back...two or three in
the interchange...*un-nee-ow, un-nee-ow, un-nee-ow*! I used to try to
see them, but they stick to the top branches so they're hidden by
the foliage.

"I remember the milkman telling me, 'Master Terry, the barbet
was once an evil money lender in a former life. He used to demand
high interest and harass poor farmers like us, so now he's being
punished for his sins. That's why he keeps crying, '*un-nee-ow*.'
That means 'injustice' in our language. See Terry,' he'd add with a
laugh, 'you'd better be a good boy. If you don't, you'll be punished
in the next life.'"

The young man smiled as he laid his pen down. Then he took
the Gideon New Testament Lionel had left with him and opened
to the tenth chapter of John's Gospel. In this quiet, peaceful setting—apart from the crowds—Terrence Pennell sensed direction.
He was to stay in Chumba throughout the week, and should the
Good Shepherd bring Marcia to the *mela*, she could spot the Australian who stood a head higher than the Garhwalis. He hoped she
would know he loved her.

## 12

# In search of Marcia

The throb of a motorcycle broke the Saturday afternoon still-ness as Vijay and Manorma sauntered home from an enjoyable hour in the nearby Botanical Gardens. She grasped his arm to ask, "Isn't that Lionel? Where's Terry, darling?"

The lone rider turned up the lane and arrived with a flourish to meet the grey-haired lawyer awaiting him. "Welcome, my boy," they heard him say. "Where's Terry?"

"Hello, uncle. Terry's in Chumba, at a *mela*."

"Is he all right?"

The newcomer parked his motorcycle, then answered, "Yes, he's in fine form. He sends his love, and he'll be coming after awhile. Here's a letter." Lionel extracted the note from his inner pocket and handed it to Kushwant Singh.

"In Chumba, at a *mela*?" Manorma said slowly.

"Did you expect that?" Vijay asked her.

"Sort of," she said with a nod. "Lionel, do you have a story to tell?"

He grinned and answered, "Yes, in fact I do."

Manorma caught Vijay's arm. "Oh! Perhaps my dream is true!"

Vijay looked at her, amazed. "What dream, love?" he asked.

She laughed lightly and suggested they hear Lionel's story first. A half hour later the opportunity came.

In the quiet of their new family room the Singhs and Lionel sipped a welcome cup of hot tea while filling up on Rani's mint sandwiches and freshly made cheese *pakoras*. During a lull, the lawyer turned to say, "Now, Lionel, let's hear your story."

"Yes, uncle."

His account of the trip brought forth much rejoicing when he told of Terry's return to faith in Jesus Christ. "He's so different," Lionel said with a boyish grin. "The Lord really did it."

"Man, that's super!" Vijay exulted. "You know something? Squirt and I pacted together in prayer that you'd give a strong testimony on your trip to counterbalance whatever else he might meet. Oh, Lionel! I'm proud of you!" Vijay's eyes shone.

Pansy's brother looked embarrassed and began examining the new wood inlay coffee table the Singhs had brought from Delhi. His finger rested on the cottage scene, ivory inlay in the walnut wood, and said, "See, family? This looks like where he rested...just north of Rishikesh. Here's the river...there's the tree...and beyond are the cottages belonging to a nearby Ashram."

Kushwant Singh chuckled, then said, "That's truly singular, especially since the table likely came from South India, not North. However," he paused, then added, "our Lord is reminding us that he hears and answers prayer."

Susheela touched his arm and asked, "Does something happen when we pray together?"

"Yes, it does, when we ask according to God's will."

Manorma looked up with interest. "I'd like to know why Mama asked. Tell us please, Mama, won't you?"

Vijay's mother shifted in her wheelchair, then said, "I'm not really sure, daughter, except that doing things together still seems strange to me. Mind you, I like it!" She paused then added with a smile, "All these years, remember, I've been very much alone in my religion. But now we do things together. Isn't..." and she looked appealingly at her husband, "isn't meeting God a private affair?"

"Hmmm," he responded. "Yes, my dear, meeting God is a private affair. As I read the Bible, we each have to find God for ourselves."

"Yes, Dad," Vijay said, "but don't forget the children of Israel. They were led corporately, and had certain inalienable rights as a nation, didn't they?"

"You've got something there, son. Manorma, what do you say?"

"I'd say both of you are right. That's what makes balance. Each of us is on our individual pilgrimage; but we're in this together. Remember when we went our own ways? We lived here under one roof, but we surely didn't mesh too well."

Vijay chuckled, and his mother murmured, "Like when I told my son he didn't dare to become a Christian."

"Exactly!" Vijay exclaimed, helping himself to more cheese *pakoras*. "But now we enjoy eating together, talking, praying and just having fun."

"I like it," Susheela reiterated.

"Cheers for Auntie Singh!" said Lionel, amid general laughter.

"What do you call it, son?" Susheela asked.

"Fellowship, Mom," Vijay said. "We strengthen each other spiritually, and find courage. But Terry? He's all alone out there. How do we know he's on the right track? Maybe he's imagining things, Dad...about Marcia, I mean. Couldn't he be mistaken?"

"Yes, my boy, unless the Lord corroborates it otherwise."

Manorma laughed, then said, "Now it's time for me to tell my story—the dream I had last night. It's been on my mind all day." She paused, then began by saying, "I do hope all of you won't laugh. It's only a dream, but I think a very special one."

Kushwant Singh chuckled, then said, "Tell us, daughter, and as the head of the family, I'll decide."

"Well, family, last night in my dream I saw a white girl in a Tibetan setting. I mean, dressed in a brown Tibetan robe. She sat in a lotus position on a prayer rug with her string of beads, and was reciting her rosary. I saw her clearly. She has dark red curly hair and beautiful hazel eyes, but they're so sad."

She paused, drew a deep breath before continuing, "The girl is in a little room with a high window. I thought she'd be reciting a mantra, but she wasn't. When I listened I heard her whispering, "Lord Jesus, send Terry. Lord Jesus, send Terry.'"

"You don't mean it, Mano!" Vijay gasped.

"Yes, darling, I do."

He gripped her hand. No one spoke, but at last the lawyer said in hushed tone, "*That*, daughter, is a revelation. It's clear enough."

Manorma choked with emotion as she whispered, "Papa, it's Marcia." Susheela wiped her tears with the end of her scarf and murmured, "Poor lass. She needs us. Let's pray for her."

"We'll do more," Kushwant Singh asserted. He rose, paced back and forth in deep thought, then turned to his son to say, "Vijay, I'm glad Terry's got the signal straight. Now, as I see it, you and Mahendra can also aid in the rescue operation."

"Oh, Dad! When? Right away?"

The lawyer smiled, then said, "No, son. Give Terry first chance to find her. It's his right, you know. If we have the facts straight—and I think we have—then the Lord has heard Marcia's prayer, and Terry will get his instructions from above."

"But, Dad, how soon may we go?"

"Wednesday morning." Kushwant Singh's eyes twinkled as he added, "We must be sensitive to God's master plan. Tuesday is also important in the Lord's agenda. You'd better stay for the civic luncheon that Kailash Rana has organized. Very admirable of him, I'd say." He chuckled.

Vijay's grimace made everyone laugh. Lionel asked, "What's the matter, Zep? Don't you like being a hero?"

"Real neat...oh, yeah? I'd rather be on the road with Squirt, ferreting out Terry. Who wants to sit through long speeches that mean little or nothing? They're building their own self-image!"

Nevertheless, on the following Wednesday morning Zep and Squirt mounted the former's newly-acquired Royal Enfield and started for Tehri City where they would headquarter with a dear lawyer friend of Kushwant Singh's. In fact, they anticipated phoning from there this evening.

The vehicle's silky purr sounded sweet as the two young men rode in the early morning through Library and Mussoorie bazaars, past Picture Palace and the clock tower, then entered Landour's narrow thoroughfare. Tantalizing odors of fresh *samosas*, spicy hot, made them stop before reaching Mullingar Hill. Each consumed four of the vegetable patties, washed down by refreshing tea, then resumed their journey. Gunning the motor, they effortlessly climbed the zigzag road, past panting coolies struggling with baskets of charcoal or wood on their backs. School children waved, and Squirt exclaimed, "Good motor, this, Zep. Your Dad advised you well."

"Yeah," Vijay answered over his shoulder, "and just broken in, too. Chappie left suddenly for the Arab Emirates, so I got a good price on it, thank God."

Soon the road leveled off on its first lap to Tehri City. With sheer drops to their right and precipitous mountainsides to their left, they passed Woodstock School and many cottages dotting the hillside. Jabar Khet lay ahead. They sped by this outpost, civilization's last, marked by the inevitable rest stop that provided a panoramic view of the snows and a welcome cup of hot tea.

Mahendra sighed and said, "This is great!" Vijay responded, "You're right, man! I love these mountains! It's like reaching out to touch majesty!"

Lofty fir-clad peaks rose precipitously to the left, with deep valleys layered in between, home of lush rain forests. On the horizon, the snowcapped giants, and in between, mountain ranges that rose tier on tier, closer ones dark green in color, then purple fading into blue in the mists that promised even higher realms. This was the wonderland that drew hundreds of thousands of visitors, not to play, but to worship.

The sheer beauty of that scintillating February day thrilled the travelers on their way to Daula Ram's tea shop near Kaddukhal Village and Sukhanda Devi's temple. "Remember, Zep?" Squirt asked.

"Remember what?"

"When Hazari Lal and we went down to the Aglar River, then we climbed Nag Tibba the next day?" He laughed, and added, "I got so sore I thought I couldn't make it...and..."

"We had to stay overnight because of wild animals prowling the area...and weren't we glad to find a relative of Hazari Lal's?"

"Sounds to me as though our guardian angels were watching out for us even then."

Three busloads of pilgrims milled around Daula Ram's tea shop. Two helpers and the busy proprietor could scarcely handle their demand for food, but Daula Ram managed a quick word with his friends. "Glad to see you," he said. "Wait for me at the table under the pine. I'll bring you a tray."

He joined them under the magnificent deodar across the road, a bit off to the side. "This is new?" Squirt asked. "I don't remember it."

Daula Ram nodded and said, "Yes, Mr. Lall, it's my trysting place with God, also a fine spot to talk with any whom he sends me."

Mahendra slapped the stocky Garhwali on his shoulder and asked, "You witnessing?"

"Yes, sir, ever since I believed."

"When, Daula Ram?"

"More than two weeks ago, sir. After reading and rereading the books you gave, one night I heard the Lord Jesus calling me to follow him—sort of like those fishermen, or that tax collector. He asked me whether I would give my tea stall to him."

Vijay leaned forward to ask, "And you said yes, friend?"

The Garhwali nodded. "Yes, sir. How can I hold back? He died for me."

"Amazing!"

"I say, praise God!"

"Has he sent anyone to you?" Vijay asked as a busy squirrel flicked his bushy tail and scuttled back and forth under the magnificent deodar. The wind soughed through the pines, part of an awe-inspiring symphony of praise to the Creator.

"Several...one especially...about ten days ago. The water's likely boiling. I'll bring your tea, and then tell you my story." He turned, and crossed the road to the stall.

Squirt took a deep breath, then whispered in awe, "Zep, the Lord just showed me a house that looks like a mountain lodge. Oh, Zep! Pansy and I...."

Vijay chuckled and said, "You sound like my Mano, Squirt. But let's pray about this."

Daula Ram approached, a tray in hand. He paused while they prayed, waiting quietly until they finished. As he placed the tray on the table he said, "God sent you today. Something happened last week, and I needed someone with whom to share." He poured out tea for his friends and served them.

Then he said, drawing a deep breath, "Since I gave my life to Jesus business has more than doubled. Pilgrims are coming all the time, and I got so tired I had to find help. So now I have a brother-sister combination from my village. It's a great relief."

As he paused, the gurgling of a nearby mountain stream came through clearly. Such a peaceful place, Mahendra mused. No wonder I sense the Lord's presence in special measure...like rarefied, penetrating fragrance.

Daula Ram continued, "Busloads have been coming every day for two weeks, and I haven't found time to talk with people, but that Monday I couldn't keep silent." He paused, then continued, "Monday forenoon a bus came filled with a group from some Ashram. Everyone wore brown Tibetan *chupas*, both men and women."

"Women?" Vijay looked up quickly as he asked.

"Yes, quite a group of women, mostly old...perhaps six or seven of them, all speaking clear Hindi. I asked where their home was and they said Madhya Pradesh, so that explained it. But two were different...one younger Indian woman, and the other a foreigner."

"With red hair?"

Daula Ram looked at Vijay in amazement. "How did you know, sir? It was covered with a shawl, but I clearly recall the fringe that showed in front. Yes, it was red, like when the Muslims come back from Mecca." He paused, then said, "The little foreigner, about my size, vomited from car sickness when she got out of the bus, so the guru said she could rest here while the others climbed the peak. They left the other younger woman to care for her needs, and that gave me the chance to serve them. I told them to stretch out on these benches until I brought them some food."

"Marcia," breathed Mahendra. Vijay nodded.

"You know her name?"

"We're searching for her," Vijay answered. "Tell us everything, Daula Ram."

The stocky proprietor nodded, then continued, "They rested for perhaps half-an-hour, then the Indian lady went to the women's room, and the foreigner was alone. I quickly took a tray of tea and biscuits and found her, head down, sobbing. I heard her saying, 'Lord Jesus, send Terry...Lord Jesus, send Terry...'"

A quick glance passed between Zep and Squirt, but they waited for Daula Ram to proceed. He said, "I don't speak English, as you know, but I understand it, and I gathered that this young woman was in trouble and was praying to my Lord Jesus for help. So, you see, sirs, I *had* to speak."

They nodded, and he paused. Finally Squirt asked, "What did you say, Daula Ram?"

"I asked whether she understood Hindi, and she nodded, wiping her tears. When she looked up I took the Gospel of John from my coat pocket. It shows Jesus on the cover, you recall. And I said, 'My sister, I love Jesus, too. Please don't cry. Why are you in an Ashram?'

"'Oh!' she said, sort of startled like, perhaps embarrassed. I don't know. But I told her that Jesus Christ loves us, that he is her Good Shepherd, and he knows each one of her needs. And I said, 'If you're sincere in your prayer, sister, he will send you help.' And I promised to pray for her, but I hoped she would tell me more."

"She didn't?" Squirt asked.

"Her friend came, and I had to leave them with the tray. But before they boarded the bus, the little white lady came to me and said quietly, 'Thank you. I believe the Lord Jesus is going to answer my prayer.' That was all, but I can't get her out of my mind." He drew a deep breath.

Vijay exclaimed, "Look, friend! The Lord is answering her prayer. That's why we're here."

"Who is Terry?" The Garhwali rose to take the tray.

"Her former husband. He's come from Australia, and he's searching for her. We're on our way to help him. See?"

Daula Ram joined his hands together in prayer and bowing his head, murmured, "Great God in heaven, thank you. Thank you!" Then he looked up to ask, "My brothers, how can I help? My home is open, and I'm at your command."

"What do you think, Squirt?"

"Man! This is terrific! Way beyond mere coincidence. I say we're well on the way to finding Marcia because the Lord has gone ahead of us." He turned to Daula Ram to inquire, "Any idea where the group lives, the ones that came by bus?"

"Yes, sir. One of the disciples said they winter north of Tehri in an Ashram and have come for the special *pujas*. There's a big procession in Chumba tomorrow. Normally they live in a monastery on the route to Gangotri."

"Ah, yes, that helps." Mahendra nodded with satisfaction and said, "Come on, Buddy. We have work to do."

But Vijay chuckled and replied, "Not so fast, Squirt. One more item, Daula Ram. We might need a disguise for the lady. You say she's about your size? Could we borrow a complete change of your clothing? I'm sure you'd recognize them if she turned up!"

The Garhwali's eyes gleamed. "Yes, sir, and she can bunk in with my family. We've been taking turns sleeping here at night, but be assured I'll stay on duty for the next two weeks so that I don't miss her."

A busload of pilgrims pulled up, so Daula Ram hastened to wait on them. Not until an hour later did Vijay and Mahendra have opportunity to get the package wrapped in newspaper and tied securely with string. Meanwhile they decided to investigate the area. "How far are we from Chumba?" Vijay asked.

"I'd put it about eighteen to twenty miles, pal. Yes, see? The road marker says 27 km. so I'm pretty close." Squirt pointed to a stone nearby.

They had walked barely a quarter mile from Daula Ram's tea shop when they noticed a two-story wooden chalet, complete with balcony and dormer windows. It sat up from the road, at the end of the ridge and thus commanded a prime view of both the snows and the foothills to the west. "Superb!" Vijay murmured.

Mahendra caught his friend's arm. "Zep!"

"What's the matter?"

"See it? There it is!"

"What? It's just a house, isn't it...albeit a very attractive one, I'd say."

"You're pretty dumb, buddy, for all your awards!" Mahendra faced Vijay and said with gleaming eyes, "Can't you see? That's our mountain lodge!"

"Are you serious?"

"Am I ever!" Squirt climbed the dozen steps to the gate that led to the house with expansive yard. Vijay followed, and together they peered in a window. "Empty!" Squirt exclaimed.

"Probably belongs to some big shot on the plains, and he summers here." Zep looked in again and commented, "Big living-dining room, isn't it? Great place for a vacation."

"What's wrong with having the entire family here—all of you and Pansy's folks? Plenty of space for guests."

"Yes? And you'd live upstairs?"

"Exactly! I seem to see some sort of study center, Zep."

"Hold it, man. I've never seen you so charged up."

Mahendra faced him and said, "I'll try to be patient, but right now, in the authority given me by my Lord, I claim this place for him. I'll be back. Mark my words, Zeppelin, I'll be back."

Vijay chuckled and suggested, "Let's find someone to show us inside. There's probably someone around, a *chowkidar*."

His friend grinned. "Zep, you keep me on an even keel. I...you know...this is the way I felt when I first laid eyes on Pansy. Suddenly I knew, I just knew she was the one for me. And now, it's the same. This is where we'll be living. The Lord will do it."

"Well, pal," and Vijay placed his hand on Mahendra's shoulder and said, "far be it from me to deter you in your dreams, or shall I say visions?" He chuckled. "But in the name of common sense, let's see if we can find the *chowkidar* to give us some pertinent information."

"Okay, lead the way."

The wooded area behind the house all but hid the two-story long wooden building that apparently went with the property. An elderly Garhwali with a slight limp came out of one room at the corner and asked, "May I help you, sirs? I'm the *chowkidar*."

"Pleased to meet you," Vijay said. "We're from Mussoorie, and noticed this attractive place. Nobody lives here? It seems empty. To whom does it belong?"

"Lawyer Basant Kumar of Tehri City, sir. He rents it out by the season to a rich Nawab from Lucknow. It's a prime location for big game hunting, if I may say so."

"Oh!" Mahendra's exclamation caused the caretaker to glance his way. He continued with a grin, "I suppose it would be. But my interests aren't in animals, but in flowers."

"Trekking? All kinds of trails around here, too."

Vijay chuckled. "You're a good salesman," he said. "Want to show us inside? And, please, the address of the owner." His warning glance toward his friend kept the latter from laughing. After all, weren't they on their way to Lawyer Basant Kumar's home in Tehri?

The obliging *chowkidar* brought his keys, during which time Vijay said softly, "Pal, he doesn't need to know our minds, but let's double check his information."

The house tour disclosed two bedrooms downstairs with a commodious kitchen adjoining the spacious living-dining room that boasted a fireplace of good proportions. Upstairs were four good-sized rooms. Mahendra quietly noted that one could easily serve as kitchen, if needed. Two upstairs bathrooms were a feature not usually found in local houses. How had it happened, they asked.

Their guide grinned and said, "Mr. Kumar knows the right people, sir. He used to practice in the Supreme Court in Delhi."

"Ah, yes, I see," Vijay responded gravely. "And that would also explain his getting electricity in this remote area?"

"Yes, sir."

Mahendra tried to sound casual when he asked, "Does the Nawab lease the house a year at a time? How long does he stay?"

"I'm not sure of the arrangements, Sahib Ji. He doesn't come until the end of April or beginning of May. If you're interested further, you'll have to ask Mr. Kumar about it."

Vijay nodded. "Yes, yes, we'd like that address."

After giving the *chowkidar* a tip they thanked him and went their way, picking up the parcel and aware that here they had met God. Mahendra said in awed tones as they sped past the house on the road to Chumba, "I'll be back with Pansy. We'll be back, dear Lord." He drew a deep breath and concluded, "Thank you for showing it to me...a mountain lodge!"

# 13

# Indradevi

Indradevi, alias for Marcia Pierson Pennell, sat demurely in the main chapel of the Ashram on a Tuesday afternoon at three o'clock. Situated in a lush area north of Tehri City, the windows were slightly ajar to let in balmy breezes with their scent of flowers from the well-tended gardens surrounding the building.

The indescribably sweet cadenzas of the Himalayan whistling thrush brought a hint of smile to Indradevi's pale face. Was heaven speaking to her weary soul? She preferred to believe that, rather than the story her friend Parvati had told.

"It's what we call *Krishanpatti*," the older woman had said. "You see, Lord Krishna fell asleep one day out in the fields, and his flute dropped by his side. A mischievous boy happened by, and as boys do, he swooped up the flute, tucked it into the folds of his cummerbund, and ran. But when Lord Krishna awoke, he was angry. He cursed the thief and turned him into a bird. But, Indradevi, the bird had learned some of the tunes, so he whistles the god's glorious music. And when he forgets, he sort of stops in the middle."

A likely tale, thought the twenty-four-year-old, seated among the other nuns, all dressed in brown, handwoven blouses, and floor-length Tibetan robes called *chupas*. Indradevi, the name given her when she took the vows of silence some eight months previous, had now come out of that seclusion to find her status upgraded from an ordinary disciple to a "living goddess"!

Was it her beautiful white skin and hazel eyes? Was it the droop of her curling eyelashes, the sad, inscrutable look that seemed always detached, foreboding? Was it her perfect features? Most surely, Indradevi couldn't remain hidden for long.

Neither the Maharishi nor his closest disciples planned to keep Indradevi hidden. The monastery needed a boost. The long winter months would soon give way to spring's freshets and warmth, and pilgrims would move northward on their journeys. Now was the auspicious time to reveal Indradevi's new position to a watching world. She learned of the Maharishi's decision through Parvati, the one person she felt she could trust.

But Parvati had gone...gone with the six elderly women with whom she, Marcia, had hoped to leave! Cursed be that sleeping potion someone had given her! Was there no great God in heaven?

She knew there was, for she had rediscovered him during her six months' silence in a small room with a high window. That window opened to the sky, and the sky reminded her of the God of her childhood.

She seemed to live with sorrow, Marcia now reflected. Born prematurely the day after her father's accidental death in Brisbane, Australia, she had never known a father's love. But her mother and she shared deeply from the time she could remember. When Mary Lou Pierson moved to North India to fill the post of matron in an orphanage school near Mussoorie, little three-year-old Marcia accompanied her.

There, during her growing-up years, she had learned about God and the Bible. Moreover, during her recent six months' confinement, those Scriptures and choruses flowed uninterrupted through her memory, resulting in a faith that daily grew within her heart. She had repented deeply and sought forgiveness for turning from the living God to Eastern philosophies.

Illusion...emptiness...striving! They surrounded her today. The girl took a deep breath as a rustle of anticipation brought her back to the present.

All eyes scanned the doorway, awaiting a glimpse of the Maharishi. The audience rose, hands joined in reverent greeting. Disciples, seekers, and visitors peered through the semidarkness to distinguish the one whom they revered, yes, worshiped. His advanced spiritual status credentialed his leadership among them. All were on a spiritual journey; the Maharishi was closer to super-consciousness and God-realization than any of them, so they adored him. Even as the crowd pushed aside to let the elderly gentleman enter, each felt a part of the circle of love that emanated from his presence.

He wore a saffron-colored robe. His hair curled around his shoulders, and his dark compassionate gaze enfolded everyone in a calm, arresting manner. The Maharishi took his seat on the raised dais at one end of the long room, and crossed his legs in the lotus-like position. Fresh flowers sat within a half-circle of burning candles that formed an altar. With a slight wave of his right hand he motioned that the meeting could now begin.

Everyone sat, spine straight, breathing rhythmically—inhale, exhale, inhale, exhale. A disciple brought a harmonium, a portable instrument with a three-octave keyboard played by the right hand while pumping bellows with the left. The result? A wheezy musical tone. "Close your eyes," the disciple said, "and allow yourself to enter the spirit of praise to our leader." One *bhajan* followed another, with voices rising and falling, subdued yet intense.

After fifteen minutes of singing, the disciple instructed, "Now join in the universal sound of OM."

The ancient word for "God" swelled unbroken, unending. After awhile the next directive came: "Open your heart to feel the energy of the life force within you. Don't judge yourself. Don't judge this experience. Open your heart still more. Let go!"

For the past three years she had done this—to sense the feeling of being in space without boundaries, a beating rhythm of light lifting her up and onward. Ah, yes, that was before she learned that evil lurked behind seeming emancipation of self, that only darkness and despair lay ahead for eager seekers after truth. Fear of that evil had pushed her to undergo a vow of silence to ensure solitude and opportunity to seek God through Jesus Christ. So now, even while surrounded by those who sought self-realization and oneness with the Eternal, Indradevi sat within an insulated realm of her own spiritual unity with the Son of God and prayed, "Lord Jesus, send Terry."

The call of the Himalayan whistling thrush sounded over the melée of sounds around her, and the girl smiled. Her Lord had heard. Terry would come, the bird song said, and Jesus was real!

At the busy little Rishikesh railway station a small-gauge train arrived noisily. It discharged its load of pilgrims, then shunted around to make the return journey to Hardwar and Delhi. Even with all the commotion, the six elderly women failed to awaken, a fact that caused Parvati to smile widely. Her sleeping potion in their tea had worked!

Now each sat cross-legged, bundle clasped in her arms, and head resting on it for a pillow. Deep in slumber, they would be there until morning. Meanwhile, Parvati had her plans.

She rose quietly, picked up her bundle and left, only to join a mixed group that had just arrived. A harried mother was trying to quiet her whining children. Parvati said, "I'm on my own. Would you allow me to help you? Where are you going?"

The woman gave her a piercing glance, and then as though assured of her honest intent, said, "Which way are you headed?"

"To Chumba for the Spring Festival."

"Are you alone?"

"Until now I've been helping a party of six elderly women," Parvati said, nodding toward the group in the corner. "They're returning to Madhya Pradesh, but my home is near Mussoorie, so I've finished my job with them. If I can help you, I'll be glad for the security of a family with which to travel. I'm Parvati."

"Yes, yes, of course. No woman should travel alone. Here, you can take some of the hand luggage." She motioned to a pile on the floor and added, "We're going to Tehri City. Is that out of the way for you?"

With a satisfied nod Parvati said, "That's very good. Chumba is up on the hill above Tehri."

"Yes, of course. My husband is on home leave, so we'll be traveling by night. You don't mind?"

"Not at all. The road is good now. We walked it this week."

"Ah, yes. Well, stay close to us, and I'll speak to my husband about you."

This resulted in Parvati's getting to Tehri by morning, an accomplishment that placed an even broader smile on her face. Now she must somehow meet Indradevi. Her news of having seen the Australian would give her friend courage!

Parvati took an auto-rickshaw to the Ashram, paying for it with the five-*rupee* note the kind family pressed into her hand. As she got out with her bundle, she entered the familiar gate and made her way immediately to the back where the nuns were busy cooking breakfast. "I've come," she said with a big smile.

"Where are the six others?"

"At the railway station in Rishikesh. They're on their way home to Madhya Pradesh today." She added with a smile, "I hope

I'm in time for the Spring Festivals in Chumba? Are all of you still planning to go?"

Several nodded, albeit rather guardedly. Then one said, "We don't know what's happening up there." She intimated the men's quarters. "They hold their meetings and make the decisions; we just carry on with our work. But I'm glad you came, Parvati. Are you going to stay?"

"Not right away. I wanted to see all of you first, and then I must meet someone in Chumba. Is Indradevi here?"

"Yes."

"Let me write a message to her. Is she still in solitary confinement?"

"Not now, but the vow left its mark on her. She's not communicative like she was before. And she's under strict diet and care."

"Oh? Who takes her tray in?"

"Would you like to?" An elder nun gave her a searching look.

"How soon?" Parvati laughed lightly, glancing at her crushed and soiled *saree*. "If I bathe immediately, and one of you supplies me with a robe, I'll be glad to take the tray. Do you mind?"

"Humph, it's a great privilege, what with her special status. I suppose you know the rumors?"

Parvati said candidly, her eyes glistening, "How should I know? I've been away the past ten days."

"Well...yes."

So Parvati carried the tray to the single cell with the high window, and to Indradevi's delight she told of meeting Terry four days earlier in Rishikesh. "He's here, just like you said. Your God brought him."

"But where, Parvati? You met him under a tree. I don't have much time." Indradevi looked up at the woman waiting to take her tray out. A tear trickled down her wan cheek and she added, "I feel it's going to happen within this week. But I know my God is going to bring Terry to take me away."

"I'll help him," the older woman said.

"Oh, bless you! You give me courage." She drew a long breath then added, "I keep reliving it...how to escape...and it's still a mystery. I'm not sure...."

"I am, but we're going to have to run a risk and tell Mata Ji."

The girl's eyes grew wide with fear. "Can we trust her?"

"I think so, mainly because she's fearless. May I share with her? Remember, if we get Mata Ji on our side, she'll be as strong as a rock. No man can stand up to her. I doubt even Maharishi."

Indradevi wiped a tear. "Do what you think best," she whispered. "I trust you, Parvati."

Mata Ji, senior-most nun in the Ashram, had a long record of maintaining strict order in her domain, but though all the nuns feared her, they knew she fought for women's rights—something novel in this man's land. Now Parvati sought a private interview with her and gained it. They walked together in the garden.

After general discussion, Mata Ji turned to look at Parvati and asked directly, "What do you want to say?"

"Mata Ji, four days ago in Rishikesh, I met Indradevi's husband, Terry, from Australia."

The grey-haired woman stopped abruptly, straightened to control herself and said quietly, "That's the last thing I expected to hear. Are you sure?"

"Yes, Mata Ji. Indradevi has been praying he would come. She doesn't want to be declared a living goddess."

"How do you know?"

"She told me today. I took her tray in by permission of the kitchen crew."

"They should have asked me. That's a digression. Indradevi is under strict surveillance." The elder nun toyed with her beads.

"I wondered...and therefore I asked her for permission to share with you."

"She gave it?" Mata Ji again faced Parvati directly.

"She said she trusts me," Parvati said, drawing a deep breath. "I assure you, Mata Ji, Indradevi is not seeking power for herself. She wants to leave."

"Hmmm...." The women paced the walks quietly, then Mata Ji spoke, "This accounts for the change in her since taking the vow of silence. It also confirms my original opinion of her, that she is an unspoiled child, not the scheming woman some infer. Parvati," the senior nun spoke decisively, "you've got to find that man and bring him here. But we have to work secretly and fast. The plans are moving ahead."

"Yes, Mata Ji."

"Since you know so much, let me say I completely disagree with this move to utilize one of us in this manner. We nuns seek seclusion, not notoriety! A living goddess? Nonsense! And why choose a foreigner? These men and their notions...."

Parvati's broad smile brought a chuckle from her companion. She said, "Go immediately and bring him here. He's to be commended for seeking his wife, and I admire the gesture. Keep me informed." She paused, then asked, "Do you have any money?"

"A little...perhaps a *rupee*...not enough to take an auto-rickshaw back. I used one coming."

"Here." Mata Ji drew a pad and pencil from her voluminous pocket, and after writing a directive, said, "Take this to Shanti Bai. She'll provide you a new *saree*, some supplies, and twenty *rupees*. Go, child, first to Chumba, then to Rishikesh. With everyone converging in Chumba this week, it's likely the gentleman will be there, especially if he's seeking his wife."

"Yes, ma'am. Any further orders?"

"Bring him here. I'll keep Indradevi secure until the last moment before the procession on *Holi* when she is to be revealed. Humph!"

Parvati joined her hands in reverence and bowed her head as she murmured, "Thank you, Mata Ji, and please pray for the success of my venture."

Less than an hour later, now dressed in the new blue *saree* and carrying her bundle augmented with food supplies, Parvati climbed into an auto-rickshaw that took her to Tehri City where she boarded a bus for Chumba. Masses of local Garhwalis, entire families, now augmented with the growing number of pilgrims, clogged the road to the town on the hill. Obviously the Spring Festival was gaining in popularity! Many groups carried framed pictures and figurines; others brought idols in gaudily decorated palanquins. Every Ashram or religious sect took part in the processions that passed through Chumba each day.

Parvati hastened to alight at the convergence of the three roads, and there she took up her vigilance, using the tea shop as her base. Surely such exposure would lead her to the tall Australian if indeed he was searching for his wife.

Terrence Pennell began to wonder whether he had missed the Lord's directive. This was his fifth day in Chumba. Despite hours of scanning every procession, no white face appeared, or if it did it belonged to a hippie half dazed with hashish, wearing dirty clothes. Terry soon sensed the disdain the general public held for such Westerners. He was glad he had allowed Lionel to outfit him in gentlemanly garb. His quiet manner, good grooming, and soft-spoken Hindi immediately brought Terry rapport with the servants at the Tourist Bungalow. Through them he kept abreast of town news.

"Sahib Ji," they said, "every Ashram is here. We celebrate for a full week, with *Holi* as the big day. And do you know? People are saying that this year a living goddess will be revealed. There's one in Khatmandu, Nepal. Why shouldn't we have one, too? She would really make Garhwal famous!"

He hadn't thought much about the report, but as the days passed, a little niggling doubt began to work within. What if Marcia was to be the living goddess? Oh, surely not! Great God in heaven! Have mercy, and let me find her, his heart cried.

On Wednesday Terry stood from morning until after lunch, scanning the crowds to no avail. A short rest in the early afternoon led to his returning to the bazaar. He hoped he hadn't missed her. Surely the heavens must open soon. "You know where she is, dear Lord," he prayed again and again. "Lead me to her."

No sooner had he arrived at the tea shop, his vantage point, when two familiar travelers drew up on their motorcycle. "Squirt!" Terry called, leaping to his feet.

"Terry! Look, Zep. There he is!"

Unashamed, Terry hugged the newcomers. With obvious delight he said, "Oh! It's so wonderful to see you! Come, come, let's have tea together."

Zep and Squirt quickly parked the vehicle, brushed the dust from their clothes and followed Terry to the table where he had sat alone. "Tea for my guests," he ordered, "and hot *samosas* and *pakoras.*"

"Sounds great," Zep said. "A fitting end to a memorable day."

Squirt chuckled. "Not finished yet, pal. The Lord may have some more goodies for us. Imagine him placing Terry right here where we couldn't help but run into him."

Just then an Indian lady dressed in blue walked by, casually placing a handwritten note in clear Nagari script near Terry. He looked up, surprised, but she made no move to stop and soon joined the crowds on the curb watching an approaching procession. A bit perturbed, the Australian opened the note to read:

"You remember me? I'm Parvati, and you're Terry from Australia. I have news of your wife, and I can lead you to her. Meet me at the back table near the big window at six-thirty. I'll wait for you there."

Terry sat stunned, then pushed the note across to his companions. Each read the message silently, and thought, is this a con game? Or, it may be true.

Vijay broke the silence. "Come," he said, "we've got to get alone. Any ideas, Terry?"

"My room at the Tourist Bungalow. I've got my thermos. We'll fill it with tea, pick up our food, and beat it. Okay?"

Two trips on the motorcycle accomplished the feat in record time, and the three were soon immersed in prayer as they sought wisdom from above. Was someone wanting money from a foreigner? Was this truly Parvati? If so, would Terry recognize her in this setting?

Both Squirt and Zep recognized it might be difficult for the lady to speak freely with any other than Marcia's husband, if such he might be called. Zep asked him directly, "Terry, are you her husband?"

"The divorce went through, but believe me, brothers, it broke my heart. She is—and always will be—my wife."

"Then, if Marcia is willing, you'll have to legalize that first marriage vow as soon as possible. But for your present purposes I can see value in your being called her husband. That gives you the right to claim her, and it appears that Marcia considers you as such."

Terry's eyes lit with joy. "Bless you, Zep! The Lord has given you great wisdom, and I'm sure your father would say the same."

"Well," Zep continued, "Squirt and I had better change plans. We can hole in here, and I'll phone Mano while you meet the lady. I suggest you bring her directly here, to establish us as being part of you. She'll know, then, that you're not alone, and that will strengthen your position. Also, we'd better do our planning together. Am I on the right track, Squirt?"

"Well said, Zep!"

Terry recognized Parvati, soon establishing the fact that she had indeed spoken to him under the tree in Rishikesh, and had recognized him from Marcia's descriptions given in detail with a picture. Within moments they took an auto-rickshaw to the Tourist Bungalow to meet Vijay and Mahendra who awaited them on the verandah. There they planned, and an hour later, they scattered.

## 14

# Ride to freedom

On that Wednesday evening gaily dressed crowds thronged Chumba Bazaar. Blaring loudspeakers from entertainment areas augmented the cacophony of sounds that marks a *mela*. Pedestrians claimed right-of-way, with motorized vehicular traffic inching their way along.

With Parvati sitting sidesaddle behind him, Vijay pressed through as best he could on the motorcycle. She grasped the guardrail for security and smiled widely at this, her first motorcycle ride. She had climbed mountains, trekked rugged valleys and welcomed new adventures, but secretly hoped that none of the Ashram personnel would see her now. She'd have some explaining to do!

Why worry, she wondered, drawing a deep breath. Sometimes one throws discretion to the winds. Time counted today. Her quick return to the Ashram would accomplish much, for her precious bundle contained Terry Pennell's instructions and a change of clothing for Indradevi's personal use.

Within five minutes Parvati had learned to sway with the driver and to keep her balance when going around corners. "You're doing well," Vijay said over his shoulder. "It's easy to see you're the athletic type."

"Due to my school training in Mussoorie, Colonel Singh."

"Ah, yes, and your life as a pilgrim since then?"

"Probably."

Except for giving directions, however, other talk remained minimal, and within the hour they approached the long road leading into the Ashram. A rather relieved Parvati alighted. "Thank you, Colonel," she said. "My coming by motorcycle with a stranger would demand more explanations than I care to give right now." She laughed lightly, then added, "The watchman locks the main gate at nine-thirty. I know the password, of course, but I think it better to arrive on my own."

"Definitely," he said, nodding. "When I return tonight, which entrance should I take?"

"This one," she said smiling. "And stop by those bushes. The path to the back door takes off from there. It is used only by the milkman early in the morning and vendors during the day, otherwise unused. But it goes directly to the back door Terry indicated in his note."

"Ah, well said, friend. You've done all of us a great favor by risking your reputation for us, Parvati. If and when you have opportunity, please look us up in Happy Valley."

"Thank you, sir," she said, then swiftly and quietly disappeared into the darkness.

Her path led through an apple orchard that skirted the high wall surrounding the women's quarters. Parvati found her way quickly with the use of her ever-present flashlight, and soon approached the back gate. As she rang the doorbell, she hoped the kitchen crew hadn't yet completed their work so that someone could let her in. If not, she'd have to retrace her steps to the front gate, and that would take additional time. Right now every moment counted! She squinted at the wan moon covered by floating clouds. "Could rain," she muttered. "That would complicate matters."

Then she heard footsteps. Someone called, "Who's there?"

"Parvati."

A big key opening the heavy padlock that spelled security for the nuns made a screeching sound. A hand pushed the door just wide enough for the newcomer to slip inside, but not before a strong light from the elder nun's torch inspected her. "Come," she heard. "You look windblown...untidy. Where have you been?"

"On an errand for Mata Ji, as you know, sister."

"Hmmm.... Pretty late for you to be out," her companion grunted. They walked up the path through the vegetable garden.

"Yes," Parvati agreed. She drew a deep breath and said, "I'd rather go directly to bed, but perhaps I'd better see Mata Ji first. It's been a hectic day. Would you kindly take a message?"

They entered the kitchen door and the elderly nun switched on the light, then turned to Parvati. "Totally irregular, all of this maneuvering. What's so important? What should I tell her?"

"Just say I've returned, and that I'd like to see her if it's suitable. Otherwise I'll wait until morning."

Her companion gave her a quick glance, then said, "Wait here, Parvati. I'll let you know."

She walked away, her keys making a jingling noise. Parvati looked around the immaculate kitchen. What a day! She felt torn apart, yet knew that for Indradevi's sake she must remain calm. She had to somehow undo the harm she had done before by giving the girl that sleeping potion demanded by the head of the kitchen crew. Parvati shuddered and thought, "I hope I'm not catching cold...or perhaps it's excitement. But, by the gods, I've done my penance, and I pray nothing goes wrong tonight!"

Parvati sank wearily on a stool, and placing her bundle in front of her on the table, she slept.

Ten minutes later a slight touch on her shoulder awakened her. She looked up to see Mata Ji bending over her. "Are you all right, child?" The voice was not unkind.

"Oh, yes, Mata Ji. Forgive me for sleeping."

"You must be exhausted. Come, Parvati."

Taking her precious bundle, she followed into the inner sanctum normally out of bounds to the nuns, and certainly to the novitiates as was her status. She looked around. Here Mata Ji meditated. A sparsely furnished room, it lacked even a window, boasting only an overhead skylight that opened to the heavens. Mata Ji motioned to a Tibetan rug, and Parvati and she sat cross-legged, facing each other.

"Now, tell me everything."

An hour later Parvati crept wearily to bed. The matter was now in Mata Ji's hands. She had done what she could.


Indradevi looked around her small quarters speculatively. It must be after ten o'clock at night, but she had no desire to sleep. Unless she was mistaken, today would be Wednesday. Days and nights had a way of getting mixed when one lives in seclusion, she mused.

Not since hearing the whistling thrush eight days ago had she been allowed the freedom of leaving her room. And once again, as during her months of solitary confinement, the girl found her every movement monitored.

But today must be Wednesday. That meant that Friday was almost here, with the acceleration of the Spring Festival honoring Kami, the god of love. She dreaded the thought, sure that it would be pivotal in her young life. Something must give before then! "Great God in heaven! Are you there?" she whispered.

For weeks she had vacillated between hope and despair, but today Parvati had been able to crash the silence. Her message of Terry's nearness thrilled the girl. The solitary hours had flown with refurbished memories of her courtship and marriage. Those were happy days. Indradevi wiped a tear.

Maharishi's advent into her life had changed everything. He slowly wove his web, masterfully treating her as a beloved daughter and showered her with praise. Indradevi shuddered. Had he even then picked her out to one day declare as a living goddess, forever under his control?

"Lord Jesus," she pleaded, "do something! You're never too late. I need you...*now!*"

Near panic gripped her. Was it useless, all her trusting the Lord for deliverance? She had sat for hours, cross-legged on her prayer mat, her beads slipping effortlessly through her fingers, her mouth moving in prayer. If anyone spied on her movements through the closed door—they had their ways of doing it, she knew, by the eye-hole—her actions would appear impeccable. But inwardly her heart burned with fire! She desperately needed help *now!*

Several minutes later Mata Ji slipped in, carefully locking the door behind her. "Indradevi," she said softly, "come, my child."

Were they going to whisk her away before Friday? Great God, have mercy!

A tear slipped down her wan cheek as she sat motionless. The voice wasn't harsh, but rather appealing. What had happened to Mata Ji? The girl listened as the older woman spoke, "Come, my child. Weep here on my shoulder. It will do you good."

Suddenly her pent-up emotions broke, and Indradevi threw herself into the arms of the elderly nun who smoothed her hair, whispered tender words and said, "I know. I am a mother. I care."

"Mata Ji...oh, Mata Ji...I'm no living goddess! I have no desire for worship and praise. I don't want it!" she sobbed.

"I know. Now, stop crying. I have good news for you."

The girl listened in wonder. She drew back, struggling for composure. How terrible to give way in Mata Ji's presence! What had happened to the years of striving to master herself? How could she ever hope for mercy now?

She watched wonderingly as Mata Ji opened a brown shoulder bag and extracted a packet wrapped in newspaper along with two notes. With a smile she handed one to the distraught girl who read, "Marcia, my love. I've come to take you away. Do everything Mata Ji tells you. Terry."

"Is it true?" she whispered, a sob catching in her throat.

"You recognize his handwriting?"

"Of course, Mata Ji. It's distinctive. I'd know it anywhere."

"In a note to me, he says he'll wait for us outside the back gate between twelve-thirty and one o'clock tonight. Would you like to go, Indradevi?"

Tears rolled down her cheeks unheeded. She clasped her hands and said, "I've prayed so long for this. I *must* go back to my husband, Mata Ji. I hurt him so badly when I left. I *must* make it right. You understand?" She paused, then added, "Please...."

"Yes, my child. Now do as I say. Take off your robe and fold it neatly on your prayer rug. Lay your beads on top. And quickly change into the clothes your husband has sent. You will be disguised as an ordinary Garhwali. I checked." Mata Ji smiled, then added, "To aid, I'll darken your skin with coffee. It will wash off. We used to do it for plays when I was teaching."

"Oh, Mata Ji, I've never thought of you as anything but a nun in a monastery."

"Now, hurry child. I'll wait for you."

Would twelve-thirty ever come? Eventually, Marcia tiptoed out, now dressed in Daula Ram's clothes, her face tinted a light brown in color, her red curls covered with a woolen cap and secured by an enveloping brown shawl thrown over both head and shoulders. Mata Ji led the way, using a private entrance into the vegetable garden at the back.

The two women crept noiselessly along the path that hugged the high brick wall surrounding the compound, not daring to shine a flashlight lest they draw attention. The wall aided in their escape. Mata Ji whispered, "Are you all right? It's a bit rough here. Don't stumble."

Marcia felt almost lightheaded, numb with suspense, but she wondered to what extent Mata Ji was risking her own position and reputation in this venture for freedom. It could even mean the senior nun's life! "Great God in heaven," she breathed, "take care of Mata Ji. This would never have happened without her."

For an anxious moment—when the door creaked as the nun pushed it after unlocking the padlock that spelled security—Marcia scarcely dared breathe. Would Terry be waiting?

What if something went wrong? Indeed, after coming all the way from Australia, would he find transportation at this hour of the night? Would he find the right path through the apple tree orchard to this gate? Her heart thumped.

She saw her superior pause, peer out, then step over the lintel to meet Terry waiting in the shadows. She wanted to run, to shout, to throw herself in his arms, but her years of self-discipline took over. Instead, Marcia waited, listening to the one voice that called to her inner depths. In clear Hindi he said, "Mata Ji? I'm Terrence Pennell. I'm glad you received my note."

"You speak beautiful Hindi," she said in low tones. "My son, I have brought your wife to you. Come, Indradevi."

Mata Ji turned back, took the girl by the hand and helped her through the door. "Go, my child," she said, handing her the brown shoulder bag in which she had placed all incriminating evidence.

The girl halted a moment then whispered, "Terry!"

"Marcia, my love, is it really you?"

She laughed softly, and the nun said, "She's a sweet, unspoiled child, one who will make you a worthy companion. Go, Indradevi, with my blessing."

"Thank you, Mata Ji. Oh, thank you!"

They turned, going down the path holding hands. The nun watched until they had merged into the darkness of the night. She brushed away a tear and whispered, "I shall never forget. I have seen Kami, the god of love, claim his own. Who am I to withhold him from his heritage?" Then she entered the compound.

Indradevi's disappearance electrified the entire Ashram. When the kitchen crew discovered the empty room they reported it to Mata Ji who personally inspected it—robe neatly folded, door locked, beads lying with the robe on the prayer mat. But as Shanti Bai pointedly said, "The goddess has gone, Mata Ji."

Indeed she had, a fact that must now become public. It was Thursday morning, almost nine, and a message had come from the Maharishi to prepare Indradevi for her journey to Chumba. Mata

Ji's cryptic note said, "Your royal highness, I would do so if I could, but the matter is out of my hands. The goddess has disappeared. I personally inspected the room to find everything in order...all but her own sweet presence."

Her face inscrutably set, she answered the summons to come in person to explain, nor did she flinch upon meeting the irate leader. "Your honor," she said, bowing low, "the goddess has displayed her powers of levitation, her transcendence of our mere human limitations. We're confined to space and time. Our Indradevi has been exalted into true freedom. How else can we explain this enigma?"

"What do you mean, she disappeared? Where were you? She was in your charge!" he shouted, his eyes flashing. The nun wondered what had happened to the emanations of love that previously surrounded him. Maharishi now looked more like a volcano about to erupt.

She bowed again, then said softly, "Your royal highness, may I remind you that this is the feast for Kami, the god of love? He has called our Indradevi to himself. His joy is our loss. But I propose we build a shrine in her honor. Let us never forget she once lived among us. We have been blessed."

"Humph!"

But that's the way it turned out, and Mata Ji's suggestion made the Ashram famous.

No eyes but Mata Ji's saw the young couple treading the lonely path to meet Vijay Kumar Singh who waited with his motorcycle at the end of the long trail. Terry and Marcia regarded the whole incident a miracle, an expression of God's unfathomable love and grace, and their interlocked fingers symbolized their intense joy. Not until they had cleared the Ashram compound did they stop to embrace, sealing their love with a tender kiss. Then Terry whispered, "Oh, Marcia, I've found Jesus through this. He's the one who brought me here."

"I know," she said, "I prayed for months that you would come. He has done it, Terry, and now we must belong to him forever."

"Yes," he murmured.

A relieved Vijay saw them step out from the shadows onto the road. "I wondered how much longer I could bear the waiting," he said. Terry grinned, and Vijay came over to the girl at his side. "Disguise notwithstanding," he joked, "I take it you're Marcia? I'm

Vijay, and you're on your way to our home. My wife already knows you, Marcia. The Lord gave her a vision of you in a cell with a high window. You were dressed in a brown Tibetan *chupa*, seated cross-legged on a prayer rug. You had a rosary in your hands and she heard you saying, "Lord Jesus, send Terry."

"Oh!" Marcia's eyes grew wide as she drew a deep breath.

"Was it true?" Vijay asked.

"Every detail. Oh, I must meet her."

"You shall, God willing. Come, jump on behind me, and Terry will sit behind you. Let's go."

Sandwiched in between the two men, she felt more like a child than a villager on a jaunt. But in any case, the stray dog barking at the moon, or the chance meeting of a creaking oxcart on its way to the city market seemed innocuous enough with Terry's strong arm around her waist. Moreover, even the merrymakers in Chumba Bazaar had wearied of the bright lights and ferris wheels that would still be there tomorrow.

By three o'clock they approached Daula Ram's tea shop, and as Vijay turned off his engine and coasted to a stop he called, "Daula Ram...Daula Ram...."

A sleepy voice answered. The proprietor cautiously opened a window, then recognizing Vijay, he hurriedly welcomed the three travelers inside. His eyes gleamed on seeing the girl. "You're wearing my clothing?" He chuckled and commented, "They seem to fit very well." He rubbed his hands together in a pleased gesture and said, "You're Terry? Welcome, sir. I have prayed much for both of you."

"Thank you."

The Garhwali laughed and said, "My pleasure, sir. Now we must celebrate! I'll make some hot tea in a moment." Still chuckling, Daula Ram stoked the smoldering embers with fresh charcoal, and fanned it into flame with a blower.

"No business tonight?" Vijay asked.

"No sir. Everyone's at the *mela*. You came at the right time. Will the girl go to my house?"

"Not tonight, thank you. We'll stretch out here for several hours, then leave by dawn for Mussoorie. I think both Terry and I will feel more secure when she's at home. Right, Terry?"

"Yes, sir!"

"And where is Mr. Lall?"

"In the Tourist Bungalow in Chumba," Vijay answered. "Terry paid his bill and checked out last evening, only to have my friend reserve the room immediately for the night. I'll return tomorrow to continue our two week's vacation."

"Very good...very good. So this is an interlude?"

"An interjection, I'd say," Vijay answered with a wide grin.

Marcia sat at one of the small tables, head on arms, almost asleep. Conversation flowed around her, like soothing background music. Terry glanced at her and asked, "Please, sir, could you spread a mat for my wife? She's exhausted. I think sleep is more profitable for her right now than tea."

"Oh, yes, yes, sir." Daula Ram quickly unrolled a thick blue rug which he placed on a grass mat in the corner. Terry picked Marcia up, carried her over and the girl thankfully stretched out. He covered her with her shawl, patted her cheek, then rejoined Vijay and the Garhwali as they talked in muted tones. An hour later the men, too, stretched out to sleep.

But early dawn saw the travelers rising to continue their journey, and by shortly after seven they pulled up to the front verandah of Kushwant Singh's home. The lawyer came out on hearing the throb of the motorcycle. He stood there, smiling widely, and called, "Vijay! Terry! You've come! You've brought Marcia?" Spontaneously he bowed his head and prayed, "Thank you, Great God! Thank you!"

Marcia looked on, amazed. Daula Ram's reaction, and now Kushwant Singh's stunned her. These were Indians, yet they loved her because they loved her Lord Jesus. She gasped when Vijay's mother came out in her wheelchair, to hold her hands and say, "Marcia, oh, Marcia! Welcome home! I've prayed much for you, daughter. I'm just a new believer, and I can't get over the wonder of having you here."

A tear slid down Marcia's coffee-stained face.

The miracle continued. Manorma came from the kitchen, squealing with delight on seeing Vijay. "Darling! I wondered who came on the motorcycle. I never expected it to be you, not this soon."

"Why not, love?" Vijay hugged her and said, "I've brought you a younger sister, Mano. Come, meet Marcia."

Manorma turned to the shy girl standing under the Star of Bethlehem on the front porch. She pushed the shawl and cap back to release a flood of lovely red curls. She placed her hands on

Marcia's wet cheeks, and with glowing eyes said, "You're already part of us, dear. I saw you almost a week ago in a vision."

Marcia nodded mutely. Her heart was too full to express what she felt.

Manorma continued with a light laugh, "Yes...hazel eyes, auburn hair with those glinting highlights. Where did you leave your rosary and your Tibetan *chupa*? Your shoulder bag and your shawl match it. They're the same color."

Marcia nodded, a hint of smile on her exquisite features.

Vijay turned to Terry standing tall and proud beside her. "Carry your bride over the threshold, man! This is a new beginning."

And in the general laughter, that's exactly what Terry did.

# 15

# The bonus

Marcia looked into Terry's eyes in wonderment. She felt his strong arms around her and heard him whisper, "I love you. I want to place an engagement ring on your finger today, darling. May I?"

She managed to nod and smile. Thinking how ludicrous she must appear in her village garb, her coffee-stained face streaked with tears that refused to stop, she said softly, "Is this real? I'm so sorry I hurt you, Terry."

"Yes, it's real. Don't worry, love. We're beginning again." As he set her on her feet, Vijay and Manorma bounded in with the backpack, shoulder bag and shawl. Vijay said with a grin, "Take her upstairs, Mano, to change. Terry and I can use the other two bathrooms. Okay?" He added, "Wait a moment until I find some clean clothes."

Just then his parents came in the front door and Terry said, "Uncle and Auntie Singh, you'll never know what you've done for us today. Thank you for taking us in. We're very needy."

The lawyer cleared his throat, then said, "My boy, family is God's provision. We're glad to offer ours to both of you. Welcome home."

"Thank you, sir. Then, please, could we meet together? Before Vijay leaves this morning, I mean? I need to discuss several matters."

"Yes, Vijay?" Kushwant Singh asked. "When did you expect to return?"

He laughed and said, "Right away, Dad, after breakfast, of course. I'm starved. But if I can be of help to Terry, I'll wait until eleven o'clock to leave. In any case, Squirt's likely watching the processions, so I'll catch up with him in time."

"All right. Breakfast at eight, and a family caucus here in the living room immediately afterwards. Now all of you get cleaned up while I tell Rani to double the amount of food."

When Manorma and Marcia entered the upstairs bedroom, Marcia stopped in amazement. "What is it, dear?" Mano inquired.

"This is yours?"

"Yes, of course, Vijay's and mine. He's had this room for years. You like it?"

"It's beautiful. My room was only about one-fourth this size, and only one high window."

"I know. The Lord Jesus showed me. Marcia, you're very special. The Lord knew just what you needed, and if he hadn't gone ahead preparing the way, you'd still be there."

"I know." Her eyes filled with tears, and she whispered, "They said I was a living goddess. Today they would have taken me out. I don't know where. Oh!" She covered her face and began to sob.

Manorma laid the shoulder bag and shawl on the bed, then took the troubled girl in her arms. "Lord Jesus," she prayed, "you've brought Marcia to us, and...oh, I do thank you! Please give her peace and quick healing. Wonderful Lord, just let her realize that all of us love her very much, and that we care."

"My head...it hurts."

"Look, dear, wash up a bit. Can you? Put on clean clothes and my bathrobe, and if you feel like it, join us for breakfast. Otherwise, I'll serve you a tray. In any case, you can sleep all day if you'd like. How's that sound?"

"Oh, thank you. Mano, is it?"

"That's what Vijay calls me...short for Manorma."

"But, but, you shouldn't trouble yourself for me. I should be caring for you." She looked at Manorma's obvious pregnant condition and asked, "When is the baby due?"

"Two more months to wait," Manorma said with a laugh. "It has to be a boy. He kicks something fearful inside me, getting ready to be a mountaineer like his dad." She looked out the window and said, "See those hills and valleys? And the high peaks? Vijay and his friend, Mahendra, have trekked all over that country...up and down...from the time they were boys. They love these Garhwal hills."

Marcia drew a deep breath. "For me they've spelled disaster; for them, hope?"

"Never mind, dear." Manorma impulsively hugged the girl and asked, "Shall I clean out the brown shoulder bag? We'll wash everything, so leave your dirty clothes on the floor in the bathroom. Here are clean underclothes, and a pretty green *salwar-kameez* that will make your red curls look glamorous. If you're too tired to get fully dressed, Marcia, you'll find a blue bathrobe hanging on the hook behind the door. Okay?"

Marcia's spirits lifted. How could she remain sad in the presence of this vibrant girl? But she laid the punjabi outfit aside and wore the bathrobe to breakfast. "Please forgive me," she said shyly, "I'll try to stay awake while we eat."

"Poor, wee lamb," Susheela commented.

"Bruised and bleeding," Vijay added.

"But deeply loved," Terry said with a smile, as he led her to a seat beside him. The trust in her shining eyes clearly showed. She could scarcely believe this was real: Terry sitting to her right, a tower of strength in answer to prayer!

After breakfast the girl excused herself. Manorma pulled the drapes, covered Marcia with a warm comforter and tiptoed out to inform the waiting family, now gathered in the living room. She's out like a light—exhausted!"

"Good!" Terry exclaimed. "It's better so. I must talk about our relationship so that all of you know what's happening. Right, Vijay?"

"Right, Terry. Go ahead."

Terry leaned against the fireplace and said, "If you don't mind, I'd just as soon stand." Susheela took out her knitting from the bag that hung on the handle of her wheelchair. The lawyer sat in his favorite spot by the window, and Manorma joined her husband on the settee. Terry looked around and thought it a homey setting, one in which he longed to find himself on a more permanent basis than as stranger or guest. He began, "If Marcia and I ever needed family, it's now. Thank you for all you've done. That five days in Delhi opened my eyes and softened my heart to bring me back to Jesus, my Savior." He paused, then with a smile added, "It also prepared me to respond to Marcia's need, thank God."

"It's all his mercy," the lawyer said.

"Yes, Uncle Singh. Well, you may or may not know that Marcia and I were divorced over three years ago. Legally, we're no longer husband and wife. But I assure you we're retaking our marriage vows as soon as possible."

Susheela looked startled. "But, Terry," she said, "what happened? I don't understand. Divorces aren't common in this country." She paused in her knitting, and Terrence Pennell toyed with the fringe of the cover on the mantelpiece before replying.

"Auntie," he finally answered, "I'd like to forget that part of my life, but I must face it...then ask the Lord Jesus to erase it from our memories. You see," and he looked at the older woman with a whimsical smile, "neither Marcia nor I were living close to the Lord then."

She nodded, and he continued, "It's not a pretty story, but I can tell you truthfully we've loved each other from the day we first met on shipboard. I was sixteen; Marcia, fourteen. Two years later we married and had two happy years. Then..."

He paused, and Manorma asked, "When did your parents die? I've heard you mention that."

He drew a deep breath, then answered, "About a month before the Indian guru showed up. I was devastated. My parents died in a plane crash, and shortly afterwards our home life became a nightmare."

"Maharishi?" Vijay asked.

"The same. Elderly...has grey, curling hair about his shoulders...a suave manner. He talked kindly, and most surely drew Marcia, but left me alone. I guess I wasn't his kind. Or maybe he had designs on her even then. Who knows? Anyway, Marcia responded and I was left alone—angry, hurting, lost." He paused, then added, "She divorced me. I began drinking, carousing, going with the wrong set. She left for India to become one of the guru's closest disciples. And ultimately..."

Vijay took up the story. "Mom and Dad, this girl has really been through it! She spent the last three years in a monastery, up on the route to Gangotri. The best of the last eight months she's been in solitary confinement, with her every action and reaction monitored and that resulted in the Maharishi declaring her a living goddess. Believe it or not, tomorrow she was to be revealed to the world during the *Holi* celebrations in Chumba."

Kushwant Singh, intently listening with his fingers evenly matched, looked up sharply. "Son," he asked, "How do you know all this? On what authority?"

"Initially Parvati, Dad. Remember her? She figured in Terry's story at Rishikesh."

The lawyer nodded, and Terry took up the tale. "Sir, Parvati came from within the Ashram group, but throughout, she's befriended Marcia. At the end, well..."

Vijay finished, saying, "She really put her reputation on the line to let us three men know how matters stood. And she's the one who enlisted the senior nun's aid, otherwise there would have been no escape."

Little by little the story became clear. Both Manorma and Susheela kept wiping tears. Kushwant Singh's probing questions brought out salient facts, and the lawyer, apparently satisfied, turned to Terry to ask, "Now what? What comes next?"

Terry chuckled, a winsome eagerness captivating his listeners as he said, "Today, sir, I'd like to place an engagement ring on my lady's finger, if Vijay will kindly give me a lift to the bazaar to buy it."

Everyone laughed and Vijay exclaimed, "Of course, man! Do you need money?"

"Thanks to Auntie Singh's sound advice, I've still got my traveler's checks, Zep."

"But why not make it a wedding ring?" the lawyer asked.

"Not immediately, uncle."

"Why not?"

"I think we need a courtship period. A lot has happened in the last three years."

"Hmmm...perhaps you're right."

Manorma spoke up, "Papa, already I've found out that Marcia comes from another world. Do you know? She's amazed at the size of our bedroom! She's coming out of a prison. What's she going to do with freedom? I think we'll have to be very tender with her."

"Yeah, you're right." Terry gave Mano a grateful look. "Vijay thought we ought to sew things up fast, but having met my Marcia, what do you say now?"

"Man, you caught me there, Terry. I guess you do need to learn to know each other as you are. But you can do that pretty fast, can't you? What do you say, Dad?"

Kushwant Singh rose and began pacing the floor. Finally he paused to say, "I think we can reconcile both viewpoints. I suggest marriage in about two weeks, after Vijay and Mahendra return. Give her the engagement ring today."

"Yes, sir, and what about other matters?"

"Well, are you staying in India or returning to Australia?"

Terry drew a deep breath, then said, "Uncle Singh, if it's safe for her to stay here, I think both of us would like that. We love the Himalayas."

"Safe? Certainly, since we're here to protect you."

Susheela exclaimed, "Yes, yes, you must stay."

Vijay chuckled and added, "You're Australian! Neither of you require a visa. Man! You could snap up any job with the soccer record you've got. Mussoorie, Terry? I know two places right now."

"Where, Vijay?" Mano pulled on his arm.

"Tibetan camps, darling, and the military camps."

"Schools?"

"Definitely. Come on, Terry, you must stay!"

The lawyer chuckled. "Well, that's settled. Now for an immediate answer. I suggest Marcia moves in with Manorma until Vijay returns; Terry can use Phulmoni's little room, and after the marriage, we'll give the newlyweds the upstairs guest room. How does that sound?"

Manorma clapped her hands. "Oh, thank you, Papa! I felt so alone last night. I'll love having Marcia for a roommate."

"You'll be good for her, daughter. It will help her to break into society again. I'd say she's sustained great pressure of late. She needs a release, but in rather small doses."

"You're right, sir," Terry said. "The adjustment may take longer than a fortnight. Meanwhile..."

"Man! Spend a lot of time with her," Vijay suggested. "She trusts you. I saw it in her eyes at the breakfast table."

"Good!" Terry said softly.

"Well, Dad," Vijay looked at his watch. "I think I should be on my way soon."

"Not yet, my boy." Kushwant Singh cleared his throat, then said, "Vijay's always given me great pleasure as a son. Now, Terry, would you also like the right of sonship in lieu of having lost your own parents?"

"I already feel like one of you."

Kushwant Singh's eyes twinkled as he said, "But the implications of my offer go much deeper than merely tasting Indian hospitality. Would you like to be my son?"

"In what way, sir?"

"As one given to us by God, our heavenly Father, through a spiritual rebirth into his family." He paused, and a deep hush fell on the group.

Terry suddenly bounded over, and placing his arm around Vijay's Dad, said with emotion, "That's magnificent!"

Kushwant Singh looked up and smiled, "That's my offer to you. You may have the right of sonship. How about dropping the 'Uncle' and 'Aunt' and calling us Mom and Dad as Vijay does?"

"Oh!" Manorma gasped.

Terry looked across at Vijay. Apparently satisfied, a grin creased his face and he nodded, saying, "Thanks, Dad. And boy, it's great to have a brother!"

Vijay jumped up, met him halfway and hugged him, then said, "Welcome, Terry! Man! This is super!"

It seemed the right moment to break up the meeting, but the lawyer had one more thing he wanted to say. "Sit, boys," he commanded with twinkling eyes. "In our Indian culture, since sons live at home, and our second son, Terry, is about to be married, I would like to announce that the house next door is now ours. I bought it this week from Tej Bahadur, who, incidentally, is in financial straits. He's been after me for a year, but I resisted until recent events placed matters in a different light."

"Dad! You bought the cottage?"

"Yes, Vijay, for an investment in privacy." He chuckled, and added, "Now I can see purpose in it. Terry and his bride can move in as soon as we get it into livable shape. How's that sound, family?"

Susheela laughed, and Manorma giggled and said, "No more Kailu? We'll miss him, won't we? He's drawn us closer together."

"Most certainly," the lawyer said amid general laughter. He added, "Tej Bahadur has used the upstairs apartment over his store as a rental. Now his family will live there. By selling the cottage he can pay off his debts, so we do him a favor and help ourselves in the bargain."

"How soon do we get it, Dad?" Terry asked.

"He promises it by the end of the month. That's next week. Of course we'll have to clean it up."

"Fun!" Manorma exclaimed.

Vijay stood and said, "Come on, family! You make me want to stay instead of leaving right now. Wait till I tell Squirt." Turning to Terry he added, "Let's pick out that engagement ring, buddy. At least I can get in on that, and Mano, I'll be taking Daula Ram's clothes."

"But I wanted to wash them first."

"Ordinarily, yes. But under these circumstances, we'd better not leave any evidence of Marcia's former life lying around. Kailu's still here, remember!"

"Oh!" The girl looked startled. "You mean it's not safe for her? Will the Maharishi hunt her down?"

"I don't know, but let's take precautions. And, by the way, Dad, perhaps you'd better caution her about following any meditation practices. Servants pick up clues quickly, and rumors go far afield."

"Well said, son. In any case, Marcia had better make a clean break with her past."

So the brown shoulder bag and shawl, along with Daula Ram's clothes returned with Vijay to the Garhwali.

Marcia slept through lunch, getting up about three in the afternoon. Much rested, she appeared in the pretty green punjabi outfit Manorma had suggested. As she stepped into the hall Terry met her. "Come, love," he said, "I'll show you my little room."

"Where?"

"Right here. See?" He took her hand and led her, opening the door to the bright bedroom that overlooked the gardens at the back. "Pleasant, isn't it?"

"But...but...we're not going to stay together?"

"Not yet, love, not until we're married." She looked startled and he said, "I have lots to share, Marcia, but the first thing I want to do is this. Come, sit down." He led her to the wicker chair in front of the small writing table. With a grin he pulled a little box out of his pocket, and said, "Finding a quiet spot to again declare my love for you is my first job—one I highly relish."

She drew a deep breath and said, "This is nice. It's more the size of room I lived in at the Ashram."

"Yes, sweetheart. Now see what I brought you." He opened the box to take out an authentic pearl ring set in twenty-two karat gold.

"Oh!" she exclaimed.

"Like it?"

Her eyes filled with tears. "For me?" she whispered.

"For you alone, Marcia. Will you marry me? I love you with all my heart."

"Are you sure, Terry? I don't want to hurt you again. I made such a mess of our marriage before." Her lips quivered.

He lifted her up, and with his arms around her, he said, "Look, love, it will be different this time. The Lord Jesus Christ is with us, remember?"

"Oh, yes."

He kissed her again and again, then slipped the ring on her engagement finger and said, "I chose a pearl, Marcia. Somehow it seems more appropriate than the brilliant diamond I gave you before. What happened to that?"

She hid her face on his shoulder and murmured, "It went to Maharishi, like everything else I owned."

"Never mind. That's past history. I'll get you what you need now. We'll be married when Vijay and Mahendra return in a fortnight, love, and meanwhile, we'll get your trousseau ready."

She looked up. "This is Manorma's outfit. Nice, isn't it? I like it better than dresses."

Later, when they sat on the front verandah waiting for afternoon tea, he asked, "You know why I chose a pearl?" He paused, then added, "It's the answer to an injury. A bit of sand or other obstruction gets into the oyster shell and irritates it. So what does the oyster do? Builds a magnificent pearl, a jewel if you please. Look at it, sweetheart. It's iridescent, glowing."

"The answer to an injury," she murmured, then turned eagerly to Terry and said, "That sounds like Jesus! Doesn't it? He suffered for us, but out of that suffering comes eternal life! Oh, Terry, I don't deserve all this. I've struggled so long for peace."

"Tell me about it," he suggested.

She began hesitantly, feeling it strange to be in the open talking to a man. Then she reminded herself that she was not in the Ashram, nor answerable to Maharishi, and she murmured, "God has been so good to us. Why should I fear?"

And within his heart Terry rejoiced, as he grasped the promise of a new life ahead.

# 16

# Chumba Bazaar

Kailu's mother, arms full of blankets and bed linens, walked past the dining room window and nearly dropped her load on that Thursday afternoon. She distinctly saw two white young people sitting on the Singhs' verandah!

Plunking everything down in the back bedroom, she said to Shanti, her teenage daughter, "Here, my back aches. Sort these and pack them in those cardboard boxes." Then she hurried back to her favorite corner to seat herself comfortably in her easy chair. With knitting in hand, she peered out and said aloud, "Now, would you know? They have company! Foreigners! Haven't seen the girl before. When did she come?" Maya Bahadur breathed a deep sigh, then muttered, "Where was she when Colonel Singh and this young man went off this morning? It puzzles me. Yesterday the Colonel and his friend rode off together. And I'll declare they packed that vehicle as if going on tour. But the Colonel's come back? Where's Lall?" She knit furiously, and said, "Kailu's father doesn't like me sending the boy over to find out what's going on, but perhaps just this once wouldn't hurt."

"What is it, Ma?" her daughter called from the back bedroom. She came and stood in the doorway. "Did you want something?"

"No, I was just wondering why Kailu is so late. It's four o'clock."

"Club, Ma. Remember? The Kailu Klub meets on Thursdays. Probably all the boys are throwing mud today in celebration of *Holi.* She paused, then said, "Ma..."

"Yes, Shanti?"

141

"Must we move? I like living next to the big house. Why do we have to go?"

"We can't do much about it."

"What, Ma?"

"I said we can't do much about it. We don't own the house any more."

Shanti walked over to her mother and asked, "We don't?"

"Humph! I suppose we ought to be glad, what with our renters leaving right now and Mr. Singh ready to buy."

"You mean *our* Mr. Singh? He bought this house?"

The woman replied sharply, "That's what I said."

"But how soon must we move?"

"By the end of the month—next week. Now look, Shanti, you've got far too much work to do to just stand and talk. Go and finish your job."

"Come with me, Ma."

The timely tinkle of Kailu's cycle bell caused his mother to jump up and say, "Your brother's come. I must talk to him. Go back to your work, girl. I'll be coming."

But the boy rushed in, calling, "Ma! I'm starved! We had club today, and do you know? That interesting Mr. Gur Bachan from the *Mussoorie Weekly* talked to us and said we're doing fine with bringing in news. That really made us feel good, so we've decided to go to Chumba, Ma."

"When and how?" said Maya, trying to keep an eye on the foreigners next door.

The boy danced around, saying, "Tomorrow, by bus. We've reserved six seats for the seven o'clock bus. Please, Ma?"

She looked at him severely. "What do you mean, please?"

The boy picked up a leftover *samosa* from a plate on the sink and munching, said, "I didn't have time to see Papa, so I'm asking you instead."

"Why Chumba?"

"Mr. Bachan says he heard a living goddess is to be declared, and we want to see her. Lots of people are going. Some went today—walking, Ma. Mr. Bachan says the busses are full, but he's paid for our tickets, so we're all right."

Maya regarded her son with a frown and said, "But Kailu, you're only ten years old! You can't go on your own. No, son!"

"Oh, Ma, please! It's important. I ride to the bazaar."

"That's different. This takes all day, and there are crowds of people. You could easily get lost. No, Kailu."

He pulled at her sleeve, his eyes pleading. "Ma, you must let me go. How can the Kailu Klub go without me? I'm the president."

"Well...we'll see. I'll ask your father."

As it turned out in both Kailu's case and with his friend, Prem, their fathers joined the expedition, each occupying the seat his son would have taken, but that seemed a small price to pay for retaining the club's reputation. Kailu and Prem stood by the window, gleefully dousing passing pedestrians with red color. Normally they would have been reprimanded, but everyone took the sport today in good spirits.

The bus stopped at Daula Ram's tea shop for ten minutes. The proprietor asked the boys, "Climbing to the top of the mountain?"

"Oh, no, sir. We're going to Chumba."

"What for? It looks like all Mussoorie is headed east."

"Haven't you heard?" Kailu piped up. "We're going to see the living goddess. And, sir, we're a news club, and we represent the *Mussoorie Weekly*."

Daula Ram's eyes twinkled as he said, "My, my! I didn't know I was serving celebrities. Here, boys, I'll give each of you an extra biscuit, and if you stop on the way back, be sure to tell me what the goddess looks like."

"Yes, sir, we will."

This bus, as all others, disgorged its passengers a mile out of town by order of the local police, to manage the crowds. Holding Kailu and a friend firmly by the hand, and sandwiching two lads between the elders, there might be some hope of not losing a boy or two in these throngs. The Kailu Klub walked in a little tight-knit group from one site to the next, following the crowds as rumors swept from one end of the bazaar to the other.

Hour followed hour, and processions proliferated, but no living goddess appeared. Finally a loudspeaker blared, "Hear about the living goddess at three o'clock on the temple grounds." Everyone pushed and shoved, making their way toward the temple courtyard that already overflowed. But the ingenious lads climbed on top of a wall. "Papa, Papa," Kailu called, "come up with us. You can sit and see like we do."

"Impossible. We can't climb."

"Yes, Papa. Come around to the back. There are some stones here, and we'll help you."

When accomplished, the Kailu Klub with their two adult escorts had grandstand seats. The temple platform and steps served as stage for a religious drama in progress. The audience stood on tiptoe, trying to see as well as hear. Kailu kept asking, "Papa, when will she come?"

"I don't know, son. The announcement said we'd hear about her at three o'clock."

"How long is that?"

"Another fifteen minutes."

At last the drama concluded, and a saffron-robed speaker with grey hair falling on his shoulders took his place at the microphone on the steps. Brown-robed disciples surrounded him, and to the wheezing sound of a harmonium, they lustily sang his praises. "Who is it?" Kailu asked.

"Shh...let's listen. Maybe they'll tell us."

After several lyrics, the singing began praising Kami, the god of love. The crowd joined in, with the leader singing the first line and the people answering in refrain. "When will she come?" Kailu asked impatiently. "I want to see the living goddess."

"Hush, boy. Be patient, and listen. You're expected to report what happens, aren't you?"

"Yes, Papa, but I'm hungry!"

Tej Bahadur smiled as he reached into his shoulder bag to pull out packets of roasted peanuts. That held the boys for the next fifteen minutes. They threw the shells over the back side of the wall and chomped loudly as they watched.

Speeches followed praising the Maharishi for having found the living goddess. Finally the holy man spoke again, this time in soft and sweet tones, "My children, beware of being caught in the illusion of that which seems to be reality. It is *maya*—not to be trusted. Only that which is spiritual is real. So I beseech you to seek true enlightenment and unity with god, even as our beloved Indradevi did. She lived among us for three years. Her beauty and purity of soul matched the graciousness of her body. Moreover, she sought and obtained self-realization with Kami, the god of love, and two days ago he called her. She followed her lover, to live forever in this *Devbhumi*, the land of the gods."

A disquieting murmur swept the audience. Kailu pulled at his father's arm to say, "She's not here? Then why did we come? Why did people say she would be?"

"Shh...listen, boy. The holy man hasn't finished talking."

Maharishi raised his hand for silence. When the murmuring had lessened, he said, "My children, we do well to honor our Indradevi, and we shall do so now. Listen...."

Conch shells blasted forth, cymbals clashed and dancers appeared from within the temple precincts. They whirled in ecstasy, portraying the wooing of Indradevi by Kami. The drama unfolded, holding the audience spellbound. It culminated only with the heroine being snatched away to forever be one with Kami in the high mountains.

"Ah," the audience said, satisfied. Now they could go home.

Late that night the Kailu Klub finally found seats on a bus for Mussoorie. When they passed the tea shop it was closed. Kailu, too, slept, this time in his father's arms.

Next day he reported, "Ma, we can't see the living goddess now. She's gone to the high mountains."

"How do you know, son?"

"I heard it in Chumba."

"Does that make it true, Kailu?"

"Of course, Ma," he said, satisfied.

In his small room at the Tourist Bungalow, Mahendra Lall spent a sleepless night praying and watching. Where were Vijay and Terry? Had the escape plans gone through? Would morning never come, and when it did, how should he fill the hours until he could anticipate Zep's return?

He rose leisurely, knowing full well that all staff would by now be in the bazaar. But he had Terry's thermos filled with hot tea, and a box of crackers in his backpack. He ate a credibly good breakfast. Then he took a long walk away from town, figuring that Vijay couldn't possibly come before noon.

On his return he decided to call Lawyer Basant Kumar in Tehri.

"Hello...hello," he heard.

"Lawyer Basant Kumar?"

"Speaking."

"Sir, I'm Vijay Kumar Singh's friend, Mahendra Lall. You'll likely remember me as Vijay's buddy who used to stop with you overnight when we trekked the area as boys."

"Yes...yes! And how are you, Mahendra?"

"Very fine, sir. At the moment I'm at the Tourist Bungalow in Chumba, waiting for Vijay. We hope to see you this evening, if that's acceptable."

"Definitely. I must have mixed the dates. I looked for you last night."

"Plans changed, Mr. Kumar. When we meet we'll give details. I thought we might meet you here at Chumba."

Squirt heard a chuckle and the answer, "Not now, young man. With the years comes gout, and with gout comes inclemency. I don't walk much these days."

"Sorry, sir, that's unfortunate. I hope we won't be too much trouble."

"Not at all, not at all. After our busy life in Delhi, we still find Tehri rather dull, so having company spices up an otherwise monotonous existence. We're looking forward to meeting you again. Any idea as to the time of your arrival?"

"No, it depends on how soon Vijay and I find each other. However, I expect him by midafternoon."

"Well, enjoy the *mela* for us, and be assured of our eager anticipation of your visit."

"Thank you. Goodbye, sir."

Bother! Squirt thought. What I really wanted to ask him was about the house. Oh, well, maybe tonight.

Hunger gnawed, so despite his desire to stay in pleasant surroundings, Mahendra joined the crowds walking into town. At the teastall where Vijay and he had met Terry, he took a small table in the back. After finishing his meal and paying his bill, he asked to sit and read while awaiting his friend.

Shortly before three he felt a slight touch on his shoulder. It was Zep, and Squirt rose quickly to greet him. "What a scare you gave me!" he said, chuckling. "Is everything all right?"

A brief nod and the gleam in Zep's eyes assured him of the success of the venture. "Come, sit down, pal. Had your lunch?"

"No...I didn't leave Mussoorie until after eleven, but I did stop for a cup of tea at Daula Ram's. Anything new?"

"In what way? Food, or circumstance?"

"The latter. Ah, here comes the waiter. I'll order, then we can talk."

While eating, Vijay sketched bare details. He spoke softly to discourage eavesdropping and said, "Squirt, I'll tell you more later. What's the lay of the land now?"

"Rumors and mounting excitement. I think every Ashram in the country is here. By the way, I phoned Lawyer Basant Kumar. He's expecting us this evening. Are we returning tomorrow? What do you think?"

"Hmmm, perhaps we should...to give a firsthand account."

"Oh, Zep, I thought you'd say that. Frankly, I'm jealous of every day. I want to hunt for a new variety of herb that's valuable for medicinal purposes. I just read about it, and I think I know where to find it."

"Okay, man, I'm weary!"

"We don't have to pull out until six o'clock. Let's go back to the room and rest."

By six, however, they rode to Tehri. The dapper little gentleman who came out to meet them looked scarcely a day older than they remembered him fifteen years previous. He wore the same style Nehru jacket, a high cut collar buttoned up, and a rosebud tucked in the third buttonhole, reminiscent of Pundit Nehru himself. There was the familiar scent of pomade, and the same meticulous hairstyle. Not much had changed, except that now he limped.

Lawyer Basant Kumar approached them, rubbing his hands in pleasure. "Vijay, Mahendra, how are you? We're delighted to have you look us up. Come, come. My wife made her best chicken curry for tonight. I trust you're hungry."

With easy chatter, he led the way. They passed through a narrow door that opened into an anteroom, which in turn led to a spacious courtyard and living quarters, all enclosed by a high wall. Potted plants filled the corners and lined the verandahs. A small fountain played in the center. "You've moved," Vijay said. "I didn't remember this."

"Ah, yes. We've been here for five years, since my retirement. Your father? How is he? Is his health better?"

"Thank you, sir, yes. He's doing very well these days, but still has to moderate his activities."

"Your mother?"

"Better than formerly. Arthritis crippled her until she became a wheelchair patient, but recently she's walking more and more. We're encouraged."

"That's good. Come, be seated, or would you like to clean up before eating?"

Mahendra could scarcely await the propitious moment for asking about the house, but it was Vijay who opened the subject. Mr. Kumar asked, "Had a good journey?"

While his pal sipped his lemonade, Vijay answered, "Yes, sir, with lunch at a new tea stall near your house."

The lawyer looked up sharply. "My house?"

"Yes, sir, the hunting lodge I believe you own."

"How did you know?"

"We spotted it while taking a walk from the tea stall. Then we met the *chowkidar* who showed us inside and gave your address."

Mr. Kumar chuckled. "You didn't tell him you knew me?"

"No, sir. I could hardly keep Squirt from blurting it out, but I decided the Garhwali didn't need to know everything. Right, sir?"

The lawyer laughed heartily. "You're a true son of your father, Vijay," he said. "If he's anything, he's discreet...and selective. A brilliant thinker."

"I think my sister inherited his qualities, not I. But Mahendra, here, he's the scholar."

Basant Kumar turned to look thoughtfully at Squirt, then asked, "What's your interest scholastically?"

"Botany, sir, particularly herbs and orchids."

"Well, well, what a coincidence." He paused, then said, "But you're a pilot! I understand both of you manned spotter planes for the Artillery. How do you reconcile that with botany?"

Mahendra smiled, and said, "Right, sir, but living in the mountains all my life has provided considerable opportunity to pursue my hobby."

"He's very modest," Vijay intercepted. "What Mahendra has detailed on orchids alone would make a thesis for a doctorate."

"You don't say...hmmm...."

The soft gurgle of the fountain as it splashed cheerily, along with the twittering of sparrows and the more distant call of the whistling thrush made Vijay comment, "Now I know I'm in the western Himalayas. This is my land!"

When the dinner gong broke into the conversation, the lawyer said, "Perhaps you surmised something is on my mind. After the meal, Mahendra, I'd like to pursue the subject."

Vijay excused himself after eating, and in the coolness of the late evening the lawyer and Mahendra Lall talked.

"I'm in the enviable position of having rented the hunting lodge to a prominent pharmaceutical firm in Geneva, Switzerland," the lawyer began as they resumed their seats in the patio. He lit his pipe and puffed on it while Mahendra tried to assimilate this new information. Finally he spoke, "But, sir, the *chowkidar* informed us that a Nawab from Lucknow comes each year."

Basant Kumar chuckled and said, "Usually, yes, but not this year. He's taking his ailing wife to the United States for advanced medical treatment, and ultimately hopes to obtain his green card." The lawyer puffed away on his pipe and said, "Nawabs, young man, don't carry the political weight they used to." He chuckled, then added, "Wealthy landlords don't carry the prestige of former days, so he's looking to the new world—but he won't find his big game there!"

Mahendra laughed. "Where's he going?" he asked. "New York?"

"Initially."

Wish he'd get on with this, Mahendra thought, but waited. After several more puffs, Basant Kumar continued, "The point is, the pharmaceutical firm is establishing an Indian base in the lower Himalayas to study rare varieties of flora, with intent of using them for medicinal purposes. Now that I consider a worthy calling." He looked directly at the young man and asked, "Are you interested in giving the next five years of your life to this?"

"I, sir?"

"You're coordinated. You're meticulous, and what's more, young man, you've got experience and don't require a visa. Add to that your association with my friend, Kushwant Singh, and you see why the scales tip heavily in your favor."

"But, sir, what does this entail?" Mahendra placed his fingers exactly together, a gesture that made the older man smile.

"It calls for living in the hunting lodge at company expense, sending detailed reports, and twice a year entertaining overseas guests. It's a lonely spot, but then, not too far from Mussoorie. By the way, are you married?"

"Engaged, sir. The wedding date is July 20."

"Congratulations, young man. May I ask to whom?"

"Captain Sydney Michael's daughter, Pansy. She happens to be a first cousin of Vijay's wife."

"Ah, I see. All in the family?"

"Fortunately, yes. Perhaps you met her father? Currently he works at the naval headquarters in Delhi."

"Yes, yes, I've heard his name. Very good family. Perhaps you'd like to talk this over with your intended bride?"

"Definitely. And please, how and where do I pursue this?"

"But you would have to leave the military."

"Pansy and I had already decided on that, sir. I'm just recovering from a serious illness. Moreover," and he chuckled, "As Vijay says, I'm basically a scholar."

"Well, that's good. I see no further hindrance."

"One item, sir," and Mahendra wondered what Basant Kumar's reaction would be. "You may not be interested in following the contact, Mr. Kumar, but I feel it's better to be straight with you. I am no longer a Hindu, and I purpose to take Christian baptism publicly before the wedding."

The lawyer laid his pipe aside, then said, "Sir, I commend you on your honesty. Had you hidden this, I could have learned of it later and would have decided you are like all others—seeking only your own gain. India needs men of integrity. I am honored, sir, to know you."

With addresses and directives in his coat pocket, Mahendra and Vijay changed plans. Instead of exploring Garhwal they returned home to get Mahendra's necessary data for his résumé, then left quickly for Delhi. A week there resulted in his appointment to the post, and both the Michaels and Singhs rejoiced at the Lord's provision.

Pansy said it most expressively when she clapped her hands and exclaimed, "A mountain lodge! Perfect! I'll even become a botanist! Oh, Squirt, I'm so happy!"

# 17

# From dreams to reality

Excitement in the Singh household mounted with Vijay's return from Delhi and the accession of the little white cottage next door. Terry moved from the small room into the guest room, thus providing Marcia with a nook of her own until her wedding day, now set for the last Sunday in March.

Next door, under Kushwant Singh's watchful eye, workmen scraped and painted inside and out, while Hazari Lal superintended landscaping.

At the big house new routines became evident, with Vijay commencing his daily trips to Dehra Dun to teach. Rani and her daughter spent long hours in the kitchen, preparing special foods for the coming festivities. "Is Miss Pansy coming?" the cook asked Manorma. "I miss her."

Vijay's wife laughed as she wiped a dish and placed it on the shelf. "Indeed she is, Rani, with her father and brother. We'll have a houseful. And don't forget Mahendra."

"But young Madame, how are we going to manage?"

"Why?"

"Well...sleeping. We can easily feed everybody."

"No problem. Men will go into the guest room, and I'll have Pansy with me. When the young couple is married we'll escort them to their new home. See?"

"Ah, young Madame, who could wish for more?"

Manorma laughed and asked, "Why the 'young Madame'? Why don't you just call me Manorma like always, Rani?"

The cook pulled her pink shawl more firmly over her head and said with a smile, "Well, it doesn't seem quite proper to address you as a girl when very soon you'll be a mother." She drew a long breath and said, "I pray every day the gods will send you a boy."

Manorma chuckled and said, "Don't worry. It's bound to be a boy. He's too active to be a girl. Bless you, Rani, I'm looking for a mountaineer, like his dad." She paused, then added, "But you know something? If it is a girl, both Vijay and I will be very pleased. Somehow, Christians think differently. We've learned that God doesn't favor one more than the other. He loves all of us, and most certainly, girls as well as boys! Why, the Bible tells us that Jesus took little children in his arms and blessed them and said that the kingdom of heaven belongs to the little ones. Isn't that nice?"

Rani wiped her eyes with her tea towel. "I wish our leaders would think like that, young Madame...I mean, Miss Manorma."

The girl hugged her and exclaimed, "You're precious, Rani. You know what? Next to Mama, you're the best cook I've ever met."

Marcia wandered around in the midst of all this activity like a person walking in a dream. She definitely felt an observer instead of the one who had caused it to happen. But with Terry's encouragement she did make a list of her needs and went with him each day to the bazaar.

He conversed while she selected small, neat prints to her liking for punjabi outfits. Then came the hassle of taking the yardage to one tailor or another in a variety of small booths in Landour bazaar. The choice of pattern, fittings, and many minor decisions at the best became a time-consuming process made easy by Terry's good flow of Hindi.

Ram Gupta, the cloth merchant, showed his obvious desire to please, with the result that Marcia gave him preference, a fact he duly appreciated. One evening he reported to his wife, Leela. They sat on the back verandah of their apartment, watching upcoming traffic on the zigzag road from Dehra Dun. He said casually, "A nice Australian couple has rented the Bahadur's house."

"Which Bahadur?" Leela Gupta asked, counting her stitches on the cable pattern of the sweater she was making for her eldest son.

"Tej Bahadur. But then, you wouldn't know. He told us in Club this week that Lawyer Kushwant Singh bought his place, so the Bahadurs have moved into the apartment above his shop."

"Oh? In Library Bazaar? They're not in Happy Valley now?"

"That's what I said, woman." He threw his newspaper down, then continued, "That Australian couple is getting married soon, and she's buying a whole new wardrobe. I enjoy their gentle manners and his good flow of Hindi."

"What are they doing here?"

"He's a famous soccer player, so the Tibetan camps have nabbed him up as Sports Director. Any school would be glad to have him."

"Hmmm...so Lawyer Singh bought the cottage as a rental? I venture he'll make a pretty sum out of those foreigners." She breathed a deep sigh.

But Terry and Marcia, all unaware of the interest their presence aroused in town, went serenely through each day, checking off items on their priority list. It included daily marriage counseling with Pastor Brown at the Union Church.

The first evening prior to leaving for the session, Terry asked Kushwant Singh, "Dad, how much shall we divulge of our past?"

"Nothing about Marcia's recent escape. That's a closed book."

"What about the divorce?"

"Certainly, without mentioning the guru. And, of course, you'll want to tell Pastor Brown about your coming to faith in Jesus Christ."

They liked the missionary's friendly ways, his seasoned advice from several decades of living in India, and his evident interest in their spiritual well-being. When Terry said, "Pastor, we're making a new beginning here, and we'd like to take Christian baptism again," Leslie Brown's eyes glowed.

"Excellent!" he exclaimed. "We can arrange that. How about having the baptismal service prior to Sunday school and church, and the wedding about one o'clock?"

"What do you think, Marcia?" She nodded and he asked, "How early should we be here, Pastor?"

"Seven-thirty, I'd say."

"There won't be many of us. Just our Indian family. You know Lawyer Kushwant Singh, and the Michaels will be coming from Delhi."

"Yes, I met them at the Christmas service."

"We hope you and your wife will join us at the wedding dinner afterwards at Kwality Restaurant."

"Why, thank you. We consider it a great pleasure."

But Rani was not to be outdone by any restaurant! She declared that her chicken curry and *pulao* with homemade relishes and *jalabies* for dessert must put the final touches to Terry's wedding day, and the family agreed.

On the last Saturday morning in March, before breakfast, the honking of the horn announced Uncle Syd's arrival from Delhi. Kushwant and Vijay rushed out, to be followed at a more sedate pace by Susheela and Manorma. "You've come!" Vijay exclaimed needlessly.

Pansy giggled and asked, "Did we beat Squirt? You know what? He's taking me to see the lodge today, Uncle Singh. I was so excited I could hardly sleep last night."

Chatter and laughter characterized further greetings, with Pansy saying, "Auntie Singh, Dad says I may stay. I hope you don't mind?" She flashed the older woman a captivating smile.

Susheela opened her arms. "Why, my dear girl, you're one of us. You know that."

Pansy leaned over to kiss her, and tears surfaced as she said, "I'm so glad the Lord has given you to me, Auntie Singh. You and Manorma are family in a special way. Sometimes I miss my mother so badly I can hardly understand why God let it happen. She doesn't even write."

Her father came over and touched her on the shoulder. She straightened to look into his eyes and realized that his pain was even greater than hers. Instinctively she clasped his hand, and both smiled. They could bear their pain together. The poignant moment passed when the Tibetan terrier spun around Pansy's feet. She bent over to pat him and said, "Yes, Sherpa, I've come home."

"Men's dorm in the front bedroom upstairs," boomed the lawyer. "Terry's in the cottage, and Marcia's in Phulmoni's small room until the wedding. Pansy, you go with Manorma until the bride moves out, then you'll have your regular quarters. We're certainly delighted to have you stay."

"Oh, thank you, uncle. Where's Marcia? Do you know, I haven't met her yet?" When they greeted each other at the bottom of the stairway Pansy held Marcia at arm's length and said, "You're beautiful! No wonder Terry followed you to India. I would too!" Everyone laughed, and Marcia's shy smile indicated appreciation for the love that flowed around her. Pansy hugged her, saying,

"How sweet of you to have me for your bridesmaid! I've never done it before. I hope I don't goof up."

The men chuckled. "Don't worry, Pansy," the lawyer said, "you can practice on this one, in the midst of your small, intimate family group. But wait until you and Mahendra have your wedding."

"You said it, Dad," Vijay commented. He added, "Hope breakfast's soon ready. Here's Terry coming across the lawn. Let's eat!"

Sherpa, the Tibetan terrier, took his accustomed place beside Pansy, hoping for the usual handouts. Suddenly his tail started thumping and the girl shrieked, "Squirt's coming! Sherpa says so. Excuse me, family." She ran to the front door. The throb of the motorcycle soon brought her fiancé into view. True, Vijay and Terry and the others followed more sedately, but the joy of the entire group flowed over as they all returned to the dining room to finish breakfast, then scattered for the day.

Susheela supervised Manorma's and Marcia's putting last minute touches to the cottage. "Terry," Manorma called plaintively to the young man who was hanging pictures in the bedrooms. "I don't seem to be able to stretch too well. Could you please help with these curtains?" Amid much laughter everything got done.

For Pansy and Squirt, astride his motorcycle and headed for the lodge, this day held special meaning. Not only did they relish being together, but it was her first opportunity to see her new home. For him, he could check through furniture piled up in one room and give directives for his coming in mid-May after the spring term concluded at the Bible College.

Pansy loved the location, and the house. Her effervescence spilled over on Sohan, the delighted *chowkidar*, who followed them. As Mahendra watched him carefully noting their preferences in a handy notebook, he decided the elderly servant would be a valuable asset, one whom he could trust.

"Now, Squirt," Pansy said, standing in the middle of the living room, "first things, first. Where do you want your study? It's the most important room in the house, so we'll build around it. Your work must be convenient for you."

"It will be more than an office...more like a lab, I'd say. So it should have easy access from the outside, and an adjoining bathroom. I can see us stumbling in, carrying loads of specimens, love.

I don't think you'd like our tracking mud, would you?" He chuckled, and she giggled in response.

"So it won't be the living room?" she said with a grin. "You're sure?" She waved her hand and asked, "Then what?"

"Hmmm...yes...how about the master bedroom? It has a door opening onto the verandah."

"And a bathroom door leading outside," Pansy added. "Well, that's settled. Now for the rest of the house, your overseas guests and Uncle and Auntie Singh...let's reserve the downstairs bedroom for them. That will be the handiest, I think."

"Right on, love. Auntie Singh can't manage steps. I've got an idea for bringing the wheelchair directly into that room with a ramp. Hmmm...have to think about that."

"Sounds good. Now, let's go upstairs and decide on those rooms."

The wide, curving stairway suggested gracious living, a feature that delighted both young people. At the top they found four more bedrooms with two shared baths. She chose the right front, saying, "Squirt, do you like this for ours?" Sohan walked over to the window and opened it, and the girl breathed deeply of the fresh mountain air. "Imagine living here!" she exclaimed. "What a glorious view of the snows. They're so close."

The other rooms were easy. "Zep's in here, close to us," she said with a wave toward the front room on the left, "and Terry's in there."

"And one for overflow," Mahendra added.

"Yes," she added, "for Dad and Lionel and who knows who else."

The tour of the house completed, Mahendra turned to Sohan and began giving detailed instructions about hiring gardeners, and the layout of flower beds, including a pool. He also suggested a service road to the back door, so that Auntie Singh wouldn't have to climb steps. Sohan noted everything carefully. Pansy giggled, and said, "It's a good thing the company is paying for all this, Squirt. It sounds pretty ambitious to me."

He grinned, and replied, "Well, we'd better do things right from the beginning. Upkeep will be easier, love."

Sohan excused himself, saying, "Sahib Ji, my wife has cooked your lunch. I'll serve you on the front verandah. And, by the way, our neighbor, Mr. Daula Ram, has sent some fresh Bengali sweets for the dessert."

"That's wonderful!" Mahendra exclaimed. "So you know him?"

"He's a fine man, sir. He thinks a great deal of you."

"It's mutual."

Meanwhile, back in Happy Valley the family geared up for Sunday, Terry and Marcia's wedding day. Mahendra and Pansy joined them in time for afternoon tea in the family room at five o'clock.

Next morning, by six o'clock, the convoy of two motorcycles and two cars drove through awakening Library and Mussoorie Bazaars to the Union Church, a direct route until the first of April. Kushwant remarked, "That saved us a lot of time; otherwise we'd have to go around by Kincraig." But with an hour to spare, they ate a hearty breakfast at a nearby restaurant.

All were aware of baptism's profound implications, although with the exception of Manorma none of the Singhs had previously witnessed the Christian rite. Susheela, so recently out of Hinduism, felt as deeply moved as her husband.

The service took place in the front of the sanctuary, with the guests seated on the front two rows. As it proceeded, Kushwant Singh found himself facing a familiar question: Why shouldn't he be baptized? But once again his reason shouted: If and when you do, this entire town will know that you, Lawyer Kushwant Singh, are no longer a broadminded Hindu, but a convert to Christianity! Are you willing for that?

No, no, his reason answered, your lifestyle is sufficient proof of God's grace in your heart. So he battled the question that refused to go away.

By contrast, both Mahendra and Vijay thrilled to the simple testimonies that Terry and Marcia gave. Terry's came first.

Standing straight and tall before them, he said, "Family...Dad, Mom, and all of you...you knew me when I arrived in India looking for peace. You saw how screwed up I was inside. I'm so thankful you took me in and pointed me to Jesus. Lionel, how can I adequately thank you for showing your love practically? You got me to cut my hair, provided me with your own clothes, and took me with you on that motorcycle trip! I saw the love of Jesus in all of you. And you brought me back to faith. Today I desire baptism to witness to Jesus Christ as my personal Lord and Savior. I love him with all my heart."

Marcia's testimony was no less moving. She said quietly but simply, "My Indian family, I need you. I have never known an earthly father. He died in an industrial accident the day before my birth, and Mother and I lived with a maiden aunt and grandmother in Brisbane, Australia. When I was three, Mother and I came to India where she took a job as manager in an orphanage. But she got cancer, so we had to return to Australia when I was fourteen. She died a year later. I was a lost lamb!"

She paused and wiped her eyes, then said, "Today I marvel at the love of Jesus, my Good Shepherd, who found me and brought me back to himself. He brought Terry to me, too, in answer to prayer." After a short pause, she continued, "I foolishly wrecked our first marriage. Today, I thank God for a second chance. And I desire baptism to witness to God's love in my heart."

The pastor's wife played "I Have Decided to Follow Jesus." The soft organ tones provided an inspiring background for the baptismal rites in a hushed and sacred moment. Mahendra pressed Pansy's hand, and Vijay Manorma's, an indication from both of the solemn intent of their hearts to follow Jesus all the way, regardless of cost.

That afternoon in a simple wedding ceremony Terry and Marcia took their marriage vows for a second time, certainly with a deepened significance. She made a beautiful bride in her white silk *saree* with hand-embroidered gold border that the Singhs had given. Kushwant and Susheela embraced the newlyweds as their own, and Mahendra and Pansy could scarcely contain their enthusiasm as attendants. Only four more months to wait!

That evening, when Rani's last homemade *jalabi* had been consumed and the sticky sweetness wiped off everyone's fingers, the family escorted the newlyweds to their new home. In the crowded living room Kushwant Singh raised his hand for silence and said, "Before anything else, let us now dedicate this house and its new occupants to the living God."

Much as a family priest would have done, he stood with outstretched hands to bless the bridal couple and their home. Wedding cake and coffee followed the dedicatory prayer, then the family withdrew. But later, in the privacy of Manorma's bedroom Pansy confessed that she and Mahendra had apple-pied Terry and Marcia's bed and hung "Just Married" signs around. Amid peals of laughter Manorma said, "You're next! Take my word for it. Vijay and Terry will pay you back double. You're next!"

## 18

# Paying the highest price

Six weeks passed with torrid heat on the plains sending hordes of visitors to Mussoorie's cooler climes.

In Happy Valley, on a hot night in early May Kushwant Singh paced his living room floor, hands behind his back. The mantel clock struck midnight. The shadows on the wall deepened as he turned the light down low.

A handwritten quote on a slip of paper lay on the side table, words that he knew by memory. Their truth reverberated as though echoing across canyons. Now he quoted them again: "Sir," his lawyer friend, Basant Kumar, had said to Mahendra Lall on hearing his witness to faith in Jesus Christ, "I commend you on your honesty. Had you hidden this, I would have learned of it later and would have decided that you are like all others—seeking only your own good. India desperately needs men of integrity."

Kushwant Singh, spiritual leader of this home, bowed his head in shame. For months he had stalled about making open confession of following Jesus Christ!

But once again, as many times before, his reason took over. A consistent lifestyle is enough, he thought. Why are specific actions necessary to validate it? Everyone knows I accept Christianity. I study my Bible openly, pray and occasionally go to church. I don't think I'm the problem.

Neither are the boys. Take Terry. He's a delightful young man...doing a great job in the camps, too. I heard just the other day of his rapport with the Tibetans. And I like the way he cares for Marcia, instinctively shielding her yet not being obnoxious about it. Yes, Terry's all right. So is Vijay—every inch a man, and the pride of my heart.

Kushwant Singh paced awhile, thinking further. Now Manorma and Marcia are doing well, but I wish Susheela wouldn't pore over that astrological chart and read her horoscope. What does it matter what color you wear on Wednesday or whether Friday is propitious for starting a journey? Pure nonsense, I'd say—a symptom of some deeper problem.

Hmmm...take the Tulsi plant in the backyard. Rani tends it religiously.

Kushwant Singh stopped pacing. With a frown on his usually pleasant face he said aloud, "You know, it's the women who uphold these Hindu ideas. Take Susheela, for instance. She still insists that Christian women can use the *tilak* as a marriage symbol." He paused, then muttered, "She says that dot on her forehead isn't Hindu, merely cultural."

His thoughts continued to flow, so did his pacing the floor as was his habit. Hmmm...whatever my wife says about the *tilak*, her reasoning is a clear case of syncretization! Where did the practice originate? Even our Manorma knows. She refuses to wear it and says, "No third eye for me, thank you. I'm not asking Shiva to protect me from evil."

But when I suggested mildly the other day that Susheela follow her daughter-in-law's patterns, she drew herself up and said, "I'm a different generation, and we come from varying backgrounds. She's Western...wears a wedding ring. I'm Indian. What's wrong with my wearing the *tilak*?"

But the problem is, I know better, and so does anyone who has studied yoga. India is full of such, so what kind of a Christian witness do we bear? Somehow, we have a flawed pattern.

The lawyer stopped pacing, stood near the fireplace and with hands folded in petition, he looked up and prayed, "Lord Jesus, what do we lack? I don't like what I see, neither do I find peace in my heart."

In the quiet hush of that midnight hour, the mantel clock measured off the moments. It seemed to say in menacing tones, "Something's wrong....something's wrong....something's wrong...." Even as once before, when Kushwant Singh had dallied in disobedience—that time with cleansing his top shelf of his sacred books— so now he knew his inner joy and peace had evaporated. "Lord Jesus," he pleaded aloud, "where are you? I need you." While the rest of his family slept, he stood alone in his living room seeking his God. But to no avail. Disconsolate, he sat in his favorite wicker chair by the window and wept. Not given to showing emotion, he covered his face with his hands and bent over as though his burden was too heavy.

After awhile he heard the Lord say, "My son, I am with you, but I, too, am weeping. I paid the highest price for you on Calvary, yet you regard your own reputation in preference to mine. Is this discipleship? No, Kushwant! I ask your all!"

Stunned, the man looked up, waiting to hear more, but silence descended and he realized he was dealing with the Almighty. Had he been bargaining with God? Holding out his paltry reasoning as a substitute for paying his highest price for Love Incarnate?

He stood, aghast at the revelation. With outstretched hands he pleaded, "My Lord! My God! Forgive...I'm an unworthy, wretched sinner, full of pride and obstinacy. Oh, God, I need forgiveness. It's not Susheela...."

He bowed his head and covered his face with his hands. Overwhelmed, he heard, "No, it's not Susheela. She doesn't have the spiritual discernment you possess. I appointed you as the head of this house, and you must lead the way. I spoke loudly to you through Terry and Marcia, but you resisted."

Kushwant Singh relived it—the young people affirming by baptism their love for Jesus Christ before they took their marriage vows. And he had felt pricked in his heart even while they witnessed to a new life. Why hadn't he and his family followed suit?

"Because of another way of looking at things," he countered.

"Whose way?"

"Mine."

"Not entirely your own. You are listening to the father of lies, the tempter. Even now he's here, Kushwant. You know he is."

The lawyer stopped. Yes, of course. There were two voices, but in his ignorance he thought the other voice was his own. Yet how could that be when he really desired the will of God! Surely he wouldn't conjure up lies against the Almighty! Hmmm....

Even now the tempter was talking, using first person. Humph! thought the lawyer. He's clever; listen to him.

Don't be foolish, like a woman. What harm comes from compromise anyway? It will take me further in the long run. I can keep the star on the verandah. Nobody needs see the Tulsi plant in the back, nor my wife's studying her horoscope while I search the Scriptures. Neither is wrong. Don't all roads lead to God? And how can I forget he's a God of love and he sees the sincere intent of my heart? Surely he won't condemn me. What's all this fuss about? I'm just being over-emotional, and I'm too tired to think straight.

The battle escalated. Finally Kushwant Singh spoke aloud, "In the mighty name of Jesus, get away from me, Satan. You have no part in me."

He sat down resolutely, turned up the light and opened his Bible to 2 Corinthians, chapter six. Beginning with verse fourteen, he read:

> Be ye not unequally yoked together with unbelievers: for what fellowship hath righteousness with unrighteousness? and what communion hath light with darkness?
>
> And what concord hath Christ with Belial? or what part hath he that believeth with an infidel?
>
> And what agreement hath the temple of God with idols? for ye are the temple of the living God; as God hath said, I will dwell in them, and walk in them; and I will be their God, and they shall be my people.
>
> "Wherefore come out from among them, and be ye separate saith the Lord, and touch not the unclean thing; and I will receive you.
>
> And will be a Father unto you, and ye shall be my sons and daughters, saith the Lord Almighty."

Kushwant Singh sat stunned at the clarity of the directive. How had he missed it before? Was it that he didn't want to see it? He looked up and said, "So help me God, tomorrow morning I'm going to find Pastor Brown and tell him our intentions, regardless of consequences. Whether anyone else follows or not in taking Christian baptism, I will lead the way."

But finding Pastor Brown wasn't as simple as Vijay's father had hoped. When he phoned the church office after breakfast the secretary said, "Rev. Brown isn't coming in today."

"How soon may I contact him?"

"I can't say, sir. He's due to attend a meeting in Poona and expects to be out of town for a week."

"May I have his home phone number?"

"You can try, sir."

He was about to dial the pastor's home when the tempter tapped him on the shoulder and said, See? You were over-emotional last night. Why make a big matter out of something so insignificant? Wait until the pastor returns.

Kushwant Singh turned slowly from the telephone, then said aloud, "No! I've had enough of you! Dear Lord, I promised I would find Pastor Brown, and I'm going to try. If you want us to see each other this morning, you have all details worked out."

He dialed, to hear, "Hello? Pastor Brown here."

"Sir, this is Lawyer Kushwant Singh from Happy Valley."

"Why, yes, Mr. Singh, and how are you?"

"Troubled, I'd say. I couldn't sleep last night. Is there a time and place when we could meet? Your secretary tells me you are leaving Mussoorie for a week."

He heard the pastor chuckle, then answer, "Plans can change, my good man. Mine now allow me an extra day here. Since I cleared my slate of engagements, I have open time. When and where would you like to meet?"

"At my home, sir? We can talk quietly, and we'd be delighted to have you join us for lunch. I need to share a family matter with you."

"Why, that's fine. Isn't this a coincidence?"

"Beg your pardon, sir, but I think not. I've been struggling spiritually for the past two months, and it's time to act."

"Give me about an hour to get there, friend. Keep encouraged and remember that God is faithful."

A boyish grin creased his features as he murmured, "Father in heaven, you're surely full of surprises! I thought I'd get a fifteen minute appointment, and here the pastor is committing himself to spending hours if necessary. What next?" He joined his hands together in prayer, and concluded, "Lord God, pardon my saying so, but you work incredibly fast, and minutely in detail. Now lead me on."

The significance of that day showed later that evening when the lawyer sat at his desk and wrote:

"My dear friend, Basant Kumar, I thank you again for your gracious care of my son, Vijay, and his friend, Mahendra. The latter is anticipating his new responsibilities and will, as you know, take up residence at the lodge by the end of the week. We are in your debt, sir, for recommending him.

"However, my main reason for writing is to apprise you of my intent to make public confession to faith in Jesus Christ as my personal Lord and Savior. This will likely surprise you, but since he has changed my life, and that of my family, it is only fitting that we publicly acknowledge his amazing grace. Therefore we propose to take Christian baptism at the Union Church in Mussoorie on the first Sunday of June at 2:30 p.m. with a reception following at 4:30 p.m. at the Savoy. Kindly join us, sir.

"My intent is to share my spiritual pilgrimage with those closest to me, and you, my friend, are high on the list.

"I remain sincerely yours, Kushwant Singh."

A dozen such letters, written personally, went to friends and relatives, including his daughter and family. Each met with varying reactions, but none with indifference. Indeed, they were treated as urgent and every invitee came. However, Phulmoni came alone. Her husband disdained his father-in-law's confession and told his wife in no uncertain terms, "You can represent the family. I'll have no part in this. He's off his rocker."

Mahendra Lall's father, though inwardly torn, resolved to see for himself and determined to pressure the Arya Samaj to action if his son also converted.

At the Singh residence the lawyer shared frankly with his wife and family, and much prayer rose for God's hand to be shown through their coming out openly. Consequences were his to determine; theirs was but to obey.

Then the Lord intervened by sending baby Singh ten days early.

On a sultry first day of June, after hours of long labor, the hearty cry of her firstborn made Manorma's sense of near panic turn to joy. In the Landour Community Hospital the red-haired missionary doctor laid the bundle in her arms with the comment, "God has given you a bonny, wee lad."

Manorma turned her head to examine the newcomer and said with a wan smile, "So you're the one who kicked so hard? And here you come...ten days early...screaming? All right, son, I say it's time you met your father."

Dr. Sheila McIntosh laughed and asked, "Shall I call him?"

"Please, doctor."

Vijay picked up his offspring as though he was porcelain, but on being assured he wouldn't break, he carefully examined the baby's wrinkled red skin and abundant thatch of blue-black hair. With a big grin he said, "Hi, wee Squirt! Welcome home."

Manorma giggled. "So he's Mahendra?"

"Mahendra Kushwant Singh," Vijay replied proudly.

Black thunder clouds rolled outside, bringing promise of an early monsoon. Billowing in from the Bay of Bengal, they rode the high winds to the accompaniment of peals of thunder. The sound brought hope that panting heat would soon give way to refreshing rain. To Vijay and Manorma and the rest of the family, wee Squirt's simultaneous arrival promised well, and they thanked God. Indians love babies, especially sons. Surely the good news of the baby's birth would help temper any adverse reactions the invited guests might harbor over the Singh family's conversion to Christianity.

Because of gentle rain that followed the thunderstorm, Mahendra didn't see his namesake until he was two days old, but philosophically, as he parked his motorcycle under the hospital portico, he said to Vijay who met him at the door, "Well, buddy, a couple of days doesn't matter all that much since wee Squirt will be staying awhile."

"Oh, yeah?"

Ten minutes later, however, the elder Squirt took the baby in his arms and on examining him said, "Misnamed, my boy...misnamed. Look at those sturdy legs and that well-built frame. Listen to that bass voice. You're more like Zeppelin than me, but we'll forget that, won't we, pal? I can see your future written all over you. You'll love these Himalayas, and run these trails. When we're together, you'll learn the various species of orchids."

Vijay and Manorma were laughing. The new father interrupted, "Wait a minute! What makes you think he'll have more mental acumen than I?"

"Easy, Zep. Look at his mother. She's smart!"

As the week progressed, Vijay sensed the undergirding the baby's birth brought his parents in the light of their approaching baptism on Sunday. He tried to encourage them, but felt it probable he might be deterred from joining, especially if Manorma and the baby would be released from hospital over the weekend. The matter lay heavily on his heart all day Friday, and he rushed back from Dehra Dun as quickly as possible to the hospital.

He found Manorma singing a lullaby to wee Squirt when he arrived. "You had a good day?" she asked. "You look tired, Vijay."

"Horrible day...one interruption after another to prevent me getting away on time. Anyway, darling, I'm here, thank God. When can you come home? What does the doctor say?"

"I told her you don't teach on Saturdays, so you could take me tomorrow, and she agreed. Okay?"

He drew a long breath, then said, "Perfect! Then you'll be there Sunday. Mind if I stay home with you, darling? I'll tell my parents to go ahead with their plans." He twirled his cap as he talked.

Manorma looked at him, dismayed. "But, Vijay," she said, "didn't you expect to be baptized too?"

He touched her, remarking, "Squirt and I have talked things over, and he thinks he should have it done at the Bible College rather than publicly here. I could join him."

"Why not in Mussoorie?"

The tall soldier walked over to the window, and before answering gazed upon the backside of busy Landour Bazaar. Over there were both friends and enemies. Christianity had been part of this hillside's culture for over a hundred years, but it had always been associated with the foreigners who came from the West. Foreigners possessed money, position, power, therefore they should be hosted graciously.

Vijay's thoughts reeled. How much did the common man in his shop know of the true gospel of Jesus Christ? Hadn't he been conditioned to believe that low caste people became Christians for the material benefits they envisioned? Where was downright integrity? How many Sadhu Sundar Singhs were there?

Mahendra's job with a foreign firm would immediately make his motivation suspect, as would his coming marriage into a prestigious Christian family. Perhaps Squirt was right to feel he should take his stand among those who knew him well, rather than negating the impact of Kushwant Singh's witness.

Vijay finally turned back to say, "Look, Mano, I can't tell you all that Squirt's going through these days, nor all that has brought Dad to this hour. You know much of it, and let me just say that for Dad and Mom, it is different than for Mahendra."

"I really don't see why," the girl said, holding her baby closer. Hadn't Lakshmi threatened all of them if they followed Christ?

Taking a chair near hers, he said, "Because of his father's attitude, for one thing. Sukhdev Lall has influence in town. I understand he's in touch with a radical anti-Christian group. He could

make this place sizzle if he chooses. Already he's blaming Mom
and Dad and me for influencing his son."

She looked up quickly. "Oh, I didn't know."

"So, under the circumstances, Mano, I'd rather wait until you
and wee Squirt can be there. It's right for Dad and Mom to lead the
way, so if you don't mind, darling, I'll stand with Squirt. That will
give him courage. He's arranging for the last Sunday in June, three
weeks from now."

Manorma drew a deep breath and said, "Do whatever you
think best."

Now, with that settled, he told her of changes at home. With a
chuckle he said, "Last evening Mom came out wearing a wedding ring! The *tilak* has gone. So has the Tulsi plant. Yesterday Dad
pulled it up and burned it. Rani may not have agreed, but she
made my favorite cheese *pakoras* for tea, so we concluded she's
weathered whatever emotions she's feeling."

Manorma smiled. "I wonder what the other servants will say."

"Dad expects to invite them into the house tomorrow evening
to tell them himself, with the hope that they will attend the baptismal service."

"Oh!" Her eyes grew wide as she said, "He doesn't leave anything undone, does he?"

"That's like Dad. He holds back until he's sure, then goes in
like a trooper. He's some man!"

"How is Mama doing?"

"Just fine, especially since my parents go to their room each
evening after tea and spend time in Bible study and prayer."

Manorma laughed softly, her eyes alight with joy. She said,
"Darling, one miracle follows another. Isn't the Lord good?"

"You can say that again, love. Bye, now, and I'll take the good
news home. I came directly here, so they're likely wondering what
happened to me."

"What time, Vijay?"

"You mean tomorrow morning? Shortly after nine, I'd say."

With a kiss for mother and son, Vijay Kumar Singh left, leaving Manorma to ponder God's mysterious ways in which he molds
a Christian family.

# 19

# Kushwant's confession

The elder Singhs and Pansy, with Terry and Marcia, were enjoying high tea in the garden that Friday afternoon, a habit now established ever since the wedding. Susheela looked at her watch and said, "Vijay's late. I hope he didn't get detained in a landslide."

"No, Auntie Singh," Pansy said with a laugh. "He told me he wants to go directly to the hospital. He's hoping he can bring Mano and wee Squirt home this weekend."

"Ah, yes," she said with a sigh.

"And if that happens," the lawyer boomed in, "we can expect slight changes in Sunday's plans. But we won't meet that until it comes."

The Tibetan terrier, seated expectantly beside Pansy, began thumping his tail. The girl squealed, "Squirt's coming! Sherpa says so. Excuse me, family!" She ran to the front entrance, the dog on her heels.

Kushwant Singh chuckled and said, "Think she'll ever grow up?"

"I used to call her impetuous; now I like her spontaneity," Susheela said with a smile. Terry chuckled and said, "Just what Mahendra needs. He's as detailed as she is uninhibited. They'll have some adjusting to do, won't they, Marcia?"

The girl at his side gave him a nod, her eyes shining with joy. "Terry helps me," she whispered. "Mahendra will help her."

By this time two motorcycles, rather than one, had turned up the driveway and Vijay and Mahendra both parked their vehicles

168

under the portico before joining the family. Pansy and Sherpa led the way with the girl announcing, "Mano's coming tomorrow!"

"Is she, son?" Kushwant asked.

"Yes, Dad. I went there first. Yes, Mano and wee Squirt will be ready by nine o'clock, unless there's a change, in which case she'll have someone call."

"You want to go, Grandma?" he asked his wife.

"I'd say yes if it was the first grandchild," Susheela said. "But since I have a full day's work mapped out, perhaps I'd better stay home."

"Mama, could I help with the baking?" Marcia asked.

"If you'd like to, I'd love it."

"Oh, Squirt," Pansy exclaimed, "let's give Mano a motorcycle escort." She giggled, then added, "You don't get a namesake every day, do you?"

"About once in a lifetime, my gal."

So Mahendra and Pansy went "just for fun," as she described it, but on the return trip plans changed when the motorcycle and car reached Library Bazaar. Mahendra suddenly spotted his kid brother, Raja, home from prep school in Poona. "Pansy," he said urgently, "could you go with the others? I must talk to Raja alone. I haven't seen him since Dad threw me out."

He flagged down both car and boy. While the teenager admired the baby, Pansy got in beside Manorma and Raja jumped on the motorcycle. "See you!" Mahendra said with a wave of his hand.

He turned to his new pillion rider and asked, "Where shall we go, kid? This is too good to be true."

"Go? Anywhere...everywhere."

"How much time do you have?" He started the motor.

"The whole day, Squirt. I arrived last evening and I simply couldn't believe what Mom told me. Dad's gone off his rocker since he turned you out! Man, Mom's all cut up about it. I wish you could see her."

"Is she home now?" He turned toward Happy Valley.

"Yeah, I think so. I just had to get out, so I told her I'd be back this evening."

"Where's Dad, pal?"

"He's meeting someone in Dehra Dun."

"Hmmm...let's check. I'll phone from this tea shop." That call changed Mahendra Lall's day. His mother awaited him and his brother out by the gate. On seeing her eldest she began to sob, clinging to him. "Come, Mom," he said gently. "Let's go into the rose garden. We can talk quietly there. Raja, how about bringing some tea for all of us?"

"Sure thing! Man! It's great to have you back, Squirt."

An outdoor picnic table and benches under the rose arbor invited lingering and provided privacy. Tears flowed down Shanti Lall's face and her son noted new lines of sorrow etched into her soft features. He took her in his arms and said softly, "I've been missing you, Mom. I needed this."

When she could talk, she said, "I don't see why your father acts so irrational instead of being grateful to the Lord Christ for healing you, Mahendra. You wouldn't be here otherwise."

"I know, Mom."

She wiped her eyes and added, "Both of us have watched you since your return from the Burma border. He knows, too, how different you are."

"Thanks, Mom." She touched his wet cheek and whispered, "Don't ever leave the Lord Christ, or that sweet Pansy. I love her. Is everything all right between you two?"

"Yes, yes, and I wish you could see the house the Lord has given me, and the job. I can't believe his goodness!"

Before long Raja appeared with a tray, checkered tablecloth folded neatly and thrown over his left shoulder. He deftly set the table, then said, "I'll be back with the tea soon. Don't worry, Mom. Isn't it great having Squirt?" He turned with a laugh and said, "The servants were wondering what I'm up to, but I told them I brought one of my special buddies and want to do the honors myself. Will I pass?"

Shanti smiled and said, "I'm proud of you. Tell the cook I'll come in half-an-hour. Thanks, Raja." He dashed back to the Swiss-style chalet set on a hill.

That unexpected interval cleared misunderstandings and set patterns for the future. Now Mahendra knew that both mother and brother stood with him. In turn, Shanti established contact on a regular basis by phone. Before he left she said, "Your father and I received an invitation to the baptism water ritual tomorrow, but your father won't let me go. He thinks you're going to be converted, too, and he's furious! I try to talk sense into him, son, but he gets stubborn." She wiped tears, then added, "It's hard. I'd like to follow Jesus, too."

"Why, Mom!" Mahendra's eyes gleamed with joy. He said, "You can, and so can Raja, but the path might not be easy. Here, take my New Testament. Put it in a safe place and read it every day." He handed the book to her. She accepted it with both hands, and lifting it to her lips, kissed it as he added, "If you ever have a chance to come and see me, let me know. I'll arrange it. And remember, Mom, Zep and I are getting baptized in Dehra Dun on the last Sunday of this month. Pansy and I are getting married in Delhi on July 20th. If there's half a chance, please come both times. Man! Wouldn't that be great?"

Her voice quivered as she touched her son's cheek and asked, "If Lord Christ can heal cerebral malaria, couldn't he do this, too?"

Mahendra flashed a radiant smile and said, "Sure thing! We'll ask him. Okay? Will you pray also?" She nodded.

After leaving, as he drove back to the Singhs, Mahendra laughed aloud and said, "Sheer impossibility! What a preposterous request, Lord Jesus! But since you rose from the dead, I believe you can do this also. Bring my entire family to both the baptism and the wedding. That includes Daya, in New York!"

He reached the Singh residence in time for Rani's late lunch that duly celebrated Baby Singh's arrival. That evening all the servants came to the bungalow to give their felicitations to Young Master, and while munching on freshly bought Bengali sweets listened to Kushwant Singh's personal invitation and testimony. Everyone loved the baby, and all but Rani decided to go to the baptismal service on Sunday afternoon.

Rani had her own reasons which she shared with her Madame. Susheela laughed as the little Garhwali said, "Miss Manorma's only a girl. What does she know about babies? You have to go, Madame, so you let me stay, and I'll take care of both Master Vijay and his family."

"Thank you, Rani," Susheela said with a joyous laugh. "You have taken away my worry."

"Yes, Madame."

After the servants had left and Manorma and the baby had gone to bed, Mahendra told the family about meeting his mother. He said, "Uncle Singh...and all of you...I feel like I'm bursting with joy. Would you believe that today I met my mother and learned

172

that both she and my kid brother are cut up about the way Dad is acting?"

"Is that so? I sent them an invitation," the lawyer said gravely. "Are they coming?"

"Dad won't let them, but Mom thinks he'll come—to see if I'm going to be converted—as she puts it."

"Hmmm...." Vijay looked across at his pal and smiled. "I'd say you got divine leading in waiting."

"Oh, yes," Pansy broke in. "At first I was disappointed, but now it seems right. Maybe the Lord's doing something special and it takes a bit more time."

Everyone laughed, but Mahendra looked at her with a grin and asked, "How big is your faith, love?"

"Why?"

"Mom asked me an interesting question. First, she told me she's glad I've decided to follow Lord Christ, as she calls him. And she admonished me never to leave either the Lord or you!"

Pansy clapped her hands and said, "See? The Lord is working."

"There's more. She'd like to attend my baptism and wedding. Now, what do you think of that?"

"You mean a great deal to her," Susheela murmured.

Pansy clasped her fiancé's hand and exclaimed, "The Lord will do it, Squirt. I know he will."

"Thanks, love. Just one more item, and then I'd like Zep to pray for this. Mom suggested that since the Lord raised me, as it were from the dead, he could also demolish the antipathy in the family and give her the desire of her heart. Now, what do you say to that?"

"Remarkable faith!" the lawyer commented.

Mahendra grinned and said, "I grant you I thought it preposterous to ask, but I can't let Mom down. How about believing with me for the entire family—Daya included—to be present at both the baptism and the wedding?"

"Isn't Daya in New York?" Vijay asked.

Mahendra chuckled and said, "So far as I know. Ready to pray, pal?"

"You bet! We've climbed mountains before. Come on, family. We've got a great God. Let's focus on him; not on faith. Okay?"

"Go ahead, son," Kushwant said with twinkling eyes. "We're in this together."

"Let's form a circle and hold hands. Mom, just stay in your wheelchair. We'll stand around you."

That prayer session again bonded the family. A hush of expectancy fell on them as they parted to face Kushwant and Susheela's big day.

Sunday dawned bright and clear with everyone but Vijay, Manorma and Rani going into town. After the morning service Kushwant was called to the phone. Vijay said, "Dad, Phulmoni just called from Dehra Dun. She's on her way by taxi and should be there in good time for the baptismal service."

"Praise God! Is she alone, or is the family with her?"

"On her own, Dad. I told her to go directly to the church."

"That's good, son. We'll keep an eye out for her. Is all well?"

"Everything's fine. I'll join you at the Savoy at about five o'clock. By that time Terry and Marcia will be back. It's good of them to offer."

"Yes, son. Thanks for calling."

Fifteen minutes prior to the afternoon service, the lawyer and his wife took their places at the front door of the church, personally meeting friends and relatives. Some had come from Delhi, and Lawyer Basant Kumar from Tehri City. Kailash Rana, the bank president, seemed somewhat ill-at-ease initially, but he lacked nothing in congratulating Kushwant Singh on his new grandson.

Just before the Singhs went into the sanctuary, Phulmoni, their daughter, arrived. "Mom and Dad," she gasped, "we almost got caught in a landslide! Boy! Was I glad we got across before a huge boulder plunged down the hillside. You must have prayed."

"We did," Susheela said.

Phulmoni leaned over and kissed her, then insisted on pushing the wheelchair and from that moment on devoted herself to her mother's needs. Susheela's day would have been momentous in any case, but this capped her joy.

Not so, Sukhdev Lall. Although Mahendra kept hoping he would come, the man didn't enter the church until Pastor Brown began speaking. Only then did he tiptoe in to take a corner seat, and having assured himself that his son hadn't yet converted to Christianity, he slipped out during the final prayer. But with his exception all the invitees joined the family at the Savoy for the reception.

Vijay's arrival eased tensions, with everyone crowding around the new father to congratulate him on the birth of his son. In this

congenial atmosphere he found it easy to also speak of his faith in
Jesus Christ, after which his father spoke. Later, when Vijay joined
Basant Kumar, Mahendra and Pansy at a window table for five
minutes, the lawyer said warmly, "Young man, your parents have
arranged a delightful occasion, and I greatly profited by his
speech."

"Thank You! Mr. Kumar."

He continued, puffing on his cigar, "You know, Vijay, for
years I have admired your father's scintillating speeches in the
highest courts of the land, but frankly, he was never so eloquent as
today. I am profoundly moved, Colonel."

Pansy gripped Mahendra's hand and squeezed it while Vijay
replied, "If you don't mind, I'll share your comments with my
father. He greatly values your friendship, and I thank you personally for coming today."

As the family gathered around the dinner table that evening,
Kushwant Singh took his usual place at the head. In his dignified
priestly manner he said, "My sons and daughters, your mother and
I have made our public confession of faith today. This entire town
now knows that we pay homage to Jesus Christ, and to none other.
Now let us pray."

At the conclusion of their meal they moved into the living
room, and at a convenient moment Mahendra said, "Uncle Singh,
I think we should celebrate. Please, would all of you, Phulmoni
included, come to the lodge tomorrow for a three-day retreat?
Fresh air, beautiful surroundings, a time set apart to praise God for
all he's done for us?"

"What a gracious invitation! How many can go? Phulmoni?"

"Yes, Dad. I don't have to return for a week."

"Great! Now, Vijay?"

"Yes, sir...special consideration for family reasons."

Everyone laughed, and Kushwant asked, "Terry?"

"Sure thing, folks. The Tibetans have some sort of *puja* on
Tuesday, so I'm free. Right, Marcia?"

"Oh, yes, Terry. I want to meet Daula Ram again. He gave me
so much courage when I needed it."

The lawyer's eyes twinkled as he asked the vivacious young
lady sitting beside Mahendra. "Pansy?"

Her infectious laugh rang out and she said, "Uncle! Imagine
your asking! You know something, family? Squirt and I walked
through those rooms and chose where we'd place every one of you,

but I didn't know it would happen before we're married. So we'll rearrange a bit, if that's okay with you."

General conversation centered on other details, then Vijay said, "I'll take three days family leave. Terry, would you like to bring Marcia on my motorcycle? I'll hoof it by bus and Dad can bring the ladies. Anyone left over can come with me. Right, Dad?"

"Excellent, my boy," Kushwant exclaimed.

The group scattered after a family prayer and planned to meet for an early breakfast, but they gathered sooner than expected.

About one o'clock that night a storm of unusual intensity struck. Lightning streaked across the sky and thunder rolled. Manorma stirred uneasily in her sleep, then awoke to howling wind and lashing rain. Vijay reached over, drew his wife and baby close and prayed, "Father, protect this house and Terry's. Surround us with angels."

The sizzle of a ball of fire flashed down a magnificent pine standing some fifty feet away. Manorma shrieked, "Oh, God! Not Lakshmi again!" Even as she said it, thunder boomed like an exploding bomb. "Vijay!" she screamed, "Fire!"

But the rain pounded down, and her husband drew a long breath before saying, "Darling, it's all right. God is here. See? He's extinguished that fireball. All of us and the houses are spared."

"Oh, how can you be sure?" She clasped the baby to her bosom. He trembled in her arms, then drawing a deep sigh, relaxed. Manorma said in wonder, "Look at wee Squirt. He's sleeping as though nothing happened. Is something wrong with him?"

Vijay chuckled and said, "Manorma, his guardian angel insulated him. See? He's relaxed. Don't you remember? 'I will trust and not be afraid.'"

"Oh, I'm sorry, Vijay. How terrible of me to doubt. Dear Lord, forgive me." She kissed the baby, laid him on the pillow and jumped up. "Let's find the others," she said.

"Now that sounds more like my brave girl. Come, darling. Bring wee Squirt."

The elder Singhs, Phulmoni and the two young couples met in the living room. Over cups of hot tea, to the accompaniment of rain and wind outside, they sang praises to the Lord for his deliverance. As soon as he could, Vijay assured himself that Terry and Marcia were all right. Plans for the family retreat would continue.

Mahendra and Pansy left early for the lodge, knowing the others would follow more leisurely. Pansy, emotionally exhausted from the night's excitement, enjoyed the early morning ride. Drawing in deep breaths of fresh mountain air she exulted in the beauty and wonder of a newly washed world. Soon they reached the newly painted white picket fence and neat little gate, and she read in wonder, "Orchid Dell."

"Like it, love?" Mahendra asked with a grin.

"It's perfect!" Underneath hung a glass-encased highly polished plaque that read, "Lt. Mahendra Lall (Retd.) Representative, Bencion Pharmaceutical Co., Ltd., Geneva, Switzerland."

"Whew!" she said, casting a saucy glance. "I'm impressed." With a light laugh she added, "I don't know whether I dare enter."

Mahendra Lall chuckled, and extended his hand, saying, "My highest pleasure."

They entered the gate to be met by several gardeners who stood and saluted. Each wore a khaki uniform with "B.P.C." embroidered on the pocket. "Building morale, Pansy," her escort said softly. "They know you're coming today. I'm sure Sohan has the whole gang out, looking their best. They've worked hard."

The compound showed it. A riot of flowers filled the front yard, and off to one side in a wooded setting, the gardeners had created a pool surrounded by rocks and ferns. Pansy's evident delight brought open smiles. "A super place to have outdoor picnics," she exclaimed.

"You can explore later," Mahendra said with a grin. "We'd better go indoors and see the lay of the land there before the gang descends."

Potted palms and plants lined the paths and verandahs. Stepping inside, Pansy saw the spacious lounge divided into several separate conversational areas. Utilizing picture windows and easy chairs, combined with coffee tables, magazines, throw rugs, cushions, and lights, the room now bore a lived-in look. Pansy squealed with delight, picking her favorite corner immediately beside a large window that looked out toward the road. "I'll be able to see you when you come," she said.

But he answered, "Unless I approach the back way, love, that leads into the kitchen."

Eleven o'clock came before the young couple had completed last minute preparations. But fortunately the guests arrived about fifteen minutes late, so all was ready. An hour later Daula Ram delivered a first-rate chicken curry, complete with *pulao*, vegetables and chutneys. "No problem," he said to Mahendra with twinkling eyes. "My brother, you've given the entire village a new lease on life by hiring our men. We thank you!"

Mahendra glanced at the bill and noted that Daula Ram offered a sizable discount. "You shouldn't do that," he scolded.

But the proprietor laughed and said, "My pleasure, Mr. Lall. After all, you're the one who brought me to Christ."

## 20

# The answer

About the same time as the family's arrival at "Orchid Dell," Gur Bachan, the reporter from the *Mussoorie Weekly*, turned his motorcycle up the driveway to the Singh's home in Happy Valley. Hazari Lal looked up from his gardening, stood and saluted. "Good morning, sir," he said, "may I help you?"

Gur Bachan stopped. "That was some storm last night," he began. "I heard lightning struck the house."

A big grin covered the elderly servant's face. "Sir," he said, "see for yourself."

"Has the family fled? It seems very quiet around here."

"I wouldn't call a celebration fleeing." The gardener chuckled. "We had a fine time yesterday, what with Mr. Singh and his family becoming followers of the Lord Christ. I must say they're in a very joyful mood, and generous, too. All of us got sweets on Saturday night, and attended church on the personal invitation of our master yesterday afternoon." Hazari Lal stretched, and with a wave of his hand said, "Please, sir, I believe you're from the newspaper?"

"Yes, my good man. It's reported that the goddess Lakshmi struck the house and wiped out the family."

The elderly servant laughed with abandon. "Please, sir, you can see for yourself. But you won't meet any of the family until Thursday. We expect them late Wednesday night."

"Why have they gone?"

"It's a spiritual pilgrimage, sir, a journey of thanksgiving because God has blessed them with a *darshan* of the Lord Christ. And, of course, the new baby."

"Hmmm, sounds a different story from what I heard." Gur Bachan took out his pencil and pad and began to write. "Your name, my good man?"

"Hazari Lal. I have served this family for the past thirty-five years, and have taken young master, Vijay, and his friend, Mahendra Lall all over Garhwal on treks. In fact, sir, I'd say they became mountaineers instead of lawyers because of the time I spent with them."

"Very good. Now...where did you say the family went?"

"I didn't say. But if you wish to know, they're at Lt. Mahendra Lall's home on the road to Chumba."

"One more question, please. Do you believe the goddess story?"

Hazari Lal laughed, and with a twinkle replied, "The report is not true. The goddess did not strike the house, nor did she wipe out the family. Both the house and family are in good condition, on eye witness report. I saw them leave in good spirits this morning!"

"No, no, my man, I mean the report about the goddess cursing them and threatening their lives. Do you believe that?"

"I take what I see, sir. Everything is fine. Not a pane broken anywhere, nothing changed except for that charred deodar. Granted that was close. But if this is Lakshmi's doings, beg pardon, sir...she hasn't learned to shoot straight."

Gur Bachan laughed, and Hazari Lal concluded, "My personal feeling is that the Lord Christ is stronger than any goddess, and I know that the Singh family has gone on pilgrimage to worship him."

And that's the story that came out in the *Mussoorie Weekly*, a report that profoundly impacted Kailash Rana, Ram and Leela Gupta, the Tej Bahadur family, but most of all, Sukhdev Lall.

Perhaps it was the combination of several factors that caused Mahendra's father to stop short when he read Gur Bachan's news report. He certainly opened the paper at a propitious time, for a telegram in his pocket told of his daughter, Daya's sudden decision to come home from New York for a month's visit. Could he meet her in Delhi? Her husband had to attend a conference in Bombay, so she had decided to see her family.

Sukhdev Lall was in high spirits. He had always favored his Daya, the petite little pixie, an energetic counterpart of her brother Mahendra.

Even as he mused, Raja, his youngest, stood at his elbow, reporting his meeting Mahendra last Saturday in town. The glowing account concluded with, "Dad, Squirt wants all of us to see his beautiful house on the road to Chumba."

"Humph...you believe that? Fat lies, I'd venture."

"No, sir. He's left the military and is working in research."

"Sounds like him...lazy sap."

The teenager challenged his father. "I don't think he's lazy. Look how hard he's worked all these years on orchids. And now it's paying off, Dad. He's got a swell job with a foreign firm."

The man threw his magazine down on the cement floor of the verandah and faced his son. "Are you trying to tell me that that good-for-nothing who leaves the army is settled financially with an overseas firm? How do you make that out, boy?"

"Dad, it's true. We can go see for ourselves. We can check him out. Chumba isn't all that far. Squirt lives between here and Chumba. We can visit him and see for ourselves." Raja drew a long breath, and added, "Come on, Dad! Squirt loves you and Mom, and he was so happy to see me on Saturday that he left everything to take me with him on his motorcycle."

"Humph...now, what do you say he's doing?"

"Working for a pharmaceutical firm based in Geneva, Switzerland as their Indian rep. He lives in a house with six bedrooms, running water, electricity, telephone. I've got his number! All of this at company expense." Raja pulled at his father's sleeve and concluded, "Dad, I was so glad to see Squirt! Please, couldn't we go to his house? We can phone first."

"You believe his line?"

"Sure thing! All I'm asking is that you check him out before calling him a liar."

"Hmmm, don't expect a quick answer. I don't make hasty judgments."

But father and son made the journey to "Orchid Dell" within the week. Sukhdev Lall turned off the car engine and got out to see his eldest running down the walk. In wonderment the older man looked at the chalet in its prime location on the hill, its well manicured gardens tended by men dressed in khaki uniforms, bearing the company's initials. Most of all, his eyes lighted when he saw the evidence of good taste and detail that had always characterized his son, Mahendra. Hmmm, he thought, that's just like him, that plaque covered with glass. That boy always did put on the finishing touches.

"Dad!" Mahendra called. "Oh, I'm so glad you've come! Bless you, Raja, for bringing him."

The two men faced each other and the elder said, "Frankly, I didn't believe this to be true. Raja finally persuaded me to check you out for myself."

"Come, come." Mahendra led the way to the lodge, and took time to show rare flowers already in place. "I have a wonderful crew," he said, grinning widely. "They're locals who know this area from childhood—great people. None better than these Garhwalis. They know the trails, and when I tell them what we're looking for, they're like hounds on the scent, Dad. Man! Am I ever glad for all the years I trekked these hills!"

"What's it all about?"

"Medical research. The Western nations are looking for herbal remedies to cure diseases, and this is a prime location for such study. Bencion has leased this place for five years, Dad. Can you believe it?"

"Hmmm, I'd say you're pretty fortunate. You're here for five years?"

"That's my contract, with provisos, of course."

"I understand the Singh family came recently."

Mahendra's face lit up. "Yes, Dad, we had a great time. They stayed three days."

"So the paper said," Sukhdev Lall commented dryly. His eldest gave him a quick glance and asked, "Paper?"

"Yes, the *Mussoorie Weekly*. Quite a report it was—some sheer nonsense about them taking a spiritual pilgrimage to give thanks for having received a *darshan* of the Lord Christ."

Mahendra laughed with abandon, making Raja come running from the pool he was investigating. "What is it, bud?" he asked.

"Nothing. How about a cup of tea inside? I'll bet you're starved. Let's go in. How about it, Dad?"

"Fine with me, son."

Mahendra Lall smiled. He knew he had won the initial contest.

With his parents bringing Raja to stay a week, Mahendra had many opportunities to quietly speak a good word for his Lord. He saw the animosity give way to genuine admiration on his father's part, though Sukhdev Lall tried carefully to conceal his pride in his eldest's social position. Working for an overseas firm on his first assignment meant something! The man lost no time informing his friends.

But the big question remained. Was this apparent change of attitude something deeper than reflected pride? Did it come from a changed heart? Was it sufficiently strong to take him and his family to Dehra Dun to see his son baptized?

Pansy and Susheela fretted, with the girl saying often, "Mano, I'm worried. I really am. We've got to pray real hard."

"Why, Pansy?" Manorma asked as she nursed the baby, sitting in her rocking chair in the bedroom. Pansy flopped on the floor nearby, looked up and answered, "Oh, it's funny. I felt so sure at first, but now that the time has come, well, I've got this sinking feeling inside that something's going to go wrong."

Manorma laughed, then said, "Bless you, you're just being human. I doubt so often, and it takes Vijay to remind me of my life's verse: 'I will trust, and not be afraid.' How about trusting instead of fearing? You see, Pansy, fear closes the door to God's workings. It's one of Satan's most effective tools."

"Hmmm, I always did say you were a saint."

"Nonsense! Just passing on something I'm still struggling to learn, dear. But seriously, let's get some things straight."

"Yes, Miss?" Pansy said with a giggle.

Manorma smiled and said, "I do sound like a school teacher, don't I? Well, Pansy, take it from me that we've got to learn how to defeat the enemy. Spiritual warfare is very real, and there are laws that govern our outcome."

"Like?" Pansy touched wee Squirt's toes and laughed to see his immediate reaction. "I do believe he's ticklish," she said.

"Cause and effect," Manorma commented. "You tickle his toes; he reacts. The enemy whispers that things are all messed up, and we lose courage. See? That's a natural reaction."

"So, what are we supposed to do?"

"Test what we hear, and believe that God never lies. He is always true to his word."

"Yes, of course, but how can I be sure he's going to bring the entire family tomorrow afternoon when Squirt says his dad has already gone to Delhi to meet Daya and his mom was scared to ask whether or not she and Raja could go?"

"That's the Lord's problem, not ours, Pansy. We don't have to figure out how he's going to answer this one, nor do we have to give him orders. See? We're asking. Sure! And, if I know my heart, I want the Lord Jesus to protect his own name. It's my part to praise him for already answering prayer, for doing what he says he will."

"You mean you really believe all of them are going to be there?"

Manorma looked at her cousin candidly and said, "I don't see why not. If the Lord could spare the house and all of us, wee Squirt included...bless him...." She stooped to kiss her son, then concluded, "surely he can round up the Lall family and get them in one place at the right time."

Pansy laughed, then said, "You make it sound so simple. So what do we do?"

"Let's try praising instead of worrying. Okay, Pansy?"

"Okay, Mano."

Next afternoon when the service in the Bible College gardens was about to start, Pansy looked around. No Lall family yet, but she reminded herself that the Lord is never too late.

The Kushwant Singh family, along with Captain Sydney Michael and Lionel sat under an overspreading mango tree near the swimming pool around which the other spectators clustered. As the college pastor announced the first hymn, an usher met Sukhdev Lall and family and escorted them to their friends. Wide smiles and nods passed between them. Pansy drew a deep breath and squeezed Manorma's hand.

The intimate group of students and faculty sang lustily, following the lyrics on the accordion played by a song leader who lacked nothing in charisma. After a ten minute exhortation on the meaning of baptism, Mahendra and Vijay gave their personal testimonies and the rite followed.

Afterwards, Kushwant Singh's extended family met with Sukhdev Lalls for high tea at Kwality Restaurant, an occasion marked singularly by freedom from past hindrances and hope of future joys. When Shanti congratulated her son, she said with shining eyes, "Your Lord Christ did it!"

But it was Daya, dashing in her red and black punjabi outfit, who told how the miracle occurred. She exclaimed, "Now I know why I had to come! Something inside kept telling me I must go home, but I never realized it might be the voice of God." Her black eyes challenged her father. "I hear Dad's even taken Mom and Raja to see 'Orchid Dell.' Raja's been telling me about it and I'm envious. I can't tell you how homesick I've been in New York."

"Why, Daya?" Manorma asked quietly.

"Oh," she drew a deep breath, then said, "it's so big! Exciting, yes, intimate, no. You can go for days without feeling needed...just do your own thing. And, for me that meant cooking, cleaning, shopping, waiting for Bobby—I mean Ramesh—to come home. Somehow, with his friends calling him Bobby, I got into the habit, too, so I hope you won't mind."

The chatter continued, with the girl telling of her desire to meet everyone, her father's sharing Mahendra's plans and her chance to see the Singhs and Pansy at the baptismal service. She had said adamantly, "Dad, you must take me! I want to be there!" So Sukhdev Lall had phoned his wife, told her to bring Raja by taxi to Dehra Dun by twelve noon on Sunday. They, in turn, had spent the evening shopping in Delhi after seeing Bobby off for Bombay, and after a good sleep, started in the early morning for Dehra Dun, thus escaping the intense heat.

"You must feel beat," Manorma said sympathetically, while Daya talked animatedly in baby language to wee Squirt.

Daya laughed and said, "Not too bad, really. I slept well on the plane, and Dad and I got some sleep last night. I wouldn't have missed this for anything." She kissed wee Squirt and said, "You're glad I came, aren't you, pudding...such an ittsie bittsie mite you are, not big like your mommy and daddy." Then she looked up and said with a laugh, "Promise, Mano? I want to take care of him during the wedding. Please?"

"Of course, Daya. Vijay and I'll be attendants. I really hadn't given it much thought, but since you asked first, I'll say yes."

Thus it happened that the entire Sukhdev Lall family came early to Centenary Church in Delhi on the afternoon of July 20, and Daya gleefully took the baby from his mother's arms to free her to be matron of honor.

Gentle rain and refreshing breezes marked that Saturday afternoon. A brightly colored canopy had been erected between the brick church and the ancient Moghul tomb just off the compound. White uniformed waiters set the finishing touches to the elaborate wedding reception that would follow the ceremony.

All was ready. Guests were beginning to gather, but much to Pansy's disappointment, her mother had not come. A flash of tears mingled with the bride's uncertain smile as she turned to her cousin and said, "What shall we do? I really expected her."

They were in the anteroom, waiting, and through the door they could hear the wedding music beginning in the sanctuary.

"No mother of the bride?" Pansy said in dismay.

"Rejoice, dear! The Lord has already provided." Manorma put her arms around her cousin and said, "Mama Singh is your answer. The Lord gave Papa to Terry, and Mama to you!"

"Of course! How could I forget? Mano...please ask Lionel to call Uncle and Auntie Singh."

They settled the matter within moments. Susheela looked pleased and warmly embraced the bride in true mother-daughter fashion. "Do you need the wheelchair?" Kushwant asked.

"No, thank God. I'll walk."

"You're sure? Lionel or I could wheel you, whichever Pansy wants."

"Please, Auntie, let Lionel walk you in. You can lean heavily on him, you know. And Uncle, sit in the front seat, but leave room for Dad to join you. You're his older brother, you know—next of kin."

"True, daughter," Kushwant said gravely, but with a twinkle in his eye. His off-white Nehru jacket with a rosebud in the third buttonhole made him look very distinguished. Auntie Singh matched him in her delicate non-crushable pink *saree* with the gold border.

Pansy said breathlessly, "Please, could you help meet the guests afterwards? I'd appreciate that, and it would help Dad to not have to do it all on his own."

"Why, of course, Pansy."

The moment came. Susheela, in the role of mother of the bride, walked with queenly gait up the aisle, leaning heavily on Lionel for support. As Pansy and Manorma peeked through a crack in the side door, the latter whispered, "It's a miracle! Isn't she lovely?"

"Yes, Mano. And look at Squirt and Zep up there in their safari suits. Do you think they're nervous? Aren't they handsome? Oh, Mano, is my hair all right? I'm beginning to feel jittery."

Manorma laughed softly and said, "You're doing fine, my dear. Pansy, your Dad is coming to take you in. Don't run. And remember, I go first."

Pansy giggled, threw her a kiss, and said, "Yes, Miss. I always did say you were a saint."

# Glossary

*chowkidar* (cho´-key-dar)—watchman, caretaker

*darshan* (duhr´-shun)—a vision, revelation, worshiping in the presence of any image

*Garhwal*: (grrr´-wall)—area in western Himalayas noted as the birthplace of the sacred river, Ganges

*Garhwali*— citizen of Garhwal

*Gur Bachan* (goor ba´-chan—{*ba* as in "*bu*tton")—newspaper reporter

*Hazari Lal* (huh-zar´-ee loll)—elderly servant, gardener

*Indradevi* (in´-druh day´-v)—goddess Indra

*Kailu* (kai´-loo)—neighbor boy

*Kushwant Singh* (koosh´-want sing)—Vijay's father, retired from serving as a lawyer in Supreme Court in Delhi

*Lakshmi* (Luck´-shmee)—goddess of wealth

*Leela Gupta* (lee´-la goop´-ta)—Ram Gupta's wife, and former friend of Susheela Singh

*Maharishi* (ma-ha´-rish´-ee)—literally means "the great holy man," the Indian guru who headed up the Ashram

*Mahendra Lall* (ma-hen´-drah loll)—Vijay's close friend and son of Sukhdev Lall, the real estate dealer

*Mata Ji* (ma´-ta gee)—honorific for "mother"

*Maya Bahadur* (my´-ah ba-ha´-door)—Kailu's mother

*pakora* (puck-au´-ra)—vegetable pattie, highly spiced, used as finger food and eaten with ketchup

*Parvati* (puhr-wuh´-tee)—Marcia's friend

*Phulmoni* (pool-mon´-ey)—Vijay's married sister living in Lucknow

*Rani* (rah´-nee)—cook in the Singh household

*Ram Gupta* (rahm goop´-ta)—wealthy cloth merchant

*Rishikesh* (rish´-ee kesh)—name of pilgrimage spot

*samosa*—a finger food, usually triangular in shape; a bit of curried potato wrapped in dough and fried in hot oil

*Sukhdev Lall* (souk´-dave loll)—Mahendra's father

*Susheela Singh* (sue-shee´-la sing)—Vijay's mother, wife of Kushwant Singh

*Tej Bahadur* (tage ba-ha´-dur)—Kailu's father; cloth merchant

*Vijay Kumar Singh* (vee´-jai coo´-mar sing)—Manorma's husband and close friend of Mahendra Lall